SUSPENSION
OF THE RULES

224

SUSPENSION OF THE RULES

A WASHINGTON STATEHOUSE MYSTERY

DON STUART

NORTH WEST CORNER BOOKS

Kenmore, WA

Northwest Corner books, an imprint of Epicenter Press Inc.,
publishes books related to the Pacific Northwest.
For more information, visit www.EpicenterPress.com

Suspension of the Rules

Published by arrangement with Epicenter Press, Inc.
6524 NE 181st St., Suite 2
Kenmore, WA 9802

Cover design by Scott Book
Design by Melissa Vail Coffman

ISBN: 978-1-60381-274-0 (Trade Paper)
ISBN: 978-1-60381-275-7 (eBook))

Produced in the United States of America

CONTENTS

CHARACTERS, BILLS, AND ACRONYMS

Principal Suspects:

Phil (Stoney) Stonington: Farmer, landowner, and founder of Washington Conservation Heritage Farmers Association

Daryl Weber: Program Manager for Agricultural Conservation Easement Program at USDA/Natural Resourced Conservation Service

Rep. Rob Thomas: Yakima County orchardist and elected Member of Washington State House of Representatives

Louise (Lou) Dwyer: Public Affairs Director for the Washington Association for Wildlife and Recreation – advocates for the Washington Wildlife and Recreation Program (WWRP)

Linda Cunningham: Government Relations Director for the Washington State Agriculture Industry Council (WSAIC)

Protagonist and his close associates:

Torrence (Sandy) Dalton: Protagonist, professional lobbyist and amateur sleuth

Francis (Fran) Dalton: Sandy's dad

Shirley J: Fran Dalton's commercial salmon troller

Carl Folsom: Sandy's farmer grandfather, his mom's father

Nancy Folsom: Sandy's farmer grandmother, his mom's mother

Susan: Sandy's deceased wife

Sherry Sebold: Sandy's close friend and Legal Counsel to House Technology and Economic Development Committee

Dean Gavick: Sherry Sebold's ex-husband

David Gavick: Sherry Sebold's son

Helen: Sandy's extraordinary Administrative Assistant

Janice Burdel: Sandy's professional lobbying associate

Lester Stonington: Stoney's son, the salmon gillnetter

Other Characters:

The victim and his family

Fortis Henry: Decedent and owner of Henry Dairy near Yakima, WA
Maryanne Henry: Fortis Henry's wife
Trisha Henry: Fortis Henry's daughter
Tony Dykstra: Trisha Henry's boyfriend
Marta Thomas: Fortis Henry's younger sister and Rep Rob Thomas' wife

Elected public officials

Rep. Robbie Flores: Chair, House Local Government Committee.
Sen. Jimmy Fang: Chair of Senate Natural Resources Committee
Sen. Lance (L.C.) Chambers: Wavering ally
Carl Browne: Governor of the State of Washington
Rep Jackson Thiel: House Speaker
Rep. Thomas Drum: Elected Member, Washington State House of Representatives and Chair of House Technology and Economic Development
Rep. Didi Harris: Elected Member, Washington State House of Representatives from Eastern Spokane County
Rep. Jerome (Jerry) Fernandez: Elected Member, Washington State House of Representatives and Chair of House Business and Financial Services Committee

Police officials

Lt. Nathan Wilson: Head of Special Investigations Unit, Washington State Patrol
Sergeant Nakamura: Washington State Patrol traffic accidents investigator
Detective Ricky Tracy: Yakima Sheriff's Detective
Lehan K. Orbison, Jr.: Chief of Washington State Patrol
P. Dumphries: Washington State Patrol Officer working Capitol Campus security

Lobbyists and legislative policy advocates

Aaron Nicolaides: Former House Speaker and Lobbyist for Fortuna Corporation

Morganthau, Staley, and Rimes: Seattle Law firm and Aaron Nicolaides' employer

Nelson Morganthau: Senior Partner with Morganthau firm and contributor to Governor Browne

Terry Moberg: Head Lobbyist for Washington Association of Insurance Providers

Ronnie Johnson: Executive Director/Editor of Truth Spotlight

Hans Fortner: President of the Washington Association for Wildlife and Recreation (WAWR) and Lou Dwyer's boss

Miles Morgan: Government Relations Liaison for Washington State Conservation Commission

Truman Harris: Didi Harris' wealthy, land entrepreneur father

Etc.

Bob Springfield: Rep. Thomas Drum's Legislative Assistant

Sarah Weber: Daryl Weber's wife

Trudi: USDA/NRCS State Office Receptionist

Lane Murray: Grays Harbor Conservation District Supervisor who beat Stoney out for a seat on the Conservation Commission

Ed Nowak: Farmer/advocate from Ridgefield, WA

Haley Powers: King County Superior Court Judge

Bills of Importance:

Budget Appropriations Bill: Threatened cuts to Conservation Commission budget

Business and Occupation Tax Reforms: Eliminate the State B&O tax

Commercial Fisheries Insurance Pools: Made subject to general insurance regulations

Conservation District Election Reform: District supervisors elected on the general ballot

Conservation Futures Tax: Increase local authority to impose tax for land protection

Conservation Heritage Priority Bill: Special treatment for farmers who adopt sound conservation management practices

Fortuna Package: Public incentives to encourage a large business investment in State

High Tech Education Bill: High tech education provided in High Schools

Acronyms:

USDA/NRCS: <u>United States Department of Agriculture/Natural Resources Conservation Service</u> – the real federal agency that helps landowners conserve their lands, soils, and environment

CDSW: <u>Conservation Districts Society of Washington</u> – a fictional private nonprofit trade association representing Washington conservation districts

WSAIC: <u>Washington State Agriculture Industry Council</u> – a fictional private nonprofit trade association representing the Washington agriculture industry

WCHFA: <u>Washington Conservation Heritage Farms Association</u> – a fictional private nonprofit association that certifies farms as environmentally responsible

WWRP: <u>Washington Wildlife and Recreation Program</u> – the real Washington State program that purchases land to protect it for environmental, recreational, and agricultural purposes

WAWR: <u>Washington Association for Wildlife and Recreation</u> – a fictional private nonprofit association that supports the WWRP

ACEP: <u>Agricultural Conservation Easement Program</u> – the real USDA program that helps local communities purchase agricultural conservation easements to protect farmland

WAIP: <u>Washington Association of Insurance Providers</u> – a fictional private nonprofit trade association representing the insurance industry

CFT: <u>Conservation Futures Tax</u> – a real State-authorized, county level tax used to fund public purchases of interests in land like agricultural conservation easements

PROLOGUE

Saturday, December 31, 10 a.m.

IT WAS THE BARKING of the dogs.

An indignant crow stalked the roofline of a nearby dairy barn. It pecked angrily at the metal roofing, bristled its feathers, cawed, and stared coldly at the four unruly dogs. Slowly, reluctantly, it spread its wings and, flapping audibly, disappeared into the gray, late December sky.

In the open barn beneath, several hundred resident cows enjoyed a morning treat of sweet timothy hay. From time to time they'd look up, chewing softly, and cast mildly curious gazes out to where the dogs continued to pace and yap from the top of an eight-foot embankment behind the building.

By just before ten o'clock this Saturday morning, the rain had finally ceased. Six invited guests had gathered in the front room of Fortis Henry's palatial farmhouse admiring the view from its perch on a gentle hillside overlooking the Yakima Valley. The Henry family's heavily adorned, post-Christmas tree filled one corner of the room. A real log fire crackled softly in a massive, river-stone fireplace. The guests had shown up at various times over the past half hour or so, most of them arriving after long, tiring, rainy drives from widely different points around the state; from Seattle,

SUSPENSION OF THE RULES

and Olympia to the west of the Cascade Mountains, and from some much smaller towns sprinkled around the state's agricultural eastside. Now they were all anxious to begin. A few had spread papers out on the dining room table and were considering possible arguments, mapping out coalitions, and otherwise preparing for the coming discussion about their strategy in the approaching session of the Washington State Legislature.

Everyone was present but their host, Fortis Henry. A dairy farmer's work is never done, especially between Christmas and New Year's when a farm crew was inevitably drawn away by family obligations.

"Wipe your feet, young man," said Fortis's wife from the kitchen door. A good-looking young male stood in the entry by the front door, unbuttoning his jacket and running a hand through his wind-blown hair. He was the expected ride for Tricia Henry, Fortis and Maryanne Henry's daughter. The day was December 31st and the two of them were heading over to a friend's house to help prepare for a New Year's Eve party. When she came down the stairs to greet him he reached out and put his hand around her waist. A nice couple. Good-looking college kids, home for the holidays.

"Got everything?" Maryanne Henry asked her daughter. Tricia held up a store bag—apparently containing her contribution to the evening's décor and refreshments.

"Mine's in the car." The boyfriend aimed a glance over his shoulder. "Stopped off on the way."

By the time the kids were gone, it was after ten. People were beginning to fidget. Where the hell was Fortis?

Maryanne, still holding a kitchen towel, glanced worriedly at the big antique grandfather clock beside the fireplace. "Crew's off on an errand," she said. "He's out back."

"Bet he forgot all about us." One of the group reached out to a coat-rack near the door and began to pull on his jacket. "Let me run on out and fetch him."

As if on signal, all six visitors, four men and two women, began donning their coats as well. Moments later they were all headed back out the front door into a now calm, cool, winter morning.

The small group stepped out onto a nicely paved walk. To the south, a shaft of sunlight had finally broken through the dark morning clouds. That's when they all first noticed the yelping of the dogs.

"Some kind of excitement," someone said above the murmur of several conversations.

They turned down the side of the house, past where their own cars and pickups were parked with several others around an ample, now-drying asphalt lot. The pavement changed to packed gravel as the drive extended beyond the house and continued down past a milking parlor and beside a huge, modern dairy barn and covered feed lot where several thousand Henry family cows spent a good part of their carefully managed lives. The modern, obviously well-run facility became a topic of impressed conversation among them.

As they proceeded, the barking grew louder. Their conversations flagged. A wave of worry washed over the group. "Fortis?" someone called out as they passed the throng of feeding, lowing cows. There was not a person in sight. A few animals looked up as the group passed. A "mooorogahh" of mild complaint came from somewhere back among the herd.

This clean, modern dairy had its characteristic odors, but the wind had calmed and, as the visitors proceeded, the increasingly rich perfume of manure made it abundantly clear what lay atop and behind the newly planted, straw-covered embankment they found in back of the dairy barn. Stepping carefully to avoid the mud, they made their way up the new, crushed-rock service road that led up the bank to where they could see the huge dairy manure storage lagoon that lay behind it.

Four family dogs were milling anxiously about at the front lip of the new lagoon. Running around the lagoon's top edge, there was a low, recently poured concrete perimeter footing that would soon become the foundation for a planned safety fence. The materials lay nearby, big rolls of chain link fencing and galvanized steel posts awaiting installation. Beyond this footing, the smooth, inner liner of the lagoon sloped steeply down into its liquid contents. There were smears in the thick slime which coated this liner; something heavy had slithered down its slippery surface. Just below, something substantial floated, hunched and motionless.

The visitors collected there, curious.

Then they stopped and stared.

There, face down and inert in the fetid liquid, was the unmistakable shape of a human body. Resting beside it, as if carefully placed there upon the lagoon's crusted surface, was a spotless white, ten-gallon Stetson hat—the well-known personal trademark of their missing host, Fortis Henry.

CHAPTER ONE

Saturday, December 31, 1:30 p.m.

Revised Agenda

OURS WAS A GRIM GATHERING AS we settled in at a Denny's Restaurant in a strip-mall next to I-82 southeast of Yakima. None of us had eaten since leaving home early that morning; still, nobody seemed to have much of an appetite.

We'd all experienced a day we'd remember vividly for a good long time.

Upon discovering Fortis Henry's body, there'd been a flurry of frantic activity. Some of us had started fumbling for phones. Others, me included, had scurried about looking for some way to fish Fortis out. After a few minutes of fruitless effort, one of our group came running back up the embankment carrying a long aluminum pole that had a hook-like gadget at the end designed, I think, for opening the skylights high up in the ceiling of the dairy barn. With this pole, we'd grappled Fortis's loose clothing, unceremoniously dragged his fouled, lifeless remains up the steep slimy side of that waste lagoon, and finally laid him out in the gravel and mud at the top of the embankment.

I picked at the cucumbers in my Dennys salad. The memory of finding his body was still too fresh: the awful smell, the appearance of his body, imagining his struggle as he fought to remain above the surface. Looking around at my colleagues' faces, I wasn't the only one. Our table was an island of gloom amid the casual retiree lunches, restful travel breaks, and cheerful family outings that surrounded us.

We'd originally come to Yakima to discuss the bill I'd been hired to lobby through the upcoming Legislature, a proposal designed to make it easier for those farmers who adopted sound environmental conservation management practices on their land to also get help in paying for those practices and in protecting their farms from development. After the accident, we'd agreed to come down here to Denny's and see what we could salvage out of the ill-fated meeting we'd planned for Fortis Henry's front room. I was the person who'd made the arrangements for us to meet that day, so launching the discussion seemed like my responsibility. As a lobbyist at the Washington State Legislature, you'd think I'd be good at putting people at ease, but I almost felt guilty for trying to open the conversation.

"So," I cleared my throat. "Should we give some thought to the proposal?"

It sounded insensitive to my own ears, but my client and employer, Phil Stonington, nodded. Stoney had hired me to represent the group he'd founded—a coalition of environmentally responsible Washington farmers who called themselves the Washington Conservation Heritage Farms Association. WCHFA is my official client, and I owed it to Stoney to give this a good try, so I stepped into the breach shortly after our orders had been served.

"Sure, Sandy." He said, reluctantly flicking open a pad of yellow paper. "One thing's for certain. We're going to need to find someone else to bring the conservation districts along."

Before today, Fortis Henry had been our lead with the State's conservation districts. He'd been on the Washington State Conservation Commission and on the Board of the Conservation Districts Society of Washington (CDSW), an association of conservation district board supervisors. Though Stoney was the founder and leader of the WCHA, Fortis was the influential figure in the tight, committed world of conservation districts.

"That shouldn't be hard," said the woman to Stoney's right. She was Louise (Lou) Dwyer, the tall, stately, but also, somehow, disheveled looking Public Affairs Director for the Washington Association for Wildlife and Recreation. Perhaps it was her tousled hairstyle. In any case, Lou's employer, WAWR, was an influential coalition of sports and environmental organizations that advocated for the Washington Wildlife and Recreation Program whose responsibility was to purchase land for recreation and environmental protection. Our bill was designed, in part, to give an edge to environmentally responsible farmers who applied to that program. Hence Lou's interest in the bill.

"I'd think the districts will easily be there for this," she continued. "Pretty much anybody from their group would do as good a job as Fortis would have." There was more than a trace of bitterness in Lou's tone. She seemed to imply Fortis Henry might not have been of much use in the first place. "Anyway, we've got you for that, Stoney. You'll do fine." In addition to Stoney's other roles, he was also on the board of the Conservation Districts Society of Washington.

Others noticed Lou's tone as well. "Or maybe a lot better," Linda Cunningham suggested flatly. Linda was Government Relations Director for the Washington State Agriculture Industry Council (WSAIC), the pre-eminent, politically active farm industry organization in our state. She was a tougher customer than Lou Dwyer; also widely respected or, perhaps in Linda's case, "feared" might be a more apt description.

"Fortis was an impressive guy," said the dark-haired man to her right, Rob Thomas. "Maybe now isn't the time to bring it up, but he did have some issues, that's for sure." Rob was the elected State Representative from the Yakima area legislative district, as well as an orchardist. He had all the makings of a politician: good looks, smooth talking, and an easy personality, I'd grown to like him. His wife was as socially active as he and was said to be a driving force behind Rob Thomas's political career. She was also Fortis Henry's sister.

Daryl Weber, who'd been silently sipping his coffee and drawing doodles in the margin on his paper, huffed in agreement.

Daryl, the sixth and last member of our group, was a Soils Scientist with the USDA/Natural Resources Conservation Service (NRCS) and worked out of the state office in Spokane. He was a 20-plus year veteran with NRCS and was as influential as he was liked, which said something. I'd asked him to attend because he was local manager of the federal program that contributed half the purchase cost of most of the agricultural conservation easement acquisitions in Washington State.

Stoney was silent but clearly agreed. He'd known Fortis for years, but he, too, raised no objections to the turn of the conversation. Clearly, there wasn't much love around that table for the recently deceased. Even I had reason to dislike Fortis Henry; I was sure most of those present knew that Fortis had originally argued strongly against Stoney hiring me to lobby for the Conservation Heritage Priority Bill.

Reluctantly, I asked the question everyone was thinking: "How do we think Fortis's accident will affect the bill?"

"Well, you do need to know, Sandy, that the commercial agriculture community probably isn't going to be able to contribute much help," Linda said, pushing a sad looking leaf of Caesar-coated lettuce around her plate. She shook her head but didn't look ashamed to admit: "You're probably lucky Fortis is gone. He made a lot of enemies on my Board."

"Amen to that," Lou added.

"He could be a real pain in the ass," Daryl said; his first contribution thus far. He did not, however, elaborate.

Why is that, I wanted to ask. But before I could open my mouth, Rob said, "There sure was a lot of talk about Fortis's damn dairy lagoon."

"I bet there was," said Linda at the same time Lou mumbled,

"Oh yeah."

Some months earlier, Fortis had secured a $110,000 USDA cost-share grant to help build his new dairy lagoon; the place where he had died. A controversy had emerged over whether he'd used his role as a conservation district supervisor to unduly influence the making of that grant.

"Not a good move," Daryl added. As an NRCS insider, he might be expected to know something more about the controversy surrounding the grant. Again, however, Daryl did not elaborate.

I was all but convinced that getting this group on track might be hopeless and admittedly, I wasn't in a mood to discuss the bill either. I was curious about Fortis, but Stoney closed the conversation down. "You know," he said, "maybe we should just give all this a rest, for now. We've got more on our minds, at the moment, than some conservation practice/farmland protection bill." He turned to me: "Sandy, maybe you could take the lead in reconvening our group at some point down the road? Or perhaps we could do some kind of an email exchange? Something like that?"

I nodded. Everyone looked relieved to end our unpleasant visit to Yakima.

As I GOT BACK ON THE freeway headed north toward Ellensburg, I considered what had just happened at our gathering there at Denny's. Of the six of us, I was the only one who hadn't in some way expressed dislike for the recently deceased dairy farmer. Each of the others were long-established figures in agriculture, government, or environmental affairs, and all of them had experience with Fortis Henry. They'd all known each other for years, had personal reputations that legitimized their views.

I was a relative newcomer to this arena. That's why I'd kept my mouth shut. My objective was to get Stoney's bill passed; I didn't have the luxury of venting.

I did, however, silently share their opinion. I knew enough about Fortis's opposition to Stoney's retaining my services to be aware that he had gone well beyond the strictly professional.

To be successful in my line of work takes more than a glib tongue and a firm handshake. You're dealing with people, with legislators, lobbyists, policy advocates, and legislative staffers, all of whom have an agenda. If you want to influence their thinking, you need to be good at reading people and at assessing their motives. Sometimes it's inspired guesswork, but if you're going to convince someone of something, you need make your case in a way that respects their point of view. It helps to have comprehensive grasp of what is going on in the world of legislative politics—the world they inhabit. But mostly, it's all about appreciating the other person's perspective.

That is a talent which, as far as I can tell, came to me naturally. It certainly isn't one I went to school to learn or that I labored to acquire. I may be wrong, but from what I've seen, I think it's something you're born with—you either have it or you don't. I have to admit, it's also something I enjoy. There's often a tingle of accomplishment when I suddenly acquire insight into someone's thinking on a matter—thinking that, very often, they would rather remained opaque.

All that is how I knew Fortis Henry had gone out of his way to put the kibosh on my services—even though he hadn't really known me. After he had failed to close me out, and since I'd been working the bill, I'd sensed his reticence to cooperate beyond what was absolutely necessary. Perhaps he was suspicious of my close connection with the commercial fishing industry and believed that the ag industry's struggles with environmental regulation to protect salmon posed some kind of conflict of interest. But I mostly suspected he just thought I was an opportunist, not someone who cared about his issues.

He was completely wrong about both of those things. Now I'd never get the chance to change his mind. I believe he'd have worked to secure the conservation district support we needed, but it wouldn't have been because he was happy about working with me.

I was fully engaged with my driving as I powered through the big sweeping curves along I-82 at Manastash Pass. I finally summited and began to relax for that long, steady grade down into Ellensburg. I began thinking more specifically about what had happened that morning and I realized that my unsettled thoughts were partly the product of a troubled conscience.

As I'd stood at the top of that embankment and looked down into that dairy pond, and when I'd realized what and then who was floating there, I'd had a brief but unmistakably spiteful reaction. It had lasted only a moment, but the fleeting thought that had crossed my mind was something akin to: "Huh, guess I won't have you to worry about anymore."

Of course, the moment had passed. I'd applied myself vigorously to finding a way to drag Fortis safely up out of that pond. That brief but unmistakable moment of personal malice was, however, something I'd need to reflect upon and come to terms with, in the weeks and months ahead.

None of it made me feel any better about myself as I chewed up the long, tedious, lonely miles for home.

CHAPTER TWO

Monday, February 13 – 10 a.m.

Busy Calendar

THE HEARING ROOM WAS FILLED WITH intense people in dark suits. Some were in urgent last-minute consultations. Others studied files they'd pulled from their leather cases. It all felt as if careers might be made and fortunes won or lost in today's deliberations of the Washington State Legislature's House Technology and Economic Development Committee.

The reality, of course, was much less profound; this event was mostly about celebrity. High-tech business mogul, Howard Oxley, was to testify here today, and both the media and Committee Members were expecting a show.

The first bill before the Committee would create a new, experimental, secondary school high-tech business education program funded by the State. The idea was that a lot of kids who could become adept at computer science and programming either dropped out or didn't go on to college. They might stay in school if they got an early taste of basic computer tech education—especially if it focused on business applications. Currently, the State's basic education funding didn't extend to something so specialized.

For the past two plus years, Oxley's huge national firm, Fortuna, had been pushing development of a massive computer

8

farm in Eastern King County—a partnership with several of the Northwest's big high-tech companies. His aggressive legislative effort to secure State incentives for the project had put him in the news and made him something of a media "darling," an emissary for the kind of high-tech economy everyone wanted to encourage in the Puget Sound area. The whole project had run off the rails a couple of years earlier, but Oxley was now back with a renewed legislative effort to make it happen.

As I entered the room and looked for an empty seat, my guess was that, with Oxley behind it, this bill had a good shot. Ordinarily it would have been referred to the Education Committee for hearing and report. It seemed quite unusual for Leadership to have, instead, sent it here to Technology and Economic Development. That they had referred it to a committee where Oxley was such a big deal suggested he must have leadership support—probably a good sign for this bill. Perhaps for his incentives package as well.

About halfway back near the windows a phone-focused blonde woman in a deep blue suit reluctantly moved her briefcase to the chair on her other side so I could sit. I'll admit I was there early partly because I was curious. The bill I had there that day, one for my fishing industry clients, wouldn't be coming up till later when most of these people would be gone and the cameras would be off. Some of my fisheries clients were already in the room waiting to testify. Sherry Sebold, a close friend and a legislative staffer for this committee, had let me know that Representative Thomas Drum, the Committee Chair, had promised Fortuna's lobbyist, former House Speaker Aaron Nicolaides, that he'd accommodate Oxley's busy schedule by hearing Fortuna's bill first; as might be expected; power begets power. I could have waited until later to arrive, but I, too, wanted to see Oxley perform.

Stoney came to the hearing as well though for no particular reason that I could see other than to take in the "event." I'd originally proposed that he and I get together later in the Capitol Dome Deli after the hearing on my fishing industry bill, but Stoney wanted to meet me here. It occurred to me that he might be curious to see how his newly retained lobbyist handled the fisheries hearing. I saw him working his way into the room through the crowded entrance. He waved and headed in my direction.

"Hey," he said, his bare, beefy head giving me a gruff nod as he drew closer. "How's it goin' so far?"

"Hasn't started yet," I said, trying not to yell over the noise in the crowded room. He prevailed upon the blonde woman to remove her briefcase and move over a seat so he could join me. She didn't look happy.

My reasons for agreeing to represent Stoney's nonprofit organization were personal as well as practical. My mom had grown up on a farm in Eastern Washington; a good-sized operation in the Columbia River Project. Her family's place had been a few miles southeast of Coulee City, a good long drive from Seattle; it seemed like a different world. As a kid, I remember being deeply impressed by everything about their farm. It had seemed, somehow, amazing to me that a person could earn a living planting crops on their own land, helping them grow, and then harvesting and selling the food or fiber they produced. There was something self-sufficient and fundamentally satisfying about that.

My mom died when I was twelve, but my dad continued to stay in touch with Mom's parents until they'd both passed away some years later. Mom's father died in the midst of one of the periodic "agriculture depressions" her family had faced over the years. As stable and successful as their farm had seemed, when everything was added up for my grandfather's probate, he and my grandmother turned out to have been so deeply in debt there was nothing left, not even the farm itself. My grandmother spent her last years in a sad, Medicaid-supported assisted living facility on Aurora Avenue, north of Seattle not far from Ballard where Dad kept the "Shirley J." My mom was an only child; with her gone, Dad and I were, essentially, the only family my grandmother had left at the end. I was maybe twelve when she died.

When my mom was alive, and during the years after she died but while my grandparents still had their farm, we'd sometimes drive over there for visits. Those visits and the times I spent with my grandfather walking the farm were deeply memorable. I had farming in my blood as well as fishing.

We weren't the only ones curious about the Oxley bill; there were plenty of familiar faces around the room. As I sat back and awaited the Howard Oxley show, I wondered just how far some of these fawning legislators would go to accommodate Oxley's wishes.

"We better get this goin' sooner rather than later," Stoney grumbled beneath his breath. As if on cue, Committee Chair Thomas Drum called Oxley's high-tech secondary education bill as the first up. After a few preliminaries, Oxley made his way to the witness table to give his testimony. I thought he seemed sincere and made a compelling case. I was impressed when the audience actually applauded a few times—something that seldom happens in any but the most charged legislative hearings.

A long list of witnesses followed him, most of them in favor, At one point, Stoney nudged my arm. "I'll be damned," he said, under his breath.

"What?" I whispered.

He pointed at the most recent witness making her way to the front of the room. "Maryanne Henry." Sure enough, a woman with light hair and familiar eyes made her way down the aisle and towards the stand; this time, instead of jeans she wore dark slacks and an expression of determination. She looked quite different from the housewife I recalled meeting that day at the end of last December.

"I'm pretty sure she's a teacher," Stoney continued under his breath. "I wouldn't have guessed she was into stuff like this."

Perhaps it was the set in her shoulders or the memory of that day that made me feel some duty to her, but I found myself saying, "We should go say hello after."

Stoney looked at me like I was crazy. "What?"

I shrugged and looked down. "Maybe offer our condolences again? It seems rude to say nothing after what—what happened with Fortis."

Stoney considered this then shrugged. "Accidents happen, Sandy. Wasn't our fault we were there at the wrong time."

Accidents happen. He was right, of course. "Accident" had been the official conclusion. Still, I wasn't sure it was the right way to describe what had happened that day. It just felt wrong.

If I had been just a bit less overwhelmed by work, a bit more willing to question what I was told by people I considered to be my friends, or maybe even just a bit less anxious to please my new client, maybe I'd have started looking into things sooner. Certainly, had I known then what I later learned, I would have reintroduced myself to Maryanne Henry that day, asked her a few questions, maybe started thinking more critically about what had happened.

But I didn't. Instead, I nodded and said, "You're right."

Still, even then, I couldn't shake the feeling in my gut that something about that day at the Henry Dairy in Yakima hadn't been quite what it seemed.

IT WAS ABOUT AN HOUR AND a half later by the time Stoney and I made our way over to the Capitol Dome Deli. The café was buried among the grey halls and alcoves deep in the labyrinthine basement of the massive Washington State Capitol Building, a marble cave in which all natural light was replaced by ubiquitous fluorescent.

Even had there been windows, however, and even perhaps some kind of sweeping view, no one there would have noticed. The Deli's patrons were fixated entirely on one another, on their policy issues, and on what might be going on a couple of floors above in the Chambers of the House and Senate or, perhaps another floor above that, in the offices of legislative leadership. Everywhere one looked, little well-dressed groups were tucked away in some corner, deep in conversation, or huddled around one of the many little tables studying some bill, map, statistical chart or, more likely, some article in the latest *Daily Olympian*.

Stoney was right at home. He was a Capitol regular; one of those activist citizens whose involvement with various groups and causes brought them frequently to Olympia. Stoney's personal interests were diverse. He owned a couple of small business properties up in Carnation, a town along the Snoqualmie River east of Seattle near the foothills of the Cascades. He was also a farmer with a big chunk of land up along the Snoqualmie River. He didn't seem to me to be all that serious about farming, but he was liked and respected in agriculture.

"Alright," he said, clapping his hands together. "Where do we start?"

I was anxious to get Stoney's thoughts and guidance on his bill, but as I began to explain to him where things stood after Fortis's death, Stoney took over the conversation.

"Son of a bitch is dead, and he's still screwing us over," he said heatedly. I looked around to be sure nobody had overheard. Thankfully, the tightly-packed Deli was noisy; people were absorbed in their own issues.

Though neither of us had spoken much about Fortis since our brief gathering at Denny's, Stoney looked ready to spew insults on his grave. Feeling the way I did, I couldn't personally fault him for speaking ill of the dead.

Fortis had been a highly visible leader among conservation districts. He'd been on the CDSW Board and also an elected member of the districts' State agency, the Washington State Conservation Commission. And he'd been active for years in legislative advocacy for district causes. He had also, unfortunately, been involved in a scandal over the conservation cost share grant he'd received to build his dairy lagoon. The whole thing had recently grown into something that was causing all kinds of political grief in conservation district country. And because of his leadership role with conservation districts, his "misdeeds" were inevitably coming back to haunt the entire conservation district cause.

His "scandal" had, for example, put the brakes on a much-needed budget appropriation for the Conservation Commission. Most of the local districts depended on annual operating grants from the State Conservation Commission. This was the money they used to keep their offices open, pay staff, and provide basic assistance to farmers trying to do the right thing in managing their land. Now that money was in doubt.

Fortis's scandal story had been initially broken by an online public watch-dog group based in Yakima called "Truth Spotlight." The group claimed on their website that Fortis had improperly used his influence as a public official (as an elected member of the local conservation district Board of Supervisors), to secure a grant of over $110,000 in Federal "conservation cost-share" money from the USFA, Natural Resources Conservation Service to help pay for the brand-new dairy waste lagoon which had been installed on Fortis's farm shortly before he died.

Unfortunately, the repugnant manner of Fortis's death had thrust his Federal cost share assistance money to the top of the local news cycle. According to the police investigation, marks in the slime that coated the steeply sloped walls indicated a desperate, minutes long struggle to climb to safety. Weighted down by heavy boots and a thick winter coat, exhausted by his struggle, and overcome by toxic fumes, Fortis Henry had finally succumbed.

Readers of the *Yakima Herald-Republic* were duly repulsed, a horror, however, that was by no means powerful enough to keep them from reading about it. Intense interest continued for several days as reporters cast about seeking new material to fuel the public fascination. Of course, the "Truth Spotlight" investigation came up and was hashed over repeatedly. Fortis's grisly death had occurred in the very same diary lagoon that he'd paid for using money supposedly obtained through improper influence.

It all became an irresistible apocryphal tale of a man done in horribly through his own wrongdoing. A particularly graphic, animated, and highly opinionated video had been posted to YouTube. Fortis's dairy lagoon project was, in fact, a good project, quite possibly better than any of the others that might have been in competition with it for the same money. Dairy waste lagoons could be sound conservation investments, both for the public and for the farmer. They allowed livestock waste to be safely stored through the winter so it could later be applied at agronomic rates to active farm fields in spring and summer at a time when vigorously growing plants would readily take up the nitrogen and other troublesome materials it contained and prevent them from being washed as toxic pollution into vulnerable nearby streams and rivers.

The problem with what Fortis Henry had done, therefore, wasn't that his was a bad project. Nor was it that he'd done anything very far out of the ordinary. It was rather that the manner in which the choice had been made was suspect. He had, of course, recused himself from the actual vote. But, as the "Truth Spotlight" folks pointed out: "Could anyone really claim Fortis's presence in the room, his participation in the discussion, his likely lobbying beforehand, and his long-standing membership on that collegial Board of Supervisors hadn't, in actual fact, influenced their decision on which project to recommend?"

It all provided grist for yet another entertaining read in the *Herald-Republic* and for the horror of Fortis Henry's death to be revisited once again, around the coffee maker at work the following day. The story had ultimately gone statewide, transported across the mountains to Washington's highly populous westside by the *Herald-Republic's* parent paper, *The Seattle Times* and then by other urban Puget Sound area papers, significantly including *The Daily Olympian*, the avidly-read paper that served the Washington State Capital.

Now, several weeks later, all that public curiosity was coming back to plague the conservation districts in their biennial legislative struggle for State funding. The Governor's Office had balked at the proposed badly needed increase in appropriations for the districts' State support agency, the Conservation Commission. It was looking like there would be similar barriers in both the House and

Senate. The resulting shortage would curtail hoped-for conservation programs and projects all across the State.

Stoney's diatribe that day in the Capitol Dome Deli suggested that, as had each of the others at that meeting back in late December, Stoney also had had a strained relationship with Fortis Henry.

For Stoney, however, the impact had been more personal. Stoney and Fortis had been fellow Board Members with the CDSW. The two of them had, in previous years, regularly gone together for visits with key State Legislators on conservation district issues. Now, Stoney could hardly walk into a Legislator's office without being asked about his colleague, the dairy farmer who'd fallen into his own waste lagoon: ". . . you know, that guy who finagled the Federal grant money."

I had to agree with Stoney; it looked like the conservation districts' appropriation was in serious trouble.

CHAPTER THREE

A Saturday in April — Many Years Earlier

Policy Backgrounder

MY DAD WAS A COMMERCIAL FISHERMAN, but, as I've said, my mom grew up on a farm. It was one of the reasons I'd wanted to represent these Conservation Heritage farmers. I loved to visit my grandparents place in North Central Washington. Even after my mom died, my dad and I still used to go over there, sometimes, for one of my Grandma's big Saturday farm dinners. I particularly recall one of the last times we did that; I was about fourteen at the time.

My grandparents' place was up off Highway 2 near Wilbur, a few miles southeast of Grand Coulee, so it was a long drive from Seattle. Dad and I got on the road early, that day; still, it was probably after eleven when we finally pulled into the dusty work yard beside my grandparents' house under a warm April sun. I was disappointed but not surprised to see no cows over in the fenced field beyond the barn. Grandma and my dad talked on the phone from time to time; she'd already mentioned to him that Grandpa had sold the cattle.

There had never been many of them, maybe a couple dozen animals, but I'd always enjoyed seeing them there. If you walked over to the fence and stood for a while watching the cattle graze in that field, the whole group of them would, ever-so-slowly, begin edging their way over in your direction. Before long, the whole herd would be standing right there with you on the other side of that fence. Maybe they were thinking they might get fed, but it felt more like they were just curious who you were and what you were doing there. If you stayed very still and spoke to them softly, they'd stick their big fuzzy heads through the fence and study you with those huge dark eyes. Sometimes they'd even nuzzle you with a massive wet nose and let you pet them.

"They're good for the soil," my grandpa always told us. He was primarily a crop farmer, but he believed in keeping a few cows. After the crops were harvested, he'd turn them out to graze on the stubble. Or he'd graze them on cover-crops in the off season. Their hooves would loosen up the soil and their waste provided natural fertilizer.

I was sad, that day, to see them gone.

When we arrived for our visit that April, we caught Grandad hard at work. As we drove in, he was over in front of the barn, still in his greasy work clothes, hunched over a hydraulic pump attached to his aging tractor. As he stood to greet us, he looked frustrated. He was holding a couple of end wrenches in one hand while shaking out the other in a manner that suggested he'd just painfully barked his knuckles. I'd have bet he'd just been swearing.

That pump was, apparently, much like the hydraulic equipment we used to drive the gurdies and anchor winch on the "Shirley J." Dad told me later that my granddad had bought the thing, used, from some neighbor three or four years before and that it had leaked oil from the start.

Dad was not always the most diplomatic of men. As we got out of the car, the first words out of his mouth were: "You know, Carl, those things aren't all that costly. You think maybe it's time to invest in a new one?"

Dad intended it as a friendly, masculine jest; a reminder of the comradeship between two men whose mechanical skills were essential to their occupations. But I could see Grandad glance in my direction and bite back his first response. Whatever that might have been, what he said was: "Well, hi there, Fran. Hi Sandy. It's great you could come." He picked up a rag and wiped his hands, as he led us over to the house. "Come on inside," he said smiling. "Nancy's cooking up a storm. Hope you guys had a good drive over."

That was typical of my grandfather. Who knows, maybe his was the genetic material that led me to become a lobbyist.

After we'd said a warm hello to my grandmother, she shooed us out of the kitchen saying she had a lot of work to do before dinner. Grandpa took Dad and me out for our customary walk around the farm. Grandpa had a route we followed that gave you a good view of most of his farming operation. I loved that walk; it followed a fence line down a shallow draw, and then turned up beside a small creek that ran along the base of a gentle, south-facing hillside.

It felt good to be walking through this carefully managed and cultivated land with a warm, Central Washington breeze ruffling your hair and nothing but the call of birds and burble of the creek to inhabit the quiet afternoon.

As we went, I noticed that the entire hillside above the creek was tilled and ready for planting to crops. This was a change from what I'd seen there in previous years. Grandpa had once explained, with some pride, why he contour-farmed that hillside and rotated the different areas between money-crops and the cover crops that renewed and secured the soil, captured sediment, and kept pollution out of the creek.

"Grandpa," I asked him. "Aren't you planting cover crops anymore?"

"Not this year, Sandy." It was all he said. There was something in his voice that kept me from asking why. My dad was a few steps ahead, looking off in another direction. Grandpa glanced at Dad, then up at that hillside, and then at me. After a moment's thoughtful pause, he nodded his head. "Come on, young fella," he said. "Duck pond's still here. Let's go take a look."

Later that night, after a nice dinner and a comfortable visit, as I lay awake in what had once been my mom's upstairs bedroom, I put it together. I was only fourteen, but my dad and I had been through enough tough times that I understood. That leaky hydraulic pump was just one of my granddad's many worries. There he'd been, on a Saturday morning, with visitors coming over, still outside in the barnyard working in his greasy overalls trying to repair some beat-up piece of worn-out, second-hand farm equipment. I knew that had nothing to do with a lack of hospitality. Or with Granddad being cheap. For Carl Folsom, making that pump last another season was a matter of necessity.

I also knew he'd been proud of those cows. He'd told me himself that they were a lot of extra work. Other than helping to restore the soil, they'd never financially supported themselves. My grandad insisted on keeping them, however, because he felt responsible for that land; said it was his duty to nurture and improve that soil for future generations of farmers.

He'd also been proud of his rotational contour farming on that hillside above the creek.

There was only one reason those cows were gone and that the entire hillside above the creek was tilled for crops. My grandparents were in financial trouble. When I'd asked about that hillside on our walk before dinner, I'd interpreted the look on his face as sadness. But later, as I lay in what had once been my mom's childhood bedroom and thought more carefully about it, I knew that look.

What I'd seen in my grandfather's face was shame.

CHAPTER FOUR

Monday, February 13, noon

New Business

STONEY MIGHT HAVE BEEN something OF a hobby-farmer, but most of his CHFA colleagues were serious growers—people who made their livings from agriculture, They were also farmers who believed in sound, environmentally responsible farm management. To be eligible for membership in their Conservation Heritage Farms Association (CHFA), each of them had been required to adopt a "full farm conservation management plan" that met the environmental quality criteria set by the USDA's Natural Resources Conservation Service.

The CHFA had been formed so it could credibly certify for its members that they had developed such a plan and that they managed their farm in "substantial compliance" with it. The farm could then use that official CHFA certification in its sales and marketing. Even some of the wholesale buyers and food processors had an environmentally sensitive customer base that wanted their food to be grown responsibly. For the smaller farmers who sold direct to the public, there was an impressive official placard they could mount near the entrance to their farms, at their booths at farmers markets and road-side stands, on-line in their websites, and in their print advertising for subscription produce sales and in other direct market venues.

A CHFA certification went far beyond the existing "organic" label that some of its members had also earned. There was a lot more to environmentally responsible farming than just avoiding artificial chemicals and pesticides. An "organic" farm, for example, wouldn't necessarily have adequate streamside buffers to protect salmon. It might still pollute streams with irrigation runoff, soil erosion, or poorly managed livestock waste. It might emit or fail to sequester atmospheric carbon, needlessly damage habitat for birds and other wildlife, worsen flooding, or waste scarce water resources.

CHFA-certified farms dealt with all those issues.

CHFA members were proud of their accomplishments, of course. They liked feeling good about their environmental stewardship. But, in the end, as with most things in agriculture, their world was driven by practicalities. What really made the difference was the market edge that CHFA certification provided.

For example, among the wholesale commercial buyers that saw the advantages of environmental marketing was a large farmer co-op food processor in the Othello area. One of the Co-op's best customers was a large, wholesale food-distributor, and among the distributor's regular clients were the cafeterias and food service providers at several Puget Sound area colleges and universities. The cafeteria managers at these institutions had met at a conference where they'd agreed to collectively ask their food distributors to provide "credible assurances" that their produce was environmentally responsible. The resulting pressure from the big distributors had, in turn, provided the Co-op with plenty of reason to encourage its farmer members to become CHFA-certified.

Not everyone was happy with CHFA, however. In lobbying this public-spirited bill, I found myself facing unusual pockets of resistance; I'd run into legislators who had questions about CHFA and about their motives. People I'd expected to be easy converts were proving difficult.

Lobbying through new legislation is never easy. I'd definitely expected some farmers to be uneasy about this bill. Most of them

22

probably liked things the way they were right now. They'd spent an entire professional career growing crops for a marketplace that rewarded production volume and that didn't much care how their crops were grown. They'd learned everything they could about how to generate copious harvests at minimum cost. When someone came along who suggested that *their* crop was better, more responsible, and maybe more deserving of purchase because it was grown to protect the environment, that wasn't going to gain many friends among these older, more traditional farmers. Many also believed all the new attention to environmental practices could end up generating a bunch of new regulations with which they'd find it costly to comply.

MOSTLY, I PUT THE PUSH-BACK I WAS GETTING down to simple conservatism—something I could overcome if I did my job right. But earlier that same day, I'd found myself in an early morning meeting with Senator Lance Chambers, an older, conservative Democrat from rural Pierce County who liked people to call him: "L.C." He was a guy I'd worked with a lot and someone whose vote and active support I was counting on when we got this thing over to the Senate.

"Yeah," he said before he was even fully seated behind his desk. "I know this bill. I didn't know you were on it though. He looked at me uncertainly. "It's a nice bill. Tight, clean, clear goals. Definitely seems like something that ought to happen . . ."

I could absolutely tell, there was a "but" coming. "But . . .?" I said.

L.C. sighed, "You know, last year, I made a big deal in my campaign about 'good government.' Ran against a real-estate broker who's been playing fast and loose with the realtor ethics for years—failing to disclose material facts, conflicts of interest, that kind of thing. He'd actually been sanctioned for it. It was the perfect campaign issue in a tough race. It worked, too. Here I am." He held out his hands to take in his small but richly furnished office in the Newhouse Senate Office Building.

Then he hesitated, but I knew what was coming. "Then you read the Seattle Times article about this Fortis Henry . . ?" I said, helpfully.

"The dairy farmer over in Yakima. Yeah. But it wasn't the Times. There's some watchdog group . . . the Truth Spotlight."

"Come on, L.C. That Truth Spotlight outfit is just a little one-man operation run out of somebody's spare bedroom over in Yakima. They probably got a dozen members, if that."

"It's all on their website, though. You've seen it, right? And there's a YouTube video."

Bless the internet, I thought. Anybody can raise hell anywhere if they've got a blog, a website, or a twitter account. "Have you even got any dairies in your district?" I asked. "Any agriculture at all?"

He nodded silently for a moment. "A couple . . . of farms, not dairies. This one guy just grows grass and sells hay. I think he's got a couple of goats. He's mostly just looking to take advantage of the agricultural current-use break on his property taxes. I do have this great little direct-market farm, though. Five acres or something along the highway into Tacoma, All organic. You can subscribe and they give you a box of vegetables every week all summer." His voice trailed off. He knew it was lame as he said it.

"One five-acre farm?" I said, "That's what you've got?"

He held up his hands. "I know, I know. But it's not about that, and you know it. Most of my constituents are urban or suburban. Office workers. Commuters who drive to Seattle or Tacoma every day. They've never heard of a conservation district. Have no clue what a conservation practice is or why you'd want to store manure in a big open lagoon in the first place."

He paused and pointed a long finger out his window to the north, in the direction of where I assume his legislative district was located. "I'll tell you what they do understand, though." He continued. "They understand graft. They know exactly what's going on when somebody who's elected to some government board pitches his own project and then sits back while his buddies vote it through knowing he'll do the same for them when their turn comes. They know when somebody is feathering their own nest with taxpayer money."

I was about to respond to that, but he got a second wind and cut me off.

"I'm sure your conservation heritage farmers are good guys. Probably deserve the help. But that dairy farmer, Henry, he had some stuff to answer for. Sounds like maybe he may have got what was coming to him. Those conservation districts you're counting on to help with all this, they have some stuff to answer for as well—this kind of thing has got to stop or nobody will trust government with anything. If I vote for your bill, at least right now, next election I'm the poor sap who's going to be standing up in front of a bunch of skeptical voters trying to explain it. Making a bunch of excuses for this guy Henry. I don't like the sound of that. And I'm not going to do it, either." He paused again, considering: "You need to find a way to get this done without using conservation districts," he said, shaking his head. "Do it through the Department of Agriculture. Or the Department of Ecology. Something like that. Maybe I can give it another look. Or just pull it. Bring it back next year—let things die down first."

He and I both knew there was no way any of that could happen. I asked him to keep the door open, and he said he would, at least until we got the bill over to the Senate. But he couldn't make any promises. I left his office knowing that was the best I was going to get until the whole Fortis Henry thing had dropped out of the news.

It all made me reflect again, as I had done several times during the weeks since he had died, on how very many people had been angry with this man and how many of them might now be secretly gleeful at his passing. I was momentarily startled at L.C.'s suggestion that Fortis Henry had perhaps "gotten what was coming to him." That was the first time I actually considered the possibility someone might have given him a push that day in December. There was, however, absolutely nothing to suggest that as possible and, as the balance of a busy day caught me in its grip, once again, I put it out of my mind.

LATER, IN THE COFFEE SHOP when I finally managed to get Stoney on topic, we were able to lay out a plan of action for the next day's hearing and for the days that followed. It needed to be good if we were to get this thing through House Agriculture and Natural Resources Committee and gain some new momentum before the next cutoff deadline in Rules.

I left the Capitol Deli that day, shaking my head. We'd been in there for nearly two hours to accomplish maybe a half-hour's work. Stoney acted like Fortis Henry had died on purpose, just to frustrate Stoney's plans.

Fortunately, at the time, at least, it all just seemed like it didn't really matter.

CHAPTER FIVE

Tuesday, February 14, 8 a.m.

Politics of Persuasion

66 **E**D NOWAK."

The Chair of the House Agriculture and Natural Resources Committee looked out over a packed hearing room for the next witness.

A large stooped man with snowy hair and a face like cracked leather had risen and was moving slowly up the aisle. He wore denim overalls and rubber knee-boots and he carried his "John Deere" baseball cap respectfully in his hands. When he sat down in the witness chair, he laid his hat carefully on the table beside the microphone.

"I been a long time in this business," he began, quietly. "It's been my life's work." He smiled sardonically and shrugged. "I been farming since I was a kid, so I guess that's sayin' something.

"Everything I got, everything I built, everything I ever cared about, it's all invested in my place, in my farm. Been right there my whole working life. My wife died there, few years back. We raised five good kids there. At this point I got grandkids, seems like, all over the country. None of them wants to be a farmer. I can understand that; it's tough work. A tough business."

The man had a presence. The room was going silent.

27

"I always treated my land as a kind of inheritance from the farmer I bought it from back after I returned from Korea in the fifties. I tried to make it a good, safe, healthy place for my family, for livestock, and for growing crops. Always kept our stream clean and safe for the fish. Left the gates open when the deer were moving through. Set up nesting poles here 'n there for hawks and such. Kept a good stand of trees that didn't need cutting. Kept hedgerows along the fence between my fields; birds 'n bees love 'em. Never used much in the way of pesticides either, not unless it was absolutely necessary. No use in killing stuff off you don't need to. And I always planted cover crops, kept the land healthy, protected the soil from washing away in the big rains and messing up the streams.

"Like I say, it's like an inheritance. My ownership there, it's just temporary. I always figured I wanted to make my place the best possible farm that it could be. Figured one day, I'd pass it along to another farmer, somebody who'd appreciate all the stuff I'd done. Somebody that'd be able to keep growing great food and who'd be better off 'cause I'd done all that.

"I'm from down outside Ridgefield. Lots of growth, down our way. Lots of homes, offices, shopping centers; lots of businesses coming in. It's all driving up the cost of land, including my farm."

The witness shook his head. "You'd probably figure that's a good deal, right? Makes my land worth more. But here's the thing. The only people that can afford to buy my land, now, are developers. I get calls from them all the time. And, you know, I'd love to sell. But if I sell to one of those guys, it makes all that stuff I've done over the years just stupid. Makes me ridiculous. Turns me into some kind of sap.

"What good was it? What was it all for? And what does it say to all those folks, now, that we're, all of us, depending on to do the right thing on *their* land today and in the years ahead?

"Those developers, first thing they'll do is 'doze off all that wonderful farm soil I've spent my life making richer. Cut down the trees I kept and the ones I planted. Knock over the barn. Barn's been there since the 1920s. You should see the timbers in that thing—big fifty footers, clear cedar. That barn, it'd be a goner. They'll build a bunch of roads, driveways, houses. Let me tell you—last thing our area needs is another freaking housing development, bunch more commuters crossing that bridge to Portland.

"Don't get me wrong, I'd love to retire." He held out his hands as if to present himself. "I need to retire. Those developers, they know I haven't got long. They'll just wait me out. One of these days I'll either give up or keel over. Doesn't matter to them; they win either way."

The audience in hearing room C was perfectly still. Even the young, digital types had put down their phones and were captivated by this witness. In the brief pauses in his testimony, you could hear the quiet hum of the air conditioner.

"So, here's the thing. This bill, this 'Conservation Heritage Priority Bill' you folks are lookin' at, this could change all that. I could apply for the Farmland Protection Program and get some extra credit for all the conservation practices I've been using all these years. I could sell an agricultural easement on my farm for enough to let me retire. And then I could sell my easement-protected farm to another farmer. A real farmer. Someone who can afford to pay the easement-restricted price and who would continue what I've started. Someone who will understand what I've done and take advantage of it, who'll keep looking out for the land and growing great local food and making it available for the people in all those houses they're building.

"That's why, when Sandy Dalton called me, couple of days ago, I decided to drive up here, today. Ask you folks, you legislators, to pass this bill. There's people exactly like me all over this state. A whole lot of us. We need this bill. I very much hope you'll pass it cause, for us, this may be the only way all that hard work, all that investment we've made over the years, investments in our farms, in the land, in what everybody now calls the 'environment,' the only way any of that makes any damn sense at all."

As Ed Nowak testified, I watched Stoney out of the corner of my eye. Nowak had Stoney's rapt attention. Stoney's feelings were obvious. Guys like Nowak were why Stoney had spent the past two years creating his Conservation Heritage Farms Association; they were the people he wanted to help. They were also my clients and they needed this bill.

Fortis Henry or not, there was just no way he and I were going to let those people down.

CHAPTER SIX

Tuesday, February 14, 10:20 a.m.

Revised Agenda

THE 8 A.M. HOUSE HEARING on our Conservation Heritage Priority Bill went nicely. After a few one-on-one meetings the previous afternoon with House Members, and then in the morning's well-attended, positive hearing, I had a good feeling about its chances of making it out of Committee. As the hearing ended, our assembled witnesses and supporters moved out into the hall for the inevitable after-action recapitulation. It was probably another half-hour before everyone had finally wound down and headed for home. I suddenly found myself alone in the downstairs hallway in the O'Brien Building. On impulse, I headed upstairs to the staff offices of House Technology and Economic Development Committee to see if I could catch up with Sherry.

Sherry Sebold and I had known each other during my early days in the practice of law before I was married. She was also a lawyer and was, at the time, clerking for Haley Powers, a well-respected King County Superior Court Judge. Sherry was the daughter of a career Army JAGC officer, and I was not long out of Navy JAGC myself when we first met, so we'd always had a lot to talk about. After law school, we'd dated briefly but our lives had moved on. She later ended up married to a biologist who worked for the

Department of Fish and Wildlife. When they moved to Olympia, Sherry had taken a job as staff counsel for several committees in the House of Representatives. I'd married Susan, lost her a year later to a drunken driver, and ultimately quit the law practice and taken up lobbying at the Legislature. Sherry and her biologist husband divorced, but she stayed on in Olympia. Sherry and I had, over the years since, become very good friends.

Sherry was one of the people, in this competitive town, whose judgment I trusted—always an island of calm in the often-frenetic legislative staff offices. From time to time we would get together over lunch to talk statehouse politics. More recently, now that her young son David was getting older and she could entrust his care to a sitter, we would also get together for dinner. It helped, in this line of work, to have colleagues whose judgment you trusted and with whom you could occasionally share policy ideas and, more than occasionally, also gossip.

I wanted to ask her about the previous day's hearing in House Technology and Economic Development. I was still curious about Maryanne Henry; I hadn't really been paying attention when Maryanne had testified on that High-Tech Education bill. I wanted to see who she'd indicated she represented when she'd signed up to speak; why had she come all the way over to Olympia from Yakima to testify on that bill. It wasn't all that surprising, I supposed. But, still, her changed appearance, the seeming "new life direction," it all just struck me as odd. I guess I just can't help it; I tend to follow up on impulses like that. Sometimes you can learn something that later turns out to be worth knowing.

Maryanne Henry's witness sign-up indicated she'd been representing a group called the Washington Association of Secondary Educators. I wasn't familiar with the group, but Maryanne's active involvement in what appeared to be a professional teachers organization suggested she hadn't quit her teaching or volunteer advocacy to run the farm herself. I wished I'd paid more attention to her testimony the day before, but I'd been more concerned about my own upcoming hearing with the fishermen and about what I needed to learn from Stoney than about what Maryanne Henry had been saying up at the witness table.

I found Sherry in her office. She was busy, as usual, but when she returned with the sign-in sheets I'd asked for, we arranged to get together at noon for lunch.

I WAS BACK DOWN IN THE LOWER HALL on my way out of the building when I glanced at the notice placard outside Hearing Room C and saw that that that the House Local Government Committee was in session. Representative Rob Thomas was a member of that committee and I realized that this might be as good a chance as any to catch up with him. Now that our Conservation Heritage Priority Bill was out of its subject-matter Committee, I was counting on Rep. Thomas to help me slip it through Rules Committee and then lead debate on the House floor. I also recalled his critical tone toward Fortis Henry at Denny's following Fortis's death and, I'll admit, I was a bit curious about what might have been behind that.

There was another reason to step inside as well. There was another bill on the Committee's calendar that I was tracking. While I awaited my chance to catch Rep. Thomas, I might as well check out what was happening on the Conservation District Elections bill. It wasn't a bill with which my clients were directly involved, but it was one that might have an important bearing on our success.

The conservation districts were a key ally on our Conservation Heritage Priority Bill. I knew they were struggling over their Commission's budget appropriation. I was already worried that their preoccupation with their budget problem might dilute their commitment to our bill, but it wasn't just the budget they needed to worry about. The districts had this other bill that was also causing them grief, a bill to reform conservation district elections.

Of the five members of each District Board of Supervisor, two were appointed by the Conservation Commission, but the other three were publicly elected. The committee hearing that day was all about how those three elected supervisors got their jobs. I took a seat in the back of the room and tuned in to see what I could learn while I awaited my chance to catch Rep. Thomas on his way back upstairs to his office after the hearing.

Rep. Thomas turned out to be one of only four of the seven Members of the Local Government Committee who had deigned to make themselves present for the Hearing. But the hearing room was nearly filled with spectators, something the absentee legislators perhaps hadn't anticipated. It looked like the conservation districts were deeply engaged on this legislation and had pulled out all the stops to kill it. As I listened to the testimony, it became increasingly clear that the districts had their hands full. Most of those present in that room did *not* see things their way. Notably, among those present was the Executive Director for "Truth Spotlight" who'd apparently driven over from Yakima to testify. And he wasn't alone; he'd enlisted the help of other "good government" groups who saw the elections bill as a chance to "strengthen our representative democracy." There were also a few individual farmers and landowners, "renegades" as the districts would see them, who wanted it to be known that they, too, supported this bill.

Clearly, reform was in the wind, and the districts weren't at all sure they wanted it.

Conservation district supervisors were not elected as part of the State's usual general elections process. Instead, district Supervisor elections were conducted entirely by the districts themselves in small, sometimes poorly publicized, local elections. Thus, you wouldn't find district supervisors listed on the general election ballot with candidates for other common positions like school board, city council, state legislature, etc. They were held on separate dates. Ballots didn't go out by mail—often, voters were required to show up in person on election day and fill out a ballot right at the district's little-known local office.

The public was often largely unaware of these elections.

Sometimes there were district elections held in communities with tens of thousands of residents, but only a few dozen people might actually show up and cast votes. A candidate could win by simply turning out their close friends and relatives. There was little or no "electioneering," little public attention and debate and, as some of the people in that room saw it, little genuine accountability to the electorate.

Needless to say, in addition to screwing things up for my Conservation Heritage bill, Fortis Henry's horrible accident, and the resulting public controversy over the use of public money to pay for his dairy lagoon, was also feeding the push for the proposed election reforms.

The bill was simple: district elections would henceforth be included on the general election ballot. District supervisors would be required to mount a campaign for election in the same manner as most other candidates for public office. The proponents argued that it was time to end the network of "old boys" that reigned over local conservation districts around the state. It was time to shed the "light of day" on district activities, activities like deciding who might get public money to build a nice new dairy lagoon.

When the Committee had completed its hearing and had moved on to another matter, the supporters and opponents of the elections bill moved out into the hall. There, the discussion became heated. I saw Ronnie Johnson, the lightly built, bespectacled, studious-looking Executive Director of Truth Spotlight, standing with his back to the marble wall facing three incensed opponents of the bill. One of them was definitely "in his face." The man was big, red-faced, and angry. He was jabbing a forefinger into Johnson's chest as he spoke.

"You should mind your own goddammed business, you stupid little shit," I heard the man say before he and his two friends turned their backs and stalked off toward the exit.

This kind of thing wasn't common at the Capitol, but I'd seen it before. The legislative process might be formal, but this place was not a church, or even a courthouse. It was all about politics. There was little pretense here of fairness. People could become overwhelmed by their frustrations. Seeing that little interchange reminded me how matters of public policy could stir up very strong emotions.

It was still well before noon when the Committee recessed. I caught up with Rep. Thomas as he stepped out into the hall through the Member's entrance. He said he was happy to talk; could take a few extra minutes before he needed to buckle down and spend some time in his office studying a few unfamiliar bills over a bag lunch.

As well as being a respected farmer from deeply agricultural Yakima County, Rep. Thomas also headed up the local, Yakima Valley chapter of the Washington State Agriculture Industry Council. There had, therefore, been two good reasons Stoney and I had invited him to our meeting that December day in Yakima: we wanted him to co-sponsor our bill, which he had kindly agreed to do. We also wanted his help within WSAIC. The approach had worked, at least partly. He and Linda Cunningham had, at least, kept WSAIC from actively and officially opposing our proposal. That was something to be thankful for.

Rob Thomas had been Fortis Henry's neighbor and his brother-in-law. Rob was also a third-generation orchardist with a spread along the Yakima River maybe two or three miles downriver from the Henry Dairy. Rob Thomas was a conservative Republican—conservative, that is, by the standards that had prevailed up until the reengineering of the Republican Party that accompanied the Trump election in 2016. Ordinarily, only a Republican would ever be elected from Washington's 15th Legislative District. From everything I could see, Rep. Thomas served his constituents well. He'd just been elected to his third term in office. None of that, however, made his position secure. Quite the contrary. In recent years, primary challenges had become common. Incumbency in Republican districts could be the kiss of death. There was no love of "government" in rural Yakima County, and no love for anyone in office even though the voters had themselves put them there.

I knew all this, at least intellectually, as I sat down across a neat desk in Rep. Thomas's office on the fourth floor of the O'Brien Building. He was one of those pleasant, clean-cut, dependable-looking guys that seem, so often, to make such great political candidates. In the past, I'd found him outgoing and friendly. Usually I'd found him confident and talkative. But today, he was mostly silent on the elevator ride up. He seemed depressed. I considered him a friend so once his office door had closed and we were in private I probably spoke more freely than I would have with someone else.

Even so, I wasn't prepared for his vehement response to what I thought was a casual, supportive comment: "Very nice win last fall, by the way," I said.

"Hah," he said with sudden passion. "Going to be my last! I'm four months in and they're already plotting my defeat next time around. I have two publicly announced challengers in next year's primary. Two! Christ's sake, this year's session is hardly even started!" He grabbed a water bottle from a little box next to his desk and took a swig. "One's a freaking radio host—big name, all talk. Right winger. Already getting money from out of state. And from some of my best contributors—guy's raised over $100 grand and the campaign's still more than a year away. Can you believe that?"

I had to admit, it seemed unusual. I guess I must have looked puzzled.

"Big anti-corruption push," he explained. "What corruption? Fortis freaking Henry and his damnable waste pond." He took another swig from his water bottle, then thumped it down on his desk and leaned back in his chair looking very glum.

In today's climate, having a well-known, well-funded right-wing primary challenger could easily be enough to send Rep. Rob Thomas back to growing tree fruit full time. His little diatribe, however, suggested that there might be more to his situation than I'd been thinking. Rep. Rob Thomas was married to Fortis Henry's younger sister, Marta. That kind of connection seemed typical, to me; an illustration of how power in rural communities often tends to run in the family. Nothing sinister there. I could, however, imagine how Fortis Henry's "scandal" might be used in a political campaign to paint a member of even his extended family. Still, I wondered if voters would really blame a person for what their brother-in-law did?

Then, suddenly, I understood. "Ah," I said. "District elections." It was one of those moments I particularly enjoy, the tiny thrill as pieces of someone's life suddenly come together to explain their thinking.

"Uh huh," he said, with a sardonic nod. "I've been trying for the past month to get Robbie to turn that damn bill down for a hearing." Rep. Robbie Flores was the Chair of House Local Government Committee. "Before that, I tried to get leadership to refer it to 'State Government and Elections.' Bill's about 'elections,' right? But no way. It's Local Government, they said. And last Friday, Robbie puts it up for this damn hearing. You heard them in there earlier. What a mess."

I was starting to see what he might be talking about. In a few days, he was going to have to cast a committee vote on the district elections bill.

"It isn't ready," he said. "Do you know what it costs for a small municipal government to have its elections on the general ballot? Can be hundreds of thousands. Could be more than the entire budget of a good many of our smaller conservation districts. Maybe most of them. For some of these districts, volunteers provide a big percentage of their labor. The State money they get to keep operating is critical for them but, for the State, it amounts to little more than budget dust. Many times, all they get is a grant or two from the Conservation Commission. They can't afford to pay for full-fledged elections. Don't need 'em. Putting them on the general ballot will put a lot of them out of business; that simple."

I must have looked uncertain, so he continued: "Elections are expensive. They're partly funded by the governments that participate, that have candidates or measures on the ballot. Think about the organizing, electronics and equipment, printing, mailing, counting, publicity, security. It adds up. Local governments pay based on their share of the cost. It gets to be a lot of money."

I hadn't thought about that. It seemed like a darn good argument against the bill.

"It also isn't needed," he continued. "There's a whole Administrative Code Title that deals with how conservation districts run elections. It's all spelled out. And the Commission has a detailed manual outlining policies and practices that make sure it's all fair and open. They're doing just fine."

I was also reasonably sure most current conservation district supervisors would prefer not to have to go through the full elections process; probably why CDSW was carefully opposing the bill.

One of the main advantages to running for Conservation District Supervisor was that it was easy. Didn't require a lot of endorsements, contributors, advertising, speeches, and campaigning. In smaller districts, you just collected the 10 signatures to put your name on the ballot and then made sure your friends showed up to vote. In larger, more urban districts, it was a bit more involved, but not nearly so difficult as running for most other public offices. Smaller districts sometimes had a hard time finding people to run as it was. Some could end up with no candidates.

Conservation district supervisors were influential people in their local communities, very often successful farmers. I was quite sure Rob would rather not buck them.

Then I remembered a conversation I'd had with Sherry over coffee a few months earlier. I'd said something, probably inane, about Rob Thomas seeming like too "nice a guy" for politics. Then I'd noticed her look.

"What?" I said. "Is there something I don't know?"

"Well, maybe just that it isn't him that actually holds that seat in the House of Representatives."

"I don't understand."

"Rob Thomas is mostly just a tie rack," she said. "You didn't know this? It's all about his wife, Marta. She runs things. She manages his campaigns, writes his speeches, decides on strategy. She makes as many public appearances as he does. She absolutely raises the vast majority of his campaign money."

"Really?"

"I thought you knew all this."

I did know Marta Thomas was an important figure in Yakima County social circles. Apparently she was also a lot like her ambitious older brother, Fortis Henry.

As I shook Rob Thomas's hand and left his office that day, the recollection of what Sherry had told me made me realize just what he was up against. Fortis's "misuse of power" scandal was, no doubt, very embarrassing for Rob's socially-connected wife. She'd be the first to understand how this elections bill was likely a direct outgrowth of her brother's "scandal." She'd probably see it as an insult to Fortis's memory. Marta Thomas must certainly be expecting her husband to vote against it.

Rob was in a box. When the Committee Chair brought that bill up in Executive Session later this week, Rob was going to have to cast a vote. If he voted to favorably refer it out, he would anger a lot of his friends among the conservation districts, people with whom he'd worked closely for years. And he would surely anger his wife. If he voted to kill it, he'd be handing his right-wing primary opponent a deadly weapon to use against him a year from now. I could easily visualize the headlines and the campaign ad: "Rep. Rob Thomas' vote fuels his family's corrupt business." An easy claim to make. A complicated one to refute.

There would, no doubt, be some stress in the Thomas household over the next few days.

CHAPTER SEVEN

Tuesday, February 14, 12:20 p.m.

Reassessing Strategy

SHERRY WORKED OUT OF A TINY SPACE tucked away in a back corner of the committee staff offices on the second floor of the O'Brien Building. Her desk was pushed up against the wall opposite the always-open door so her back was to me when I arrived. She kept a neatly organized work-space with her laptop in a little docking stand that allowed her to use one of those ergonomic keyboards when she was at her desk. A small charging cradle for her phone stood next to her computer. There was some section of the Revised Code of Washington up on her computer screen. She was hard at work when I arrived, oblivious, I think, to the time or to the fact that I was a few minutes late.

"Hard at it?" I said.

She looked up at me, glanced at her watch, grabbed her phone and stood. "Sometimes harder than it ought to be," she said smiling and pulling her jacket off a rack behind the door. As we stepped out of her office, she glanced up and down the hall. The place was deserted during the lunch break. "I'm supposed to advise these committees on the anticipated legal impact of proposed legislation," she said. Then, lowering her voice, she added: "But sometimes they'd really rather not know."

41

Sherry worked for the State Legislature but, in practical reality, she answered to the Committee Chairs. She'd managed to keep her job through both Republican and Democratically controlled Legislatures; no small feat. She didn't elaborate and I didn't ask for an explanation. She knew I knew enough to fill in the spaces. It was one of the things that made our get-togethers enjoyable; something we both understood.

During our short walk down Capitol Way together, I must have seemed distracted. "Hey," Sherry said with a smile, tapping her forehead and then pointing at mine. "What's going on in there?"

I laughed. "Sorry," I said. "Not much, probably. I just had a couple of odd meetings. Reminded me of that ugly business last winter. Fortis Henry. Guess I'm still not over it."

"I wouldn't be," she said. "Not something that happens every day."

"I didn't care for the man, but his dairy farm was something," I said. "After the accident we ended up standing around a lot and got a good look at the operation. Amazing place. Every cow has a tracker that transmits its exact location to a computer. You can tell how much time each individual cow spends eating. How much milk it produces. Its weight. Where it goes and how active it is. They're all recorded on video so you can find them and see what they were doing during any particular part of the day. You can click on any individual cow and it will bring up graphs showing everything about it. With all that, you can tell how healthy it is and deal with issues before they become problems. All very cool."

We were inside the little coffee shop by then. Sherry nodded as she tossed her bag on the seat beside her and sat down at the narrow booth. "Sounds very cool," she said, grinning at me like she often did when she teased me.

The menus were all decorated with hearts and cupids in celebration of Valentine's day. I saw Sherry glance at it and then pointedly ignore it. Both of us were single, but we'd kept our relationship comfortably professional. Neither of us really wanted to change that.

"Speaking of cool," I said, teasing her back, "what's going on in the fascinating world of Technology and Economic Development? Is the Fortuna package still on track?" Most of what I'd been thinking about for the past few weeks was Fortis Henry and this bill; I could use the change of topic.

"Looks like it," she said. "Aaron Nicolaides and my boss are certainly tight. I'm pretty sure Drum will move anything Nicolaides asks for." Several of Fortuna's legislative incentive proposals for their big computer center in Eastern King County had necessarily passed through Sherry's Committee. Smart lobbyist and former House Speaker that he was, I would have bet Nicolaides, who was again leading Fortuna's effort, would have made sure he had her Economic Development Committee Chairman, Rep. Thomas Drum's, support sewed up before he ever got started.

"They're persistent, I'll say that. When Fortuna's incentive proposals fell apart a couple of years back, I figured the whole thing would disappear."

"So did I. Business opportunities in high tech tend to be fleeting. Not this time, I guess. It's always nice to get a boost from the government."

I was silent for a moment, looking out the window at some passing pedestrians. Sherry took a bite of her sandwich and glanced thoughtfully in my direction. "You know, the fact that you didn't like somebody, doesn't mean you're required to feel guilty when they die," she said in a perceptive change of topic.

She'd read me like a book; knew immediately that my "interest" in Fortuna was just cover, that my mind had wandered back to Fortis Henry. The more I tried to avoid thinking about that December day in Yakima, the more I kept picturing him floating in that lagoon. It was difficult to erase recalling my uncharitable reaction to it. "It's true, I never liked the man," I said. "All about his own agenda. I knew we had to work with him on Stoney's bill. Part of the reason Stoney and I decided to suggest meeting at Fortis's dairy was to keep him feeling important while making it easy for him to join us. But I'd have avoided him if I could."

"I can't imagine what you could have done to change what happened."

She was right, but the whole thing just kept nagging at me. "He did try to talk Stoney out of hiring me." There wasn't much I hadn't discussed with Sherry of late. Her level-headed practicality helped me think things through, both professional and personal.

"Even so."

"He told Stoney to steer clear of someone who worked for people that earned their livings catching the same salmon that farmers were being 'put out of business to protect.' Thought I'd have a conflict." What Fortis Henry had apparently not understood, but Stoney had—maybe because his son was a fisherman—was that both farmers and fishermen had an interest in healthy salmon runs. It might be for different reasons, but problems for both increased as those runs declined. Both faced regulations designed to prevent those declines. Both had an interest in the success of those regulations. And, anyway, my brief for the commercial fishing industry had never included working environmental preservation. My fishermen worked those issues for themselves.

"Uh huh." Sherry was playing me—getting me to talk out what was bothering me. I ignored it. Or, maybe, I just fell for it.

"At least I wasn't alone in disliking the guy." I'd already told Sherry about our unsuccessful meeting at Denny's following Fortis's death.

"Speaking of which," she said. "I guess you know, Lou Dwyer's in my mystery book club."

I did. "Women of Mystery" they called it.

"I don't think she liked Fortis Henry at all."

"She say something to you about it?"

"Not really. But after you and I talked about that accident, I mentioned it to her. It was just a brief exchange, but she said something like: 'Couldn't have happened to a nicer guy.' Sarcastic, you know. A bit mean; she's usually a lot more tactful. Considering the circumstances . . . I just don't think she liked him at all."

I'd largely forgotten about Lou Dwyer's reaction that afternoon at Denny's. I wondered what Fortis Henry and Lou Dwyer could have had going on to put them at odds. A lot of conservative farmers didn't like the Washington Wildlife and Recreation Program. It was more a matter of principle than of self-interest; WWRP was the State agency that made land purchases for recreation and the environment. Conservatives just didn't like public purchases of private land—whatever the reason. Or maybe she and Fortis had crossed swords somewhere—Lou tended to get quite involved in local politics, backing legislative candidates that supported WWRP. Anyway, I'd believed Fortis was more of a moderate than that. It didn't really make sense.

"Eat your sandwich," she said. I hadn't even seen it arrive. I took a dip, and a bite. The French dips were usually quite good, but I hardly noticed. Once again, I'd been drawn into thinking more about the day Fortis Henry died.

"I will say, the man ran a tight ship," I said, remembering their perfect family home, the clean paved drive and parking lot, the carefully tended feed lot and dairy barn, the high-tech livestock tracking, and that spiffy, brand-new dairy lagoon. "He dressed like a dude. At least whenever I saw him. Him and that classy hat. That day had been the first time I'd ever seen his home and dairy farm. Really nice place." I took another bite.

"You've got nothing to feel bad about. You know that, right?"

There had been something about that day, about finding Fortis Henry's body, that had been niggling at my subconscious ever since. Suddenly it hit me: "He was wearing his damned hat even when he died," I said. "It's strange. Who does that? Who the hell wears a $600, white Stetson cowboy hat to do some chore out in the back lot of a working dairy farm?" I said. "Just stupid. Vain."

"Uh huh."

I gave it some more thought. "Thing was spotless. When he fell in the lagoon, it landed upright. Pond wasn't covered yet; it was open to the air. Even with the rain, it had this crusty, ugly surface. It could have come straight from a hat shop. Not a spot on it."

Sherry gave that some thought. "What's his wife like," she asked.

"I don't know. Nice, I guess. Very homey, comfortable. I was a little surprised that she showed up at that hearing yesterday; it's why I was curious to see your sign-in sheet. She looked a lot more, I don't know, professional than I'd recalled. Still, she does keep a clean, orderly house, I can say that."

"Seems like she might have had something to say about her husband wearing his good clothes to work out in the barn."

"You'd think. He was, of course, expecting us, expecting company. Maybe just went out there to deal with some simple chore at the waste lagoon. I met the daughter; seems nice. His crew were mostly off. The couple of guys that were at work that day were out on some errand."

"So, he grabs his best Stetson hat to go out to fix something at his waste pond?"

"Doesn't feel right."

She took a sip of her lemonade and then reached over to touch my hand. "Shouldn't make too much of it. People are strange," she said.

It was enough to make me relax. "I guess they are," I said, grinning. "Even people you think you know." Then I steered the conversation around to more comfortable, less troubling topics like the upcoming operating budget negotiations and, for a few minutes at the end, about Sherry's young son David and our dinner plans for the weekend after next.

We were back on the hill by just after one.

CHAPTER EIGHT

Tuesday, February 14, 4:30 p.m.

Off-Calendar Encounter

DESPITE A BUSY AFTERNOON, I found myself unable to push aside my troubled thoughts about Fortis Henry's death. There was the manner of his demise, of course. No one could have seen his lifeless body dragged up out of that horrible waste lagoon and not have been affected by it. There was my personal guilt over my own troubling reaction to his death in the moment of his discovery. I was bothered by the strangeness of that spotless, white Stetson hat I'd seen resting on the surface of the filthy pond.

Maybe I should have seen it all sooner. In my own defense, when we found him, that day, it seemed so obviously an accident. The police thought the same thing. There wasn't a single reason to suspect otherwise.

It was, however also, somehow, unsettling to consider how the man had been so universally disliked. Apparently, Lou Dwyer was not a fan. I recalled Lou's unfavorable comment at our gathering at Denny's after Fortis died. And, from what she'd said to Sherry, it sounded like Lou might harbor some serious animosity.

I liked Lou. Despite my worries, she and her organization had turned out to be a solid ally in our fight to pass our Conservation

Heritage Priority Bill. Her employer, the Washington Association for Wildlife and Recreation (WAWR), was one of the preeminent groups that supported and fought for the Washington Wildlife and Recreation Program. We'd have been nowhere without them.

Fortunately, Lou and her colleagues had seen a solid political benefit in our bill. If it passed, certified Conservation Heritage Farmers would be taking increased advantage of WWRP's farm-land protection program and she'd have secured their likely future support, a new political beachhead for her organization within the ag community.

Lou and I had been in close contact over the past couple of months. Even so, I might have forgotten all about Sherry's comments over lunch if I hadn't run into Lou herself later that same afternoon. I'd scheduled several appointments with Members of the Senate Natural Resources Committee regarding a commercial fisheries bill I was working. The last of these meetings was at 4 p.m. with Senator Jimmy Fang who'd taken over as Natural Resources Chair when Abel Mortenson died a couple of years earlier. As I stepped out of Senator Fang's office up in the Cherberg Building, there was Lou, seated in the hall, awaiting her own appointment with a Senator in the office next door. As usual, she somehow looked slightly disheveled—maybe it was her vaguely offbeat hair-style. In every other regard her appearance was conservative and impeccable. She also looked very solemn with her face buried in the back pages of *The Daily Olympian*.

"Bad news?" I said, pointing at the paper.

She looked up and grinned. "Of course," she said. "Politics is always bad news for somebody. Even when you win you figure it cost too much."

I could hear muffled but intense-sounding voices emerging from the next office. The Admin wasn't there, had maybe gone home for the day. "Headed in there?" I asked.

"I hope so," she replied, glancing at a clock mounted on the wall. "Doesn't sound like it's going be any time soon."

"Gets serious around here sometimes."

"Could be worse." She looked around." All things considered, not a bad place to earn your keep."

I couldn't help comparing my clean, comfortable work life with what many of my farming and fishery clients did for a living. "With any luck," I said, "We won't be finding any bodies today."

That generated a quick, strained snort of laughter. She pointed at the closed office door from which we could still hear what sounded like a contentious discussion. "Hopefully not," she said with an exaggerated eyebrow wiggle.

"Speaking of which . . ," I said, sitting in a nearby chair. "I guess we all had some issues with Fortis Henry. I gather you two weren't on really great terms."

That caused her to lay down her newspaper, She looked surprised, maybe at me bringing it up. Then she considered. "Not so much," she said. She didn't ask me how I knew. Maybe her feelings weren't much of a secret.

"I've been thinking about him, lately," I said. "His death, and some of the stuff he was up to before he died. It's still having some impact."

She leaned back with a sardonic laugh. "I've heard. Gotta say, didn't surprise me."

"What was it all about? Your issue."

She glanced at the wall clock, then at the closed door. Then: "He didn't like having the farmland program in WWRP. You know we've got this percentage limit, right? In the statute."

I did. There was a formula for how much of total WWRP appropriations went for farmland protection. It was something like 9% of appropriations over $50 million. Of late the typical appropriation been at about $100 million, so that provided roughly $4.5 million for protecting farmland each biennium. Not a lot, but a great deal better than nothing.

"He thought it was much too little," she continued. "He wanted to create a new, completely separate program under the Conservation Commission or in the Department of Agriculture. One that would be solely about protecting commercially valuable farmland. They could then grow their program in the future without being constrained by some fixed percentage share of our appropriation."

"And your Association didn't like that because . . ." The minute I asked, I knew the answer. A new, separate program would spawn its own, separate, supportive constituents—some of whom could be peeled away from Lou's Association; including the very same farmers her group had counted on to help them support WWRP in rural communities. If Fortis's new program was successful, it would almost certainly become a competitor for scarce State land conservation dollars, drawing financial support away from WWRP in the biennial appropriations battles. A new program could also look very much like a model to other groups and interests within WAWR, people who, given a successful example to follow, might also decide to split away and go it on their own. It could all end up fragmenting the powerful collaboration that had been so successful, over the years, in providing political support for WWRP.

She watched me figure it out. "Yeah," she said. "Not great for the acclaimed Washington land conservation coalition."

"My impression was he was with us on the Conservation Heritage Priority Bill," I said.

"He'd have backed it," she said. "Just thought it was a baby step. Wanted to do a lot more. And without farmers having to adopt a bunch of conservation practices. Thought his farmers could get conservative, farm community support for new, separate state money for farmland only. He figured he could get some votes from both sides of the aisle and make it happen."

Personally, I thought it sounded like a great idea. I didn't say so, however.

She motioned at me with the folded newspaper she still held in her hand. "Your friend Stoney? You know he's a long-time member of American Farmland Trust. Their whole mission is protecting agricultural lands from development. I'm sure they're with you on your bill, right?"

"They are. Terrific organization. They're a big help."

"Well even they are a part of our WAWR coalition. They'd love to have more money for agricultural easements. But they know they'll need our coalition, ultimately, to get it."

"But not Fortis, apparently."

"If Fortis had been interested," she continued, "I'd have actually helped him work within our coalition for a larger percentage. He had some political capital to offer. That's something I could see. But that wasn't what he wanted. If he'd still been around when this year's Session started, and if he hadn't been discredited like he was over that dairy lagoon thing, we'd definitely have seen his bill pop up somewhere. As it is, it looks like the bill died with him, if we're lucky."

"Hell of a thing," I said. "Finding him in that damn waste pond was not one of the finer experiences of my life."

"Me neither. Did you drive over that day from Seattle?"

"Yeah. Miserable drive. How about you?"

"Same. Only I had to come from down here in Olympia. Would have gone over highway 12, but it was closed with the snow. I was probably on I-90 same time as you. When'd you get there?" She asked.

"Quarter to ten. Something like that."

"I was ahead of you, there by half past nine. I think I was first."

"Did you see Fortis before he disappeared out back?"

"Just missed him. Maryanne brought me a cup of coffee. She said Fortis had been down the hill to a grocery in that little cluster of businesses by the freeway exit. Picked up a few snacks for our meeting, came back and left them for her on the dining room table. Then he'd apparently gone out back for some reason. It had stopped raining by then. Made myself comfortable on their nice warm sofa by the fire and that incredible Christmas tree and drank my coffee. After that miserable drive, I was just damned happy to be there."

I'd had a shorter drive that she had. Still, I knew how she felt. With all the rain, it had been an unpleasant way to spend what might otherwise have been, for both of us, a nice stay-at-home, New Year's Eve Saturday morning.

And it had all ended up being a waste. By the time Fortis's body had been removed and all the official stuff with the Sheriff's deputies was over, we'd been well past noon. Given how we all felt, it should have been obvious that meeting at Denny's was going to be a failure.

It had been a better day for us, though, than it had turned out to be for Fortis Henry.

MY OFFICE IS IN AN OLDER HOUSE I own in a residential district in Olympia. I recently rented out a remodeled upstairs apartment and run my lobbying operation out of the main floor. It serves the purpose nicely. The living room makes a great waiting and reception area. The dining room is perfect for a conference table where I can meet with clients. There are three downstairs bedrooms that serve as offices. And it's just a couple of blocks away from the Capitol Campus. Now that I have a young couple as upstairs tenants, I'm getting a good chunk of my mortgage payments covered as well.

That evening, I was late getting back to the office and then worked well past dinner. I ordered in Chinese and, rather than make the long drive to Seattle, I stayed over on the bed that's tucked in among some filing cabinets in a back bedroom. That gave me an early start the next day. There was a lot going on, and Wednesday flew by as well. It wasn't till late Thursday that I finally managed to finish early enough to head home to Seattle for the evening. I was on the road just in time to catch the worst of the northbound evening traffic.

CHAPTER NINE

Thursday, February 16, 7 p.m.

Strategic Advice

MY HOUR-LONG COMMUTE between Seattle and Olympia was not my favorite time of the day. When the Legislature was in Session and I had to work late or attend an early meeting, I frequently stayed over in Olympia. But our Legislature only met for three to five months each year. The rest of the time I worked out of the small home office in my urban condominium in Seattle's Belltown area.

I liked Olympia. But during the majority of the year, when the Legislature was not in Session. there was no real reason I needed to be there. Besides, Seattle was slightly more convenient to my clients and their business. There were also, of course, some advantages to living in a large, urban center. I'd never quite convinced myself to move down to the Capital permanently.

Another reason I made my home in Seattle was because of my father.

My dad was getting older, maybe a bit too old to be driving that big, heavy, 42' commercial fishing boat solo to Southeast Alaska and back every year. It was a thousand miles from Seattle to Northern Southeast where my dad liked to fish. At eight knots, and if you anchored up at night, it was a rugged ten-day trip. That assumed the weather was reasonably nice. which it never was. He generally figured on about two weeks of travel, but some years it ran to over three. That trip, plus all the fishing, would be a big deal for anyone; but it was especially tough for a man over seventy.

I'll admit, he had it all down to a science. He'd done it year after year, since before I was born. I, sure as hell, wasn't going to change his mind if he was determined to keep at it. Of course, if everything went right, I knew he could keep fishing for some years to come. That did not, however, keep me from worrying. My dad was the first to teach me that things don't always go as planned at sea— or anywhere else for that matter.

It'd been awhile since I'd seen him and I decided it would be good to check in.

He had the boat hauled out at a marina on the Ballard waterfront. It was getting dark as I walked into the boatyard. The "Shirley J" was easy to spot, cribbed up high-and-dry at the far end of the paved yard. She's a typical West Coast commercial troller, wood, an Ed Monk design. She may have been a bit stodgy by modern, pleasure boat standards. But, with her modestly flared bow, her upswept, nicely curved transom stern, and her perfect seven-window, curved-front pilothouse, she was nothing less than "sweet" judged as a commercial fishing vessel.

But then I'd known her for as long as I'd lived. So, OK, maybe I was biased.

There was my dad, standing under the stern, the area around him all lit up by a string of bright work lights. Typical. He never let something like a dying sun slow him down. He was bolting new zincs to the sides of the steel rudder. The big, powerful, bronze propeller was all polished up and I recalled that he'd planned to get it looked at after hitting a chunk of drift on the trip down through Canada last fall. The bottom of the boat was freshly coated in bright red antifouling paint. I knew Dad would have done that job himself; there was no way he'd hire something like that out if he didn't have to.

You couldn't tell he'd been painting, however, from looking at him. As usual, hardly a drop had gotten on his overalls. He is an amazing craftsman and mechanic; can do almost anything with his hands. But for me, his most amazing talent is that he'll do the messiest, most difficult tasks and, somehow, never get dirty. It's a trait that was decidedly not passed on to his son.

"You think it might be time to call it good for the evening?" I said, nodding westward toward the fading glow of a fallen sun.

He took another tug on the wrench that secured his new zincs, squinted at the sky, took up a rag and wiped his hands. "Your timing's perfect," he said. "Eaten dinner?"

"Nope."

He reached up over his head and knocked a couple of times on the wood hull. "This thing's here till morning. Not all that, uh, 'habitable' at the moment. How 'bout the Salmon Bay Café?"

Just a couple of blocks up the Ballard waterfront, the Salmon Bay Café was a local institution. Great food and a "real deal" commercial fisher/maritime worker hangout.

Dad motioned for me to wait, climbed up a ladder to the deck of the boat, a good ten feet above the paved yard, and was back down a moment later. The only thing I could see that he'd changed was his hat, a nice fresh, clean "General Motors Diesel" baseball cap to replace the identical but older, well-worn one he'd been wearing to work on the boat. Now that he was properly attired, he was ready to go. We walked the couple of blocks up Shilshole Avenue to the restaurant.

"So, what brings you by, son," Dad asked me once we were settled. "Got something on your mind? Or are you just checking up on your old pop?"

Both, I thought. I took a sip of my water, studying the clean "GMC Diesel" baseball cap beside his plate. "You ever think about getting a nicer hat?" I said.

He looked at me strangely. "Why the hell would I want to do that?"

I shrugged. "I dunno, just to wear something nicer maybe? Like if you were getting dinner with your friends or something?" I suppose I wasn't asking this right, so I got more specific. "Why would you change your dirty work hat if you're just putting on another baseball cap?"

Dad played with the wedding band he still wore on his finger, a habit when he was pondering something. "Well, sure, I guess I could get another hat. But that other one, that's my work hat. I don't want to wear that going out somewhere," he said looking perplexed. "In public and all. It's a greasy mess—just like me when I'm on the boat." The fact was, Dad's overalls were mostly spotless. He leaned in closer, setting down his beer. "What's this about, son?"

I thought back to Fortis Henry and his perfectly white Stetson hat. He'd been so wrapped up in his work he'd supposedly gone out back doing chores right before we'd all come for our visit. But wearing his nice hat *while* doing dirty work? That didn't sound right.

I laid my half-eaten burger down on its plate, trying to understand. "You remember me telling you about that guy that died, a few months ago?" I said. "Fell into the waste lagoon?"

"Sure. The dairy farmer."

"There's another line of work that gets its hooks in you," I said. I was puzzled; trying to think it through as I spoke. "You've got a bunch of cows that have to be fed, milked, and tended to every single day. All kinds of complicated, expensive equipment requiring attention. Massive amounts of feed and livestock waste to deal with. Constant clean-up. He was a tough guy, but there's no relief from the constant work. You know, wherever he went out in public, he *always* wore this classy hat. A big white ten-gallon Stetson. Kind of a trademark."

"So, what, you figure I ought to get myself a cowboy hat?"

Even distracted, I had to laugh at that. "Nah, you better stick with the 'Jimmy Diesel,' Dad." I shook my head, picking my burger back up. "Forget about it, I'm just thinking out loud."

I wanted to ignore the look he gave me—raised eyebrows and pursed lips. I set down my burger and sighed. "Well, the guy, the dairy farmer—his name was Fortis Henry—when he fell into that waste lagoon he was wearing his fancy hat. He was shorthanded. I guess he'd gone out there to do some chores before the rest of us showed up. I'm just wondering, why the hell would he have been wearing some $600 spiffy white hat to do chores in one of the messiest workplaces on the planet. It doesn't really make sense, right?"

It was Dad's turn to laugh. "Not to me." I was pretty sure my dad didn't think a $600 hat made sense no matter where you wore it. His hats were free promos from the local G.M Marine dealership.

"Well, here's the thing," I said, finally realizing what was troubling me and putting my thoughts into words. "What if he wasn't alone? What if he wasn't doing chores? What if, instead, he was out there, I don't know, maybe with someone—a visitor? He was maybe showing someone around. Or just having a private conversation."

He shook his head. "You think you'd put on a $600 hat for something like that?"

I thought more about it. Maryanne Henry had told Lou Dwyer that Fortis had been out getting a few groceries and had returned shortly before Lou arrived. He left the groceries on the table and then, apparently, had gone directly out back. I was becoming more confident in my own thinking.

"I think he might have been with someone," I said. "Maybe one of our group was turning into the driveway just as Fortis was returning from the store. Fortis steps inside the house for a moment to drop off the groceries. Then the two of them head out back. He's showing someone around, or they have something private to talk about, something like that. It's the only way it makes sense. He's been out in public, wearing his good hat. He's in the company of a visitor. They're just going out back to take a look or to talk before the rest of us arrive. That's the only way it figures. I think maybe that's why he had on his best hat."

Dad still looked puzzled. "Seems sensible to me," he said, but he said it with a look that asked why it was so important.

My stomach was churning as I put the pieces together. "The thing is, Dad, if one of us was with him when he went out back, why didn't they mention what had happened? Nobody said 'boo.' And if he was with someone when he fell, why didn't they try to help him? Or come inside to get help? Or say something about it?"

We both sat there for a moment, our food growing cold on our plates as we thought about that. Then my dad shook his head. I knew we were both thinking the same thing.

Had I just stumbled onto a murder?

CHAPTER TEN

Thursday, February 16, 8 p.m.

Amended Strategy

BY THE TIME WE RETURNED TO OUR FOOD, my bacon cheeseburger was stone cold, though I barely remember getting it. Instead, I was reliving the day of Fortis Henry's death, seeing it all in a new light. And I was rethinking what I'd learned since. My dad ate his meatloaf in silence, letting me think.

"You know," I said, finally. "There's something else about that day that I haven't mentioned. The people who were there, at the dairy for our meeting, none of them liked the man. Some had serious issues with him. Even me."

He raised his eyebrows at that, so I continued: "Fortis Henry was against me being hired to represent the Conservation Heritage Farmers. I only got the job because Stoney fought for me."

Dad knew Stoney Stonington. Stoney's son Lester was a Puget Sound gillnet fisherman in addition to working on his father's farm. It was because my Dad and I knew Lester and we'd both met Lester's father, Stoney, that I'd ultimately ended up with the Conservation Heritage Farmers as a client.

The whole time I was talking, my dad was looking increasingly uncomfortable.

"I get what you're thinking, Dad. Believe me," I said.

"You don't really know anything for sure," he said. "You understand that? It's all guesswork. You do know, once you open this box, you're going to end up in it yourself? Up to your ears again."

I saw his point.

"But you're still thinking you should explain all this to the police. I can see it written all over you. Who we talking . . . the police over there in Yakima?"

"I don't know what to think. If I do that, it's going to cause a lot more foofaraw in the press. There's a bit more to it than just some guy who died." I proceeded to tell him about the misuse of office scandal over the money that paid for Fortis Henry's dairy lagoon and how that had become an issue in the current Legislative Session. And in the media.

Dad just shook his head. I looked at him quizzically, not sure what he was thinking.

"Boy, that place is a snake pit," he said, pointing a thumb over his shoulder in the general direction of Olympia. "I really don't know how you do it."

For once, I tended to agree. "Bottom line is: if I start bringing all this up with the local Sheriff, it's going to cause a huge mess. Best outcome would be if they just don't believe any of it; laugh me off. Could happen; I don't have much. If they do take it seriously, they'll investigate. A whole bunch of added hassle and grief for the Henry family. Maybe big worries for all my friends and colleagues who were there that day. Includes Stoney, my client. Me too. Any of us could have done it."

"If you believe your theory about the hat . . ," he said, thinking, "Wouldn't it have to have been whoever arrived first?" he said.

'Yeah," I said, giving that some thought. "Maybe someone who got there just as Fortis was pulling in from his errand to the grocery store. But that could have been anybody. Even back at the time I don't think I could have told you who was there when I arrived and who came later. Not for sure. I think that could be tough for any of us. Maybe we could remember some of it, but at this point, it's been nearly two months; would be hard to reconstruct. Anyway, the killer could have been there early, went out back with Fortis, and just came inside later to join the rest of us after Fortis was dead. Maybe acted like they'd just then driven in."

"Their car would have been there when you came in and parked."

That was true, but it didn't hold up when I thought about it. I shook my head. "Bunch of pickups and sedans. I don't know what any of the rest of those people drive. The lot was bigger than just for a normal home; it served the farm and the farm crew as well. I think four or five of the vehicles already in that lot belonged to the Henry Family or to the farm business. At least a couple probably belonged to members of their farm crew, even shorthanded as it was. Maybe some of them might possibly know what car one or another of the others drove. I seriously doubt any of us is going to be able to swear what cars were and weren't there in the lot when we arrived. After over two months? No way." I could see that it might be worth a try to ask but, to me, it seemed hopeless.

I continued to think. I needed to keep in mind that if I let this slide and the matter was later investigated, the fact that Fortis was opposed to Stoney's hiring me would surely come out; several people knew about it. As Dad had pointed out, I was going to have a motive and be in this stew right along with everybody else.

Also, if the police became aware that I'd been conscious of possible wrongdoing and hadn't come forward, I'd look all that much worse. Somebody I'd already questioned might be wondering, even now, what I was thinking given some of the questions I'd been asking.

My dad contributed his own view: "All on account of the man wearing a nice hat."

The whole thing was depressing. I had enough problems, and enough work to be done, without getting wrapped around the axle by something like this.

My dad wiggled his bushy eyebrows. "I will say, Sandy, you might want to make sure your friends are keeping up their life insurance."

Dad was referring to the murder case I'd been caught up in two years before but his humor wasn't helping. I said, "Maybe I just need to forget about it. There's nothing, really, that says there was a murder. Nothing solid."

"That's true," my dad said thoughtfully. "You got me convinced, though. I'm not sure, if I was that Sheriff, that I wouldn't want to know about it. How you going to feel about it if, knowing what you do, you still just remain silent?"

Now he was playing devil's advocate. I had to think about that. "What am I supposed to do? I don't even know if I'm right about there being foul play." I rubbed my eyes, remembering Detective Wilson, the State Patrol lieutenant with whom I dealt last time around. "Seems like a good possibility they aren't even going to be interested in this."

My dad didn't grace that with a response. Instead, he said: "You could, maybe, look into it a bit further, on the 'QT.' On your own, without letting people know what you're up to. That make sense?"

I thought about that. I was surprised that he'd suggested it. Maybe he'd been more impressed with my performance two years ago in the Abel Mortenson murder than I suspected. "Maybe I could have a chat with my colleagues who were there that day, the ones with whom I haven't already discussed it since. See why they seemed to dislike the man so much. See if maybe they could remember when others arrived."

It all sounded farfetched, but it was all I had.

My dad stared out the window, across the lot in the direction of some commercial boats moored in the neighboring marina. Then he turned and looked me in the eye. "You'll figure this out, Sandy. You always do." He smiled and again turned his eyes thoughtfully back out through the window toward the boats and toward the Lake Washington Ship Canal beyond. That Canal led to the Hiram Chittenden Locks and, beyond that, to Puget Sound and, ultimately, to the wide open, free, unobstructed waters of the North Pacific Ocean.

Then he turned back to me, smiled, rose from the table, picked up his "GMC Diesel" baseball cap and pulled it firmly on his head. "Well," he said, decisively, looking around the busy working man's restaurant. "Least I won't ever have to worry about getting fish blood on some $600 hat."

CHAPTER ELEVEN

Friday, February 24, 9 a.m.

Regular Order of Business

VERY YEAR THERE WERE, LITERALLY, THOUSANDS of bills
filed in the Washington State Legislature. One of the services
I provided my clients was tracking legislation as it moved
(or didn't) through the process. Fortunately, the Legislature published detailed records. Once you've identified a worrisome bill,
keeping an eye on it wasn't all that difficult. Just a bit boring. Janice
Burdel actually liked it, and I was lucky to have her periodic "bill
status reports." She let me know, every day, what was happening
on my clients' issues, reports I summarized and sent out to them
weekly during Session.

The toughest part of tracking, however, wasn't just following a
bill as it moved through the Legislature. It was also about identi-
fying the ones that were a threat. But Janice was good at figuring
out which bills were the ones to watch, which was half the battle.
"Report's on your desk," she called to me as I walked in. "Shout if
you have questions."

I tried not to sigh at the chore of scanning through the amendments that were emerging on bills we were tracking, and writing up
my weekly status reports. I hadn't been at the task long, however,
before I ran across something interesting. One of the bills Janice

had flagged and that we were watching from a distance was one that would increase the dollar authority of local counties to levy Conservation Futures Taxes (CFT). Local counties were allowed to impose this tax to raise money specifically for public acquisition and conservation of local lands. This tax was the main source of local dollars that were needed to match money from state land conservation programs like the Washington Wildlife and Recreation Program (WWRP). And those combined dollars, in turn, helped provide the match needed to get yet further funding from the federal Agricultural Conservation Easement Program (ACEP). That federal program was the one Daryl Weber administered.

The bill had been sponsored by Representative Didi Harris, one of those rare Democrats who managed to get themselves elected from conservative Eastern Washington. Didi Harris's legislative district included parts of suburban Spokane, but it also reached well out into ag country. It was a tough district for a democrat. Harris's success in politics, there, had apparently turned on her widely respected family history in farming and her leanings as a conservative Democrat. She was said to be financially secure and easily able to support her political hobby out of personal finances. I'd never seen it myself, but I'd heard that she was extremely aggressive in her politics, someone you didn't want to anger. She'd managed to secure and hold onto a Democratic seat in a red district through three terms in office. You had to admire that; it had to take some serious grit to pull that off in rural Spokane County.

Janice was walking by as I began studying the Spokane area on Google Earth. Since she was still in her late 20s and I had crossed over 40, she was convinced I can't possibly know how to use a computer.

"Here, let me give you a hand with that," she said. I didn't object as she replaced me behind my laptop and, as I looked over her shoulder, brought up the Spokane area from above. It was enough to provide some perspective on Rep. Harris's bill to increase the CFT. "Look at this," she said, scanning the Spokane suburbs.

Not that many years ago, the Spokane population had been largely concentrated in and around the city itself. Even today, the majority of Spokane County was still agricultural. But the city of Spokane had steadily grown and sprawled. Especially to the east toward Coeur d'Alene and to the north toward Newport. Former farmland within commuting distance from town was being rapidly bought up at development prices and converted to residential and commercial uses.

Didi Harris's CFT bill would be appreciated by her elected local government colleagues and other growth-management-oriented constituents in Spokane County. Increasing local Conservation Futures money could help local governments, land trusts, and growth management advocates in her community compete in securing that State and Federal money for the protection of local environmentally sensitive and agricultural lands. Since slowing development with purchased easements was voluntary and required no growth management regulation, it was probably a popular approach for her to take with her conservative landowner-constituents while also being a mild achievement to offer her more liberal Democratic supporters.

The bill was relevant to our Conservation Heritage Priority bill, if only indirectly. It was worth watching. I'd asked Janice to attend its Senate hearing the previous week. What I found mildly surprising was Janice's note that Daryl Weber had testified at that hearing. It reminded me of Daryl's negative reaction to Fortis Henry during our meeting at Denny's following Fortis's death.

As the NRCS administrator of ACEP, I could easily see why Daryl might like Didi Harris's bill; it could help increase local demand for his program. It was a bit unusual, however, for an NRCS employee to get this involved in a State legislative issue. He had come all the way over from Spokane to Olympia on a working weekday to testify, presumably on NRCS's dime. That the Bill's prime sponsor, Didi Harris, was from Daryl's home district suggested she might well have been the person who asked him to do so.

It all got me thinking that I should have a chat with him about our upcoming Senate work on my bill. I might also slip in a few questions about what had happened that day over in Yakima. Maybe he'd remember something I had forgotten.

Helen was my incredible Admin who ran my office. Her desk was just outside my door. I could never hear her working, but she knew everything that went on in that place and I suspected that she listened to everything I said and did. "Helen," I said. "Would you ring Daryl's office for me? I have a few questions."

There was no reply from the desk outside my door, but there never is. Like clockwork, however, a few short moments later I heard, "Line 1! It's Trudi, Daryl's office receptionist." Helen's a bit like Siri—say her name and what you want, and it just sort of happens.

I picked up the line and said, "Hi Trudi, it's Sandy."

"Hey, Sandy," she said, her voice sounded distant, as if she were multitasking while talking. It was always busy in their office. "I'm sorry, Daryl's not in today. If it's urgent, though, he's over on your side of the mountains again—I think he's briefing some of the Westside offices in the Black Lake office."

It would be a lot easier if Daryl and I could talk in person. And here he was again, right in my back yard. "Fantastic," I said. "I'll call him there."

"Uh, you'd better hurry," she answered. "His meeting is over at eleven. He's got a flight out of SeaTac at 12:55."

I looked; it was almost eleven. Daryl could already be on the road. "Trudi," I said, trying for an overtly dramatic sotto voice: "You think you know me well enough to trust me with Daryl's precious cell number? I've probably missed him at Black Lake. It would be nice if I could catch him before he's too far out of town."

I'd had trouble getting personal numbers before, but Trudi, bless her heart, relented. I caught Daryl in his rental car while he was still on Highway 101 approaching the I-5 northbound on-ramp south of Olympia.

"No sweat," he said. "I'll reschedule the flight. There's Horizon flights all afternoon. Where to you want to meet?"

The easiest place I could think of was a nearby state office building cafeteria. It was close to the freeway, had parking for him, and was easy walking distance for me. The food wasn't too bad and we'd be arriving safely ahead of the lunch crowd so it would be easy to find a table.

I grabbed a jacket, told Helen I'd be back in about an hour, and headed over there.

CHAPTER TWELVE

Friday, Feb. 24, 11 a.m.

Surprising Backstory

T HE CAFETERIA IN THE BASEMENT of the Natural Resources Building was still largely empty when I arrived. I picked up a coffee and found Daryl already seated and working his mobile while nursing his own tall coffee and a big pink-frosted cookie.

"Thanks for switching things around for me," I said, feeling embarrassed for inconveniencing him largely on a whim.

"No problem. I swap things out like this all the time. They put me on a flight at two-twenty. Plenty good. Actually, I'd just as soon spend the hour here drinking coffee and shooting the shit with you as sitting in my office behind a keyboard writing reports." Daryl had been with NRCS for something like twenty years. It showed.

"Well, I appreciate it. I know you're a busy guy. Personally, I hate last minute travel changes."

He shook his head, smiling easily. There were a few crumbs on his shirt as he leaned back in his seat. "I've been on the road with this job so long it's all on cruise control. Don't think I'd know how to do anything else."

"Well, let's hope you don't have to," I smiled back. "I'm very glad to have you on our team with this Conservation Heritage Bill. It's going to be a close one."

"Worry not. I'm not going anywhere." Then he paused with a flip of his eyebrows and added: "With any luck, anyhow."

"You ever think about doing anything else?" I asked, curious. "With your knowledge and experience, seems like you could easily do some kind of consulting."

"Not really." He laughed. "I was actually serious when I said I probably wouldn't know how. I do have a lot of knowledge up here." He aimed his eyes upward. "But it's all specialized, very specific to my work. Kind of like a highly skilled zeppelin pilot, you know. I met a Boeing engineer, once, who'd done years of intensive study with wind tunnels. Now most of that stuff's on a computer. I'm really good in my job, but I'd be completely irrelevant someplace else."

"You could always farm," I said, joking. Most of his work, over the years would have been with farmers. I was sure he knew better than most how tough *that* business was.

But then he surprised me. "Well, as it happens," he said with a broad grin. "That's exactly what I'm doing."

"What?"

"Farming," he said, as if it was obvious. "Wife and I are buying a place up east of Spokane. Eight acres with a nice house and a great little barn. Just four or five acres that's farmable, but it's got water. And decent soil. There's even part of an old irrigated orchard. We're growing some fruits and vegetables for sale at farmers markets in Spokane and Coeur d'Alene. Been thinking about this for years."

"Wow," I said. "Sounds exciting." I studied him for a moment. He looked to be maybe a bit under fifty. But, aside from appearing a bit tired, he seemed in good health. "You must have farmed before?" Farming was a lot of work; it would be tough to run even a limited operation and still hold down a full-time Federal job. I tried hard to sound positive.

He did, however, detect the whiff of skepticism. "Worry not," he said. "I grew up in Iowa. My dad grows corn; he's just turned eighty and still at it. Him and my brother. I been on farms and working with farmers my whole life. Before I got into this agricultural easement stuff, I was a farm conservation planner out of the Spokane area Service Center. I've probably written half the farm plans in Spokane County. It's in my blood."

"You ever consider going back there? To Iowa? Pick up where your dad leaves off?"

"Oh God, no way. He already has my brother for that. The two of them, they're full speed ahead. Anyway, I'd hate growing some big commodity crop; all land and no money. That, now, *that* is a tough business. Nah," he said grinning. "I'm the second son, the one that goes off to college and ends up working for the government. What I want to do now is try out some of what I've been learning and preaching all these years. A small operation, multiple crops, direct market. Just grow some good, wholesome food and sell it directly to neighbors that appreciate it."

Backed up by a Federal job now, and Federal retirement down the road, it sounded like a reasonable plan, if he could make the time to pull it all together. Meanwhile, if the farm brought in some extra money, he'd be so much the better.

I'd noted that he had said he was "buying" his farm, not that he had "bought" it. I hoped that didn't mean he'd needed to borrow a lot of money. Land near Spokane could be expensive. Buyers were paying development prices on land that was further and further away from the urban center. A good deal of traditional wholesale agriculture was slowly being displaced by suburban housing.

"So, what's this all about," he asked, with a glance at a clock on the cafeteria wall. It was past 11:30. "I don't suppose you asked me to join you at this classy establishment just for the aesthetic experience." The molded plastic chairs and Formica topped tables around us were already beginning to fill up for the lunch break; the room had taken on the echoing quality of institutional eateries everywhere. Most of these would be folks that worked for Natural Resources, Fish and Wildlife, Agriculture, and the other State Agencies housed in the several floors of offices directly over our heads.

"Yeah, well, you're right. I didn't." I knew what I had to do but was unsure how to start. "I was just wondering: I know you've been with NRCS here in Washington for much of your career, you've been at the State Office for several years now. I was just wondering if you had ever previously worked with Fortis Henry over that time. I mean, I assume you knew each other what with his connection to the conservation districts. You ever work with him on anything in particular?

"Oh yeah," Daryl said. "I knew him forever. I ran into him a lot. Fortis was up-and-coming as a force in State conservation district politics. He was full of ideas; wanted to change the world and everybody in it. He was always one of those people who's absolutely certain that *all* of our environmental problems could easily be solved with voluntary, incentive-based private landowner conservation. Hated regulation, of course. A one hundred percent true believer in the conservation district cause. Recent years," Daryl shook his head. "He just became, I don't know, 'political'' I guess."

"Political?"

"Yeah, you know, only thing that mattered was getting things done his own way. Working the angles. Whatever the cost. 'Political.'"

That would not have been how I'd have defined it, but I didn't try to correct him. "You like the man?" I said. It didn't sound like it.

He furrowed his brow. "No," he admitted. "Can't say I did. We crossed swords a few times over the years. But it was more than that. I think he never really trusted NRCS. He was all-in with the idea of the 'conservation partnership' of federal, state, and local folks working together for the common good. But NRCS is still 'gov'ment' after all." He put air-quotes around the word. "Worse yet—he wiggled his eyebrows, 'Federal gov'ment.' He was convinced there had to be some ulterior motive, some hidden agenda behind everything we did. As an NRCS employee, I couldn't be trusted either. He was a guy who was awfully sure of things that fit with his world view, but never very willing to ask the harder questions about stuff that didn't." Then he paused. "What's this all about, anyway?"

At that point, I pulled out the "explanation" I'd concocted and crossed my fingers. "You've heard about the difficulties with the Commission budget and all. And about Fortis and his NRCS-funded dairy lagoon? I'm wondering if you might know and be able to share any insights into that? From inside NRCS maybe?" It was all I had to offer Daryl as a halfway reasonable explanation for why I was asking all these questions without owning up to my growing suspicions of murder and even, perhaps, suggesting that he might be under suspicion himself.

It was a huge relief when Daryl seemed to accept it. "Not really," he said. "Not specifically. Generally, I can say that district supervisors have always had an advantage in gaming the system; it's just the way it works. Mostly, they're pretty conscientious in how they go about it—they could take a lot more advantage than they do. In many places, including here in Washington, they also have some standard best practices. It's not like there are huge sums of money involved. Washington is actually one of the better states; in many places around the country, conservation project funding opportunities can get very little publicity so the only people who really know about them are the Supervisors and their friends. We don't have anywhere near enough funding for all the projects out there, so there's not much point in seriously advertising the programs. As long as the projects the districts recommend seem sound and worthwhile, NRCS often doesn't get all that critical about how they were chosen. We pretty much try to do what the local district recommends. It's the way it is. I've never liked it. But Fortis didn't do anything out of the ordinary. Or even anything particularly dishonest. His dairy lagoon was a reasonable project. Well worth funding; worth getting done."

"I guess," I said. "It has certainly created a stir."

"Who knows, Sandy," he replied. "On the positive side, maybe this whole mess will open some eyes in district leadership. I think they sometimes resist change without thinking much about appearances. About the kind of trouble this kind of sloppiness can cause. After having to deal with this elections bill, maybe they'll clean up their act some."

"NRCS ever take heat about something like this before? Maybe elsewhere in the country? Have they ever considered a policy change that would help them somehow better second-guess a district-recommended project that might seem dodgy or unethical?"

Daryl looked at me with mock amazement. "And poison the precious district-NRCS partnership?" Then he smiled but became serious. "No way. Never. I mean, we make our own independent decisions. But, you know how it works. Nobody likes the Feds. The districts, with their locally-elected Supervisors coming right out of the local farming community, they're another matter. They're local leaders, respected people in their communities. They're our 'in' with local farmers. We'd never, *ever* do anything to damage that relationship."

I really didn't have much more to ask him; at least not without explaining my probably-wild suspicions. I wasn't yet prepared to go there. Instead, I went back to his plans for farming.

"You already going with this farm?" I asked.

"Oh yeah," he said, brightening up again. "We moved in last year. My wife and son are working the farm full time, already. They're even more gung-ho than I am. It's really more their project than it is mine. We opened up the roadside farm-stand last fall. Didn't have much to sell, but what we did have sure disappeared in a hurry. This year we should be selling direct to the public by mid-summer. Have a website, the whole bit." He dug through his wallet and handed me a card. "We call it 'Daisy Valley Farm.' You should let me know next time you're in Spokane. I'll drive you out there, Meet the family. Sarah will fix us a home-grown lunch."

When I got back to the office, I was still thinking about our conversation. There were two points in our brief meeting that stood out. One had happened right at the beginning when he'd talked about his work with NRCS. It had sounded to me like there might be some kind of problem with his employment. The other disconnect was when he'd described his relationship with Fortis

Henry. He'd tossed off his answer a bit too lightly, I thought. It felt like there could be something more personal there than he was letting on. He'd also subtly diverted me away from further questions along that line. It had all given me the distinct impression that Daryl's dislike of the man was somehow more complex and disturbing than he was letting on.

I had an hour or so before I needed to get back to the hill, so I decided to feed my curiosity. I typed in the web address for "Daisy Valley Farm" from the card he'd given me and came up with Daryl's website. The site was a bit amateurish, but it nicely reflected the passion of its owners and the inherent charm of their enterprise. There was a mission statement: to provide "healthy, tasty, environmentally responsible, and affordable farm-fresh produce." There was contact information and a map. And there were pictures of a little farm stand with a few colorful vegetables laid out, pictures of crops coming up out of the ground, and one of Daryl, his wife, and their adult son all smiling happily and standing at what looked like the farm entrance beside a "Daisy Valley Farm" sign. Their freshly-painted house was right behind them. It all reflected the emerging, real-life fulfillment of a happy family's wholesome dream.

Seeing that picture reminded me that Daryl had once told me they still had their adult, developmentally disabled son living with them. There would be medical costs associated with that—probably covered by Daryl's USDA-NRCS health insurance. Daryl had told me that his wife stayed at home and looked after their son. It seemed like this farm enterprise might be providing her with a welcome new outlet in life, and maybe one for their son as well. In addition, hopefully, to some added income.

On impulse, I pasted the farm's address into Google maps. There were "street-view" materials available so I did a virtual "drive by," curious about what it all looked like from the road. I ended up seeing the same property shown in Daryl's website, but as it had appeared two or three years earlier when the last Google camera-car had driven by. Obviously, this was before the Weber family had purchased the place. In these old "street view" shots, it didn't look all that great. There was a big, commercial "for sale" sign staked in the yard in front of an older, sad-looking house surrounded by open fields and a few scattered trees. Judging from the pictures on their website, Daryl, his wife, and son had transformed the place over the past year or so.

When I zoomed in on "street view" for a closer look at the house, the big "for sale" sign also became even larger and something else caught my attention. The details at the bottom of the sign were hard to read, but there, in big letters across the top I could easily make out the statement: "Offered by Truman Harris Properties." That caught me by surprise. I believed I remembered that this was the same part of the world where Rep. Didi Harris' family had their farm. I believed I'd heard the name Truman Harris before. Would this be Didi's father?

That prompted another on-line search for "Truman Harris Properties." And I brought up another website. This one was very professional with vague but important-sounding descriptions of the firm's seemingly far-flung enterprises. On careful reading, however, and based on what I'd heard, I believed that most of what they did was develop and/or sell-off undeveloped land located in the Spokane Valley, land that been the beneficiary of some expansive rezoning in recent years. The "About Us" page unashamedly bragged about the Harris family and included a bio and photos of their successful, politically connected daughter, Washington State Representative, Didi Harris.

After a few moments of thought, I made one more search. This time on Spokane County's real property "parcel search" page. It was easy to find Daryl's property. Posted on the Recorder's webpage was the real estate tax affidavit for the recent sale to Daryl and Sarah Weber of their new farm property. The transfer document was a real estate contract. The seller/lender was Truman Harris Properties, LLC. And the sales price was $535,000. The Zillow website backed that up and had pictures from the time of the last sale. For that money, they could have purchased a lot more land further from town. But, then, that might have made Daryl's commute less possible. As Daryl had mentioned, there were a couple of decent looking outbuildings. And the house showed better on the inside than it did out. I could see that the purchase price might make some sense, but it certainly wasn't cheap. That the Weber family was in debt to the seller suggested the possibility that they'd been unable to secure a bank loan; not a good sign of financial health.

In all this searching, I'd probably stumbled upon the source of the Harris Family's wealth—and it wasn't agriculture. Truman Harris was, apparently, engaged in the long-term, systematic sell-off of pieces of their very large family farm in ever smaller parcels as those properties happily gained market value through the periodic rezoning driven by Spokane's sprawling growth. Daryl's new farm property had been recently re-zoned to R-5 which allowed one dwelling per 5 plus acres. Daryl's newly purchased home had been on that land for many years, but the surrounding, newly-subdivided five-acre parcels were selling off for new home, "rural residential" construction. All of it was going at per-acre prices that would have been impossible under its previous twenty and forty-acre zoning. My guess was that Didi Harris' dad Truman had been engaged for years in an ongoing "dance" with emerging zoning laws while juggling parcels and land values for the long-term financial benefit of this new family business. Farmer-turned-developer, a natural evolution unwittingly driven by our State's sometimes-schizophrenic but often predictable local public policy on land use.

$535,000 seemed like it might be a heavy lift for someone with Daryl's income, especially if it was the sole income for a family that included a disabled child who might have special medical needs. Even government medical benefits wouldn't cover everything.

Still, none of what I'd learned in the past couple of hours seemed especially relevant to my objective in speaking with Daryl in the first place. I had confirmed that Daryl, like the rest of us who were there the day Fortis Henry died, hadn't much liked the man. I had learned nothing specific, however, to suggest that Daryl might truly have wanted him dead.

CHAPTER THIRTEEN

Thursday, March 2, 10:30 a.m.

Enemy of My Enemy

LINDA CUNNINGHAM'S EMPLOYER, the Washington State Agriculture Industry Council, WSAIC, was a powerful coalition of farm organizations, commodity commissions, professional service providers, ag industry contractors, seed, fertilizer, chemical, and equipment suppliers, and other ag support businesses.

As their Director of Government Relations, Linda led one of the most robust ongoing lobbying efforts in the Legislature.

She wielded a lot of power. On one occasion, late the previous summer, I'd attended a meeting of the WSAIC State Board to make a pitch for their legislative support. While I awaited my slot on their agenda, I'd seen Linda at work. I watched the Board walk through a list of legislators who were seeking the group's endorsement in the coming elections. They had a rating system: "5 stars" down through "1 star." They also had a list of some 30 legislative floor votes from the previous session, plus a great many key votes on issues in committee. To get a "5 star" rating, the candidate needed to have a perfect voting record; that is to say, they needed to have voted in the way recommended by WSAIC every single time. To get a "4 star" rating they were only allowed two unapproved votes. Given the broad nature of the issues on that list, even that seemed like an incredibly high standard. Certainly, no Democrat would ever qualify no matter how conservative they were or how supportive they might be of agriculture.

Even so, a good many legislators had met that standard. And there were several others, candidates for re-election, who were present at the meeting hoping to explain their "misdirected" votes. In a couple of instances, they actually succeeded. But that WSAIC Board was very tough. These candidates might have been important elected public officials when they were over on the other side of the mountains casting votes in Olympia, but there at that board meeting in Othello they were just supplicants. Watching them humbly pleading their case with these tough farm industry board members was very educational. If they wanted the endorsement of the organized agriculture industry, they had to toe the WSAIC line.

Through the entire process, it was crystal clear that Linda Cunningham was driving this boat. Her thoughts were sought on every major point of discussion. Her opinions were respected. As the Board exchanged views and engaged in discussion, she could be seen moving about the room. From time to time, she'd draw one or another member aside to have a private word. Clearly, she was orchestrating the votes; no-one seemed bothered by that. She might be mere "staff" to this organization, her views might be nothing more than "recommendations," but she was their professional lobbyist, the person they counted on to protect their interests and who was familiar with the political territory. Her views were respected. Anyone watching, definitely including the several State Legislators present, had to know that Linda was the power in that room.

Considering what I'd seen at that event, I had cause to wonder. Could Fortis Henry have represented a threat to Linda's extraordinary power? Even before Stoney had hired me, I knew who Linda was, of course; she was a familiar figure in Olympia. In his initial briefing, Stoney had mentioned that Linda had disappointed Fortis and the conservation districts a few times and he and Fortis had let her know about it. But carefully. He referred to her as "agriculture's Genghis Kahn," someone who "took no prisoners." Both Stoney and Fortis had agreed, however, that her support for our Conservation Heritage Priority Bill was essential. Fact was, if WSAIC had opposed our bill, it would never have come out of Committee. If she and her organization had decided to actively support it, passing it would have been a shoo-in. In the end, we didn't get their enthusiastic support, but they didn't oppose us either. That, at least, gave us a shot. It was my job to make the best of that.

Linda and I had never previously worked with one another. I'd occasionally see her in one or the other of the natural resources committees. We were usually there on different bills. That we'd also never crossed swords was partly a result of my practical guidance to my fishing industry clients which mostly steered them away from large-scale involvement in purely environmental issues. Even though protecting salmon runs was in my fishery clients' long-term self-interest, I did what I could to keep them out of those fights.

Suffice it to say that, unlike the agriculture industry, my fisheries clients' survival depended on them keeping their powder dry and, unlike Linda Cunningham's farmers, we stayed away from large scale environmental issues. Incidentally, if we'd been involved in those fights, there's also little doubt we'd have also found ourselves at odds with Linda Cunningham—a place we'd never want to be.

The reason my new farmer clients hadn't ultimately secured WSAIC's robust support was, like most things in Olympia, a bit complicated. Unlike my fishermen, WSAIC got involved in many broad, statewide issues. It did that to maintain its credibility with its membership as the preeminent industry group representing a huge, diverse industry. Agriculture came in second only to aerospace in economic impact in the state of Washington. WSAIC could find it difficult to focus on minor issues like a small group of conservation-minded farmers when they were dealing with other huge issues that affected millions of people and involved a broad, statewide coalition including many industries.

Among larger the issues distracting WSAIC's attention away from our Conservation Heritage Priority Bill was a tax controversy that had begun in a previous legislative session. It had started with Fortuna's all-out effort to pass their package of State incentives for their computer-farm investment. While that earlier effort had been on hold for well over a year, the publicity surrounding it had stimulated a continued public discussion about Washington's unusual tax system.

Language in our State Constitution, previous statutes, and rulings of our State Supreme Court had effectively prohibited an income tax. We had a long, painful state political history of failed efforts to change that. Instead, Washington relied heavily on sales taxes, property taxes, and our arcane, rough-edged Business and Occupation Tax that was deeply despised in the business community.

When Fortuna had temporarily placed its efforts on hold it had, with considerable public fanfare, cited our Business and Occupation tax as one of their reasons. This led the business community and anti-tax activists to decide it was time to take on that tax; to try to rid our State of this "unfair, heavy-handed" burden on business forever.

The fact was, farmers themselves were exempt from the Business and Occupation tax; they only paid it if they were engaged in direct retail sales. But their wholesale purchasers, support and supply businesses, and food processors did pay it. And those support businesses hated the tax with a passion. So, despite the limited impact on agriculture, WSAIC had decided to become deeply involved in repealing it. There was a bill working its way through the current session that would place a repeal referendum on the ballot in the next election.

Meanwhile another group, "Citizens for Tax Equity," an organization with more liberal leanings, had initiated their own new effort. They were gathering signatures for an alternative ballot measure which would also eliminate the Business and Occupation

Tax but would, in its place, amend the State Constitution to allow a new, graduated income tax which would reduce Sales and Property taxes as well.

WSAIC, of course, strongly opposed a new income tax. Such a tax *would* , have affected farmers.

WSAIC had become one of the leading organizations supporting the referendum to simply abolish the Business and Occupation tax. That outcome would, of course, have left the State with a huge tax deficit and no good way to make it up, not an outcome that much bothered most conservatives. All this was taking place at a time when Legislators were under order from the State Supreme Court to fully fund primary and secondary education in accordance with another mandate in the State Constitution. And it was all keeping WSAIC and Linda Cunningham fully engaged.

Thankfully Linda, personally, appreciated what we wanted to do for the Conservation Heritage farmers. We probably owed her our thanks for keeping WSAIC out of it. I decided that was the excuse I needed to call her and, incidentally, pose some questions about her history with Fortis Henry and about the day he'd died. When I called her WSAIC office that Friday afternoon I was surprised to learn she was out on sick leave; hadn't been in her office for nearly a week. In her absence, her legislative duties were being performed by other members of WSAIC staff. She was, I was told, working from home in Olympia.

Linda answered the phone immediately: "You know, my assistant is handling everything," she said when I told her who was calling. "I'm out of commission for a while."

"Actually, Linda," I said. "I'm looking for something else. Any chance you've got a few minutes to spare?

"Nothing but time," she said. "I'm in a cast with a broken foot. Trying to work from home, but not going anywhere for a good long while."

"I'm sorry to hear that. I hope you don't mind the call." I was just what she needed, someone asking her about how much she liked Fortis Henry. But I wanted those answers. "Any chance we could get together. I have a few questions about our bill."

"You sure you don't want to talk with one of my staff at the office?"

"Absolutely sure," I said. "What I need is some background. Maybe I can buy you a coffee, a pastry, something like that. Make it worth your while."

She laughed at that. "You know what, Sandy, you're on. But I meant it about being stuck. I'm on crutches for another month. After that I'm in a boot. Would you be willing to join me here at my condo? I'd absolutely kill for a latte. And, seeing as how you're offering, you can also get me one of those coconut-almond bars they have at the downtown Starbucks."

She gave me her address and minutes later I was in my car. A latte and a coconut-almond bar seemed well worth the answers I hoped she'd provide if, somehow, at odds with the tough, take-no-prisoners impression I'd formed of her. It was probably a break for me that I'd be able to catch her in a relaxed home environment.

CHAPTER FOURTEEN

Thursday, March 2, 11 a.m.

Shaky Alliances

66 I'M INTRIGUED," LINDA SAID AS I stepped through the door to her comfortable apartment on West Bay Drive in Northwest Olympia. As she'd said on the phone, she was on crutches. The fiberglass cast on her left foot was patriotic red, white and blue; a far cry from the heavy white plaster I recalled from when I was once hurt as a kid. She smiled when she saw I was carrying the little Starbucks bag with her latte and the pastry. "You brought my bribe. Must be important."

"Well, I've got a few things I wanted to ask you that I hope will help with our bill," I said. "And about Fortis Henry."

"Ah," she said, pivoting and crutching her way awkwardly over to a dining room table near the front window. "It's a good bill. Glad to help."

I stepped past her, put the Starbucks bag down on the table, and pulled out a chair for her.

After propping her crutches against a nearby wall, she sat and peeked inside the bag. "Breaking it didn't actually hurt much," she held up her casted foot, "but wearing this thing's a real bummer."

"I can't imagine being out of the office during Session," I said, pulling up a chair. "I'd go crazy."

"Crazy has been my middle name since I've been in this thing," she said, munching her pastry bar. "Like I said on the phone, with being out of the office, I'm mostly out of touch on the particulars, but if all you want is some history, you might as well make yourself comfortable."

I nodded, cupping my hands around my coffee. "So, it sounds like you're OK with our bill?"

"Absolutely. What's not to like? It's all voluntary; no regulation. It leverages existing State spending on WWRP, so no new taxes. Maybe it'll pry some of that money away from environmental stuff to help a few farmers protect their land and investments while improving their liquidity. I'm all for it."

"Can I ask how it went down with your Council?" I said, leaning in. "I mean, we haven't seen any support from them—they seem awfully quiet."

"Yeah. Well, you should maybe just settle for that, OK? I mean, nobody on my Board really likes WWRP. Anything that helps government buy land, especially interests in ag land, is always going to run into a lot of skepticism at WSAIC."

"Maybe I should be thanking you that they're staying out of it?"

Linda smiled, broke off another small chunk of her bar, and popped it in her mouth. "You just did," she said, swallowing. "Damn these things are good."

"That day, last December, at Fortis Henry's place. You already knew that's how it would go down, right? That your Board wouldn't go for it?"

"Seemed pretty likely."

Despite her organization's involvement in a host of issues, Linda still, apparently, knew which fights to pick and which ones to stay out of. "So, why'd you come? Why bother meeting with us that day at all?"

"Almost didn't. I was at my parents' place over in Colfax for a few days over Christmas. Needed to head back to Olympia anyway; Yakima's right on the way. I would have helped, if I could.

And Fortis Henry may not have been my favorite guy, but he was influential in our Association. Maybe you knew, he was President of our Chapter there in Yakima County. There's a growing segment of our WSAIC membership that sees things differently, these days. I try, at least, to stay in touch with it."

She took a large sip of her latte and continued. "You probably know, even if my guys had agreed to help you, it wouldn't have amounted to much. Not this year. We got this Business and Occupation tax deal. The forever fight over water rights. And there's that damn Fortuna stuff. My Board hates that Fortuna package. It's political payback by the Governor, helping out his contributors. No way we're ever going to let that happen."

There it was, again. The WSAIC getting involved in political fights that, to me, seemed extraneous to the immediate interests of agriculture. It was the way they played the game.

Linda wasn't all that far off the mark about Fortuna, however. Governor Carl Browne, a Democrat, was leading the Fortuna campaign. Fortuna had hired the big Seattle Law firm of Morganthau, Staley, and Rimes to handle their political effort; the firm's senior partner, Nelson Morganthau was known to be a heavy-hitter in Democratic politics and had contributed heavily to the Governor's last campaign. The firm's head lobbyist, and the man leading the Olympia push for the legislative package, was former House Speaker Aaron Nicolaides, also a Democrat, someone intensely disliked by Republicans. The Fortuna Package might have been all about easing the way for a large business investment, but it definitely had a Democratic flavor.

"You said Fortis was influential," I said. "If he'd lived, do you think he might have had some sway on our bill with your Board?"

Linda paused and moment, then: "No. He was a pusher. He might have tried. But it wouldn't have changed the outcome; might have made it worse. He'd made a lot of enemies on my Board. It's not much fun for those of us on staff when there are quarrels among board members. And none of it makes friends, you know what I mean?"

"Quarrels? Over . . .?"

"Fortuna, for one. Fortis liked it." I recalled that Maryanne Henry had testified in support of Howard Oxley's tech education bill; apparently, she and her husband shared views about Fortuna.

"Huh. Any particular reason?"

"He didn't need a reason. Just always knew best. Arrogant. Thought it was a good thing, I guess. Kick start the regional economy. Kept taking issue with the rest of the Board over it, even after they'd taken the vote. You know, you piss a bunch of people off and then you're surprised when they don't want to help you."

"Fortis needed WSAIC help on something?"

"Duh! District elections."

I thought about that. I'd been under the impression that the District Elections bill was recent; that it had materialized in the Legislature. Linda was telling me it was something that had been gathering force much earlier, apparently before Fortis Henry died.

She saw my confusion. "You're familiar with the bill, right?"

"Yeah, sure. But I thought it was, you know, recent."

"Nah. That issue's been simmering for years. When Fortis got himself in trouble over that damn waste lagoon, it just gathered steam. You know how it is, people sense weakness. Fortis's little scandal over his sweetheart cost-share deal created the perfect storm. Put the conservation district elections issue right up on the front burner. We all knew that bill was coming. He was over here last November begging our Board to help him kill it. Most of my guys don't really care much about conservation districts, or their elections, one way or the other. Still, they might have helped Fortis out if he had been more willing to play the game. In the end, they just froze him out. Got what he deserved, I'd say."

That startled me a bit.

She noticed. "Oh, no. No. I didn't mean that," she hurriedly corrected herself. "I don't mean the accident. Just, you know, when they blew him off on the elections bill. God no. Nobody deserves to end up like that. Awful!"

ON MY DRIVE BACK THROUGH TOWN to my office I reflected on that. At the time she'd said it, it had sounded to me like she'd actually meant he'd deserved to die. Maybe it was just my imagination given what I knew or suspected. In any case, Fortis Henry had definitely been a problem for her, but it seemed to me like it would take a good deal more than an obstreperous board member to have given Linda Cunningham a motive for murder. It also seemed possible there was more to it than she was saying; that Fortis had been undermining the amazing power position she'd developed with her board and, ultimately, in State legislative politics.

CHAPTER FIFTEEN

Monday, March 6, noon

Political Undertow

OUR BILL FINALLY PASSED THE HOUSE.
It was none too soon; the official cutoff for passage in the first house was Wednesday. Stoney had come down to Olympia for the event which had taken place shortly before noon. We'd had some serious doubts. And there had been opposition. But, in the end, the bill had cleared the House with a comfortable margin. We were in a solid position for our upcoming struggles in the Senate.

It was in this spirit of celebration that, after the vote, Stoney suggested lunch. Sherry and I had planned to get lunch together but I was sure she wouldn't mind if Stoney joined us. He's something of a character. I thought she might get a kick out of meeting him.

As it turned out, however, Sherry already knew Stoney. He'd apparently testified on several occasions before her committee. He was also a good friend of one of her fellow House staffers so she'd seen him around the committee offices several times. The three of us made a comfortable group as we headed downtown in decent spring weather.

"So you're Sandy's insider in House Committee staff?" Stoney said as we walked past the Tivoli Fountain toward Capitol Way.

"More like his unpaid informant," Sherry said. "And sometimes the wall he bounces ideas off of when he's already decided what he want to do but he needs somebody to tell him he's right."

Stoney looked us over. "So, you two an 'item' or what?" he said. Then to Sherry: "Seems like high time some good-looking woman like yourself took this fella in tow."

Sherry and I both laughed at that. "No, no," we both said together. Then she added: "Just colleagues. Both of us are far too old and selfish to get involved in some personal relationship."

It was something on which she and I were in perfect agreement. But Stoney didn't seem convinced. "Yeah, right," he said, with something of an eye roll.

WE WERE ALL IN GOOD SPIRITS as we took a table at Ramblin' Jack's on 4th street.

"You getting what you need from the conservation districts in all this?" Stoney asked me as we were scanning our menus.

"They've been great," I told him. "Thanks to you, the districts have been there with testimony, as you know. They've also been actively lobbying our bill right alongside the rest of their work. Getting the word out to their members and in their newsletters. You saw that Miles Morgan came in for our hearing." Miles was the Legislative Liaison for the Conservation Commission.

"I should bloody hope so. This isn't one the Commission should be sitting out."

"I think they're making an effort, especially given their struggles with the budget this year."

"This is one of the reasons I ran for that damn seat on the Commission."

His suddenly bitter tone contrasted with the positive vibe we'd shared so far. This was also the first I'd been aware that Stoney had run for a Commission seat. Three of the State Conservation Commissioners were actually elected by the district supervisors at their annual meeting of the CDSW. "I didn't know you'd run for the Commission."

"Last year. Lost. Fortis freaking Henry."

"Fortis Henry? But he's from Yakima. How'd you end up running against him." The three elected Commissioners were elected from three regions of the State: East, Central, and West. Stoney would have run for the West region position. Fortis Henry's seat would have been "Central."

"No, it was Lane Murray. From Grays Harbor. But Fortis was behind it."

Our pleasant lunch conversation had suddenly turned serious. Sherry seemed unsure of the conversation, but I leaned in.

He continued, "It was the way it happened. Underhanded. Lane's a good guy, but I should have won that seat. I only lost because Fortis had organized an under-the-table campaign to support Lane. Convinced Lane to run. Then Fortis pulled out all the stops with all his buddies. Him and his friends sent out personal letters to all the West Region supervisors and made a bunch of phone calls with subtle slams. I didn't know anything about it till too late. I didn't even know I'd have an opponent till the last minute."

This was all news to me. The election had taken place the previous year, before I'd come on board. It sounded very much like this might touch on some deeper rift between Stoney and Fortis Henry. It certainly helped explain why Stoney ignored Fortis Henry's advice and hired me anyway. I wanted to think he'd hired me because I was so wonderful. But maybe not. Who knew, maybe he did it to spite Fortis.

At this point, the waiter would soon be showing up to take our orders. Sherry glanced at me, and then, I'm sure in an effort to redirect the conversation, she said: "Well, Stoney, you guys did get your bill through the House. It seems like congratulations are in order." Then with a decisive pause, she looked back down at her menu: "So, you've eaten here before. What's good."

That got the rest of our discussion off in other directions. But I'd learned enough to see that there was more to the Stoney-Fortis relationship than I'd previously been aware.

CHAPTER SIXTEEN

Friday, March 10, 4:30 p.m.

Hail Mary

A S WE MOVED INTO MARCH, several of the "problem bills" my clients faced had been dealt with. Our Conservation Heritage Priority Bill was still alive and kicking. Lacking anything further to go on, I'd tried to put my suspicions about Fortis Henry's death on hold, focusing, instead, on the day-to-day work in what had turned out to be a busy session.

One Friday, the second week in March, Janice and I were working the Hill early on a matter that had come to our attention recently. The Senate was in Session with a full calendar and one of the items on that calendar for passage was a bill that I'd been asked, at the very last minute, to step in and kill.

At this point in the process, that was a very big order.

Among my fishing industry clients were several cooperative marine insurance pools—small, independent, fisherman-member-owned and funded organizations that could offer very low rates on vessel casualty and liability insurance. Typically, insurance on commercial fishing vessels was hugely expensive. It was, after all, a risky endeavor. The actual risk of loss, however, depended greatly on the experience and personal good sense of the operator. The pools carefully vetted applicants for membership, effectively eliminating the questionable risks. Nobody got into one of these pools unless they were recommended by two other respected fishermen members and then approved by a very savvy and connected Board. Irresponsible operators need not apply.

Unfortunately, there was a single but powerful State Representative, Jerome (Jerry) Fernandez, Chair of House Business and Financial Services Committee, who disliked these pools. He'd prime sponsored a bill that would subject them to standard insurance regulations—hugely cumbersome auditing, operating, reporting, and reserve requirements designed for much larger, corporate, commercial insurers selling coverage to a much broader and less-informed public.

In real-life, Fernandez was a pharmacist who owned a successful local drug store in the town of Carnation—nothing to do with fisheries. My first inclination was to try to talk him out of it. I'd arranged an appointment almost immediately.

"So, you're here about that insurance pool thing," he'd said as we shook hands at the entrance to his office. It was like he was already preparing to shoot me down. He waived me to a chair and took his seat behind his desk.

"Well, sir, I was hopeful there might be some other way we could address your concerns."

"I doubt it," he said. That was certainly blunt.

"Could I ask if there are some particular issues that led you to file this bill. Maybe you have some constituents we could work with. We'd be quite willing to do what we can to address any problems that have arisen."

He was just shaking his head; not having any of that. "Those pools are a public menace. They skate along the edges of the insurance law, but they're insurance companies, plain and simple. They need to be regulated just like the rest of the insurance industry."

This was going south fast, but I needed to make my best effort: "I guess you're probably aware that not one of these pools has ever failed in some 60 years of their existence. Not a dime of member money has ever been lost. Nor has there ever been any suggestion of impropriety."

"Doesn't matter," he said. "Horses and barn doors, you know what I'm saying. Fact that it hasn't happened yet has nothing to do with it."

"I guess you have some constituents that . . ."

"I don't need to have constituents to tell me there's a problem here. Any fool can see it if you take the trouble to look."

I sat back and looked at him. His arms were folded tightly across his chest. He was sitting ramrod straight in his plush chair. His look was grim. I could see nothing for this but to back off so that's what I did. I was out of his office a few minutes later knowing nothing more about why he wanted this bill, but absolutely sure he was going forward with it no matter what.

Rep. Fernandez's District was in rural King County, up toward the Cascade foothills east of Seattle. Stoney, as it happened, was a Fernandez constituent. The district was landlocked and, other than Stoney's son Lester, my dad's gillnetter friend, it contained very few commercial fishermen. Fernandez wasn't an avid sports fisherman either, so he'd never been a factor in any of our periodic sport-commercial battles over who got to catch the fish. When I was asked to kill the bill, I'd given Stoney a call to see if he or his son Lester might have some idea why Fernandez seemed so opposed to insurance pools.

It turned out that one of Stoney's business properties in "downtown" Carnation was right next door to Fernandez's Pharmacy. Stoney's tenant knew Fernandez well. Pharmacists, the tenant told Stoney, also faced substantial costs for insurance; they had a lot of professional liability exposure for potential errors in filling prescriptions. Fernandez had, apparently, once invested in a cooperative insurance scheme with a group of his fellow local pharmacists. The plan had gone bust, along with a significant initial investment by its early participants. From what Stoney passed along to me, Fernandez also had a reputation as a hothead and as someone who carried a grudge. Sometimes it didn't take much to give someone with a taste for power an excuse to throw his weight around.

He had the same reputation in the Legislature.

The rest of the insurance industry seemed mostly ambivalent about his bill. I supposed my client's pools might be competitors for some of the larger marine insurers, but it couldn't have amounted to much of their trade because they didn't seem to care either way.

As Chair of the House Committee dealing with insurance, however, Fernandez was in a position to do a lot of damage even if the bill was just his own personal bright idea. It was going to be difficult to stop him. By late Thursday afternoon, Fernandez's bill was out of Committee, through Rules and headed to the Senate floor. It looked like I'd been called in too late to stop it. I'd been told that, if it passed, the Governor would probably sign it; I wasn't sure why, but that decision appeared to have been made. By end-of-day Friday, my clients would be in serious trouble. Janice and I were the only thing standing in the way.

I was worried. Despite our best efforts, I thought the bill likely to pass.

Over the past several days, Janice and I had completed a series of meetings with key Senators, but at this point, all we could do was work the Senate doors, texting and emailing senators, sending in notes, occasionally catching them in person as they came and went. We did what we could to orchestrate our few supporters at the last minute. Janice was over working the Republican side, and I was working the Democrats.

Because our situation was so grave, I decided, late on Thursday, to take a serious gamble.

I stopped by the offices of the Washington Association of Insurance Providers, the principal insurance industry trade association in our state. It was late in the day. Much of their lobbying staff was on the Hill, but I managed to catch up with Terry Moberg, their chief lobbyist. He was in the office making a flurry of last-minute phone calls to key Senators' offices on another bill also coming up the following morning. It was close to five-thirty and most of those offices were closing for the night, so as things slowed down I had a chance to brace Terry with my proposal.

The bill Terry was fighting was a much more important one than mine; a substantial overall reform in insurance industry regulation. Terry's organization had lost control of the bill mid-session to a new but vigorous public reform activist group based in Seattle and with the ear of the Seattle press. The group had secured last-minute amendments that had transformed some carefully drafted, relatively modest initial reforms into much more threatening measures that Terry's industry group was now desperate to kill. His bill was also too close to call.

What I proposed to Terry was a merger.

I'd managed to muster a solid and committed minority of opponents to Fernandez's bill, but I knew I didn't have the numbers to kill it in a straight floor vote. The Members I'd enlisted, however, seemed firmly opposed. Partly that was because Rep. Fernandez wasn't much liked, and partly it was because several of them represented districts with a significant commercial fishing industry constituency and my marine pool clients had made their voices heard. Rep. Fernandez, however, had a head start. He'd convinced his friends, acolytes, and the ill-informed to go along. His support might be mild, but he had the numbers to win.

Given the right pressures, however, I thought some of his weaker supporters might falter. On the other hand, I was confident that the opponents I'd enlisted were seriously invested and would stick to their guns.

For Terry, a merger was a matter of percentages. Several of the firmly committed Senators I'd enlisted to oppose Fernandez's bill seemed to be leaning toward support of the bill Terry was opposing. Or they were undecided. Terry and I walked through our lists. Several of his "marginal yes" Senators were my bill's stronger opponents. If the two bills were merged together, we believed they might decide to vote against. Some of the strong opponents of Terry's bill

SUSPENSION OF THE RULES

seemed to be mild supporters of Fernandez's bill. They, too, would probably vote against a merged version of both.

On balance, it seemed like merging these bills would gain both Terry and me a few additional negative votes. If we threw in together, we might have a shot at killing both bills.

If this was to happen, however, it needed to be done procedurally, on the floor, at the last minute. And it needed to be done by consent; any opposition would prevent it. We were sure Leadership would like the idea; neither of these bills was partisan. Both were on the same general topic, so they'd appreciate the chance to speed things along—get two bills moved off the floor with just one vote.

There was also a good chance the new, relatively inexperienced non-profit citizen-activist group pushing Terry's bill wouldn't be prepared for something like this. They might just see such a merger as a procedural expediency, one that might seem like a positive sign, the joining of two bills, both of which were a shoo-in. Not a strategic threat.

The more likely problem would be Fernandez himself. He was influential in the House, but I suspected his reach in the Senate might be limited. Still, if he was personally attending to this matter, he might easily nix the idea by asking his Senate supporters to refuse consent. If that happened, we'd be back to square one and, I was reasonably sure, my insurance pool clients would be out of luck. Nonetheless, both Terry and I were desperate. It seemed worth a try.

The Senate can move very slowly. Little had gotten done in the morning session. It ended up quite late in the day, pushing up against the evening recess, before our two insurance regulation bills had finally worked their way, side by side, to the top of the calendar. Terry's bill came up first and Senator Packer, who was backing it in the Senate, rose to speak in favor. Before Packer spoke, however, the Lieutenant Governor, who, in Washington, serves as President of the Senate, recognized the Senate Democratic Whip and Packer returned to his seat. Let me just say, Terry and I had called in a favor or two to make this happen, but the Whip moved, "in the interests of time," that this bill be amended to include within it the full contents of the next bill on the agenda—Representative Fernandez's bill. We were approaching evening recess, the whip argued. Both bills were on the same topic and should, logically, be considered together. They had nearly identical titles and could easily be dealt with as one.

I was up in the Senate Gallery holding my breath. As a matter of Senate consent, if any Member of the Senate raised an objection at this point, the bills would remain separate. Both Terry and I had spent a good part of the past 24 hours or so working Senate Leadership and bringing our key supporters up to speed. If this worked, I thought we had a chance. If not, I was reasonably sure we were screwed.

From my perch, standing in an aisle up in the Gallery, I could see Representative Fernandez below. He was clearly visible at the far side of the Senate Chamber, standing in the lobby area. Unlike lobbyists and the general public, Members of the House and Senate had courtesy access to each other's chambers during Session. Fernandez had obviously come over to the Senate Chamber to shepherd his bill, to offer encouragement to the bill's supporters, and to watch its passage. From where I stood, I could clearly see his surprise and momentary confusion at this unexpected consent motion. He'd seen me up there in the gallery and I saw him glance up in my direction. Perhaps he realized this might be something I had orchestrated. In a flash of inspiration, I ignored his glance and instead looked down toward another part of the Senate Floor, shook my head vigorously, moved my hands back and forth, palm outward while I mouthed a silent "no."

From where he stood, of course, he had no idea that I was looking at the back of some unknown Senator's head.

Out of the corner of my eye I could tell that he saw me but was still undecided. My ace, here, was that Fernandez probably had no clear idea just where the vote might stand on either of these two bills. He was, after all, a busy legislator with a lot to deal with. It was lobbyists like Terry Moberg and me that tracked the details.

Then I saw Senator Packer stand again as if to potentially raise an objection to the merger. This had doubtless come as a surprise to him as well. Before he spoke, however, Packer looked over and made eye contact with Fernandez. Packer held out a hand, palm up, as if to ask: "Is this OK?" It appeared that Packer had the OK to merge from the proponents of his bill, but was prepared to prevent the merger if Fernandez didn't like it.

It was very late in the day. Fernandez probably knew his bill was looking reasonably good. But he also couldn't be sure what I'd been up to in the past few days. I very much doubted he had much of a vote count. And he also had to be anxious to see his bill move, not happy to see it pushed up so close to the very end of the day's calendar at the end of a week, vulnerable to further delay that might give me further opportunity to kill it. He might be seeing a chance to get it passed as a part of a much larger bill that probably looked to him likely to pass. Hopefully, he now believed I was unhappy with this proposed merger amendment. So, he shrugged, nodded, and made an uncertain "thumbs-up" sign.

Packer sat back down thus signaling to both bill's supporters that the merger was OK. And, with that, the deed was done. The first and larger bill was successfully amended by consent to include the full contents of Fernandez's bill in its entirety and Fernandez's bill was then stricken from the calendar.

When the resulting merged bill was presented for a vote, it died by the narrowest of margins. It would be at least another year before any of this could come up again. Who knew what changes would occur by then? We now had a full year to think through a sound strategy and to prepare the public and political support to prevent this from ever happening again.

I scrupulously avoided looking again in Representative Fernandez's direction; I very much did not want to make eye contact with the man. Instead I slipped back through the crowd and out through the gallery entrance into the upstairs hall. As I did so, I heard the President of the Senate call for the evening recess.

I hurried down the steps to the floor below and then quickly slipped through the usual crush of lobbyists and interested constituents congregated near the main floor entrances to the Senate Chamber. As I headed toward the Capitol Building's south entrance I looked back just in time to see Representative Jerry Fernandez come out of the Chamber door, pause a moment to look around at the crowd, and then hurry over to the stairs heading up toward the Gallery. I had no doubt whatever that it was me he was looking for. Judging from his face, he was positively enraged. I was very glad he had missed me because I was reasonably sure he knew perfectly well that he had just been snookered. I'd made an enemy there. Fortunately, his Committee wasn't one I usually had to face. I'd gained another year for my insurance pool clients, a very long time in the legislative world.

As I made the short walk back off campus toward my office, I forced myself to suppress the crystalline memory of Representative Jerry Fernandez's enraged face as he'd bulled his way out that Senate Chamber door looking for me. Instead, I got on my phone and made the welcome call to some thoroughly delighted clients. I earned some considerable respect with my work that day. I'd lay out the details in my weekly report but, unfortunately, I'd never really be able to discuss the subterranean device I'd used to win, however nice a story it might have made.

Nonetheless, I happily took my victories where I could find them.

CHAPTER SEVENTEEN

Thursday, March 23, 4:30 p.m.

Agency Liaison

TOWARD THE END OF MARCH, I had a slow Thursday afternoon and decided, late in the day, to drop off and see if I could catch Miles Morgan, Legislative Liaison with the State Conservation Commission.

The Conservation Commission is in the same building as the Department of Ecology, a modern, multi-story structure in Lacy, just off I-5, north of Olympia. I didn't have an appointment but, when security called Miles, he turned out to be in. I was given a visitor's badge and directed down a long, open hall to the Commission's offices on the ground floor.

Miles had been with the Commission for at least 20 years. He was happily married and was one of those friendly, well-liked, comfortable people that find their niche early in life and then just stick with it, rolling with the punches, and doing a solid job without seeming ever to make any enemies. It is a valuable life-talent, one I wish I shared.

The Commission collaborated with WWRP in administering WWRP's farmland protection program. The Commission was also the lead State agency responsible for conservation practice incentives in agriculture. They were important to us on both counts.

I'd made a presentation on our bill at one of the Commission meetings late the previous fall, so Miles was familiar with my bill and had already been supporting our efforts. Still, it seemed like Stoney's misgivings about their diverted focus might be justified. Aside from helpful testimony at the hearing in the House and a few lobbying contacts, I hadn't seen much out of them in the past few weeks. I wanted to be sure they'd be there beside us as we moved our bill through the Senate.

After Miles had assured me that they were still our allies in this fight, I guided our conversation to Fortis Henry—a hidden agenda that was driving most of the meetings I'd had of late. "You seeing much fallout, this session, from the Fortis Henry cost-share payment situation?" I asked Miles.

He shook his head. "Ever since that article in the Times, it's been like climbing Mt. Rainier for us," he replied. "Nobody cared so long as it was more or less contained over in Yakima County. Politically, it's another matter when it shows up in the Seattle and Olympia press."

"You think you'll get your budget?"

"Actually, at this point, I'm not at all sure." He took a sip from what looked like a cup of cold, dead coffee on the corner of his desk. And then made a face and set it back down. "On top of that, we have that damned elections bill. Nobody wants to kill a reform bill when the public thinks the current system is corrupt."

"Is the bill that bad?"

"Oh, yeah. It really sucks; way too costly. Districts hate it. The ones in the larger, wealthier communities will do OK; a lot of them have local assessments from their Counties that can cover much of the expense. But most of the smaller ones will be in a lot of trouble. And, even for the richer ones, it takes a lot of money away from their work on the ground."

The "assessments" he was talking about were small (typically five dollars per parcel) property taxes that sometimes were imposed locally to support conservation district work. State law authorized the local county councils and commissions to adopt this small levy to help support their local conservation districts. Most of the smaller and more conservative rural county commissions were very slow to do this; they disliked any property taxes. Many of those rural districts could only look enviously on as their colleagues in the more "progressive" counties used this property tax "assessment" money to grow their programs. Moreover, even in the counties that had levied the tax, the authorizing county governments, in exchange for the assessment money, tended to impose unwelcome demands on the local conservation district; sometimes extracting concessions that diluted the actual benefit the district's farmers got out of the new money.

The whole thing was the subject of much painful discourse in conservation district country. But, after watching that contentious hearing on the elections bill in House Local Government Committee a few weeks back, I'd actually been giving all this some thought.

"I've been wondering," I said, hesitant to tinker with such a sensitive issue—not entirely confident I knew all the facts. "The reason the taxing authority is given to county government rather than to the districts themselves is probably because the districts aren't really all that accountable to the voters. Suppose you included in the bill an amendment that provided that, once their elections are on the general ballot, the districts would then have authority to pass a local, per parcel, assessment themselves? Or, maybe, they could be authorized to place it on the ballot for voters to decide? As a local initiative?"

Miles looked a bit startled at this. "Hmm," he said. "That's a thought." And think about it he did for a moment or two. "You know an awful lot of our district supervisors wouldn't want their elections decided on the general ballot anyway. They just don't like the idea." He considered it some more. "And they're a pretty conservative lot. Many of them would never want to impose a local property tax anyway. Taxes just aren't in their blood. Know what I mean?"

"Well, you know, Miles, you could make the whole change voluntary. Make the thing optional for each district. The ones that want to do it could opt to be elected on the general ballot and, given their increased voter accountability, they'd get the authority to levy the assessment or to propose it as a ballot initiative. The ones that didn't want that, could stay with the current system. Maybe the Commission could adopt a new code of ethics for local district supervisors to address public concerns. Something like that."

"Huh," he said again. "Not sure how the districts will see all that but we could have something a hell of a lot worse crammed down our throats if we don't come up with something soon."

I wasn't entirely sure if Miles's response to what may have been my hare-brained ideas was just tact or if he seriously thought they might help. But I took it in anyway.

"I guess Fortis Henry's little scandal hasn't helped with any of this," I said.

"You'd think, with Fortis gone, all his mess would go away as well," Miles replied. "I have to say, though, Fortis was a guy who made an impression."

His comment made me recall what Linda Cunningham had said about Fortis's contentious participation within WSAIC. "So, were you having other problems with him as a Commission Member? Or was this dairy lagoon cost-share deal just a one off?"

Miles smiled grimly and shook his head. "If only," he said. "Guy was a constant menace. Injected himself into everything. Late last year he got all upset about one of our candidates for local district supervisor. Over in Spokane County. Had the Commissioners all cranked up about that for months. Those of us on the staff were running in circles, trying to sort it out."

Spokane? "You're not talking about Daryl Weber?"

"Yeah. Daryl. You know about that?"

"I'd just heard that he's applied for a Commission appointment as supervisor there. Just wondering."

"Daryl's a great guy. Terrifically qualified to be a supervisor.

Spokane CD is really fortunate he's interested. Having him there will help them and us—help cement our partnership with NRCS. Big plus."

"But . . ."

"But Fortis was all upset because Daryl's application specifically claimed that, said he'd be able to help strengthen the district's relationship with NRCS, that he knew from the inside how the Agency works and could help us deal with them. All to the good, far as most of us were concerned. But, as Fortis saw it, he was using his official NRCS position to advance his own interests. Daryl's application letter was actually on NRCS letterhead; apparently that's a no-no with the agency. Who knew? Who cared, you know?"

Miles response almost made me laugh. "So you're saying that Fortis Henry, the person accused of misusing his position to secure a hundred some thousand bucks in cost-share benefits from NRCS was actually upset about Daryl Weber's use of NRCS stationary to get a position as a conservation district supervisor?"

"Yep," he said. "Rich, right? Keep in mind, Daryl had already obtained the OK from his boss to do this, to become a local conservation district supervisor. It's a bit unusual, but Daryl's NRCS responsibilities, most of the time, don't really intersect with local district issues. When they do, he can recuse. Supervisor is just a volunteer position, you know. There's no money involved. It's non-partisan."

"Did Fortis do it?" I asked. "Did he ever actually notify NRCS about Daryl's use of the letterhead?"

"Nope. Unless he did it without telling anyone. When Darryl heard the complaint, he actually resubmitted the same application on personal letterhead. Fortis made a big deal of it here at the office and with a couple of the other commissioners. But his next public chance to bring it up would have been at the Commission meeting in January where Daryl's boss, the State Conservationist, would have been present. I know he got push-back from some of the Commissioners. That was just before Christmas. As you know, he died on the day before New Years'. I don't think he ever actually sent in his complaint; we'd have heard if he had. None of the rest of us cared."

On my drive home to Seattle, that evening, I considered the fact that Daryl had become something of a political "player." He was far more involved in political issues than was typical for most Federal Government employees. I wondered if that had gotten him in trouble in the past. I also wondered about the vague similarity between Daryl's claimed misuse of his official position and the case that had been made about Fortis Henry's.

So, on a hunch, when I got back in the office the next morning, I pulled up the website for the "Truth Spotlight" and then got on the phone.

"That'd be me," was the reply when I asked to speak to the organization's Executive Director. "Ronnie Johnson, at your service." From their website I knew Ronnie Johnson had a staff of one. Him. I recalled the young, slim, spectacled, committed-looking young man I seen in the O'Brien Building hallway after the hearing that day a few weeks earlier.

After introducing myself and explaining my interest in their Fortis Henry story (my version did not mention any suspected murders) I got to it: "So, I assume you must have had informants on that story, right. People who came forward to tip you off?"

"Absolutely. We talked to several people."

"I'm wondering about initially. About what got you interested in the first place. I can understand if you need to protect the confidentiality of your sources, but it would be very helpful if you could possibly let me know who that was?"

"So, again, you're interested in this because . . .?"

"I'm representing a group of farmers on some legislation in Olympia" I said. "It's a bill that would make it easier for them to use sound conservation management on their farms and then protect them from development. I need to drill down and get some more details on your story. It's having an impact on our legislative efforts." I could appreciate his caution, but I didn't really want to get into a lot of detail, so I kept it vague.

"Um. I guess I see. As it happens, there's no confidentiality problem at all," he said. "We didn't name sources in the article itself, but we wanted to have some of them ready to back us up publicly, if the need arose. They were OK with that. Was kind of surprising, actually. I'd heard nothing about this thing, and then, over a few days last Fall, I had a number of spontaneous calls. Kind of like several people were thinking along the same lines at the same time. I had a lot of help working up the story from Linda Cunningham. Maybe you know her; she's with WSAIC. She's very knowledgeable about how this stuff works. But initially, we got a tip from a guy who's with the Federal Government, with NRCS. Over in Spokane."

"Are you talking about Daryl Weber?"

"Yeah, that's right, Daryl Weber. He knew all about it. Said it was wrong and we ought to do something about it. Why? You know him?"

"Oh yeah," I said. "I know him well."

CHAPTER EIGHTEEN

Friday, March 24, 10 a.m.

Direct Approach

DARYL WEBER! AND LINDA CUNNINGHAM!
I was particularly troubled by Daryl. He and Fortis Henry had been in some kind of feud. Daryl had been in the perfect position to know of Fortis's substantial cost-share payment. NRCS Local Service Center Team members typically attended their District's board meetings, all of them were Daryl's colleagues and friends. And the financial information would all have ultimately passed through the State Office where Daryl might see or learn about it. Presumably the feud started with Daryl's call to Truth Spotlight. Then Fortis had countered with his threat to report Daryl to his bosses for violating federal "misuse of position" rules and misusing NRCS stationary. As innocuous as that might seem at first glance, after I took a look, on-line, at the Federal rules themselves, it did seem like a possible problem. The rules were quite rigorous.

In Fortis's case, his Federal cost-share assistance grant had been perfectly legal. The decision to give him the money had been made in a way that was no different from how thousands of such decisions were made around the State and across the country every year.

As an elected member of the Board of Supervisors for the local conservation district, Fortis had, of course, recused himself from the vote on the district's recommendation concerning his project. But he'd definitely been present when that vote was taken. He'd been there and had participated in the entire Board discussion leading up to it. The rest of those Supervisors were also, of course, good friends, colleagues, neighbors, members of his local community.

Darryl and Fortis obviously had reason to intensely dislike one another. Each was willing to do the other damage. What was most troubling was the casual manner in which Daryl had deflected my interest. When I'd asked, he'd gone to some lengths to downplay the seriousness of Fortis's "misdeed." That he hadn't been more forthcoming made me wonder what he might have had to hide.

Still, misusing a letterhead and exaggerating one's apparent influence in an application for a volunteer public appointment, while it might technically violate the rules, didn't really seem all that serious. Maybe he might have faced some administrative discipline, but it probably wouldn't have amounted to much.

Then I remembered Daryl's odd comment in connection with his work. He'd said something like: "with a little luck" in reference to his future with NRCS. I'd just ignored it at the time. Now I began to wonder what he'd meant. That plus the fact that he'd clearly been sufficiently bothered by Fortis's threat that he had avoided telling me about it when I had given him the opening, it all made me wonder what else might have been in Daryl's NRCS personnel file.

How could I find that out? I could think of only one way.

"Hi Sandy. What can I do you for today?" said Daryl. Faced with his friendly voice and bright attitude, I almost lost my nerve. I was feeling increasingly uncomfortable with not reporting my suspicions to the police. I'd come to a point where I needed to act.

I had to know.

So, I dove right in: "Daryl, a couple of weeks ago, when we got together over here in Olympia, we talked at some length about Fortis Henry's little cost-share boondoggle. But you failed to mention that you were the one that tipped off the Truth Spotlight folks about what he'd done."

"Well," Daryl said cautiously, "I guess I'm not sure what difference it makes, Sandy. Does it matter?"

Daryl was asking a good question. My only real answer would reveal what I suspected about Fortis Henry's death. I could equivocate or make something up. But I was by then reasonably sure I needed, soon, to have a conversation with someone at the Yakima County Sheriff's office. When that happened, it would all become public. And Daryl was going to look back on our conversation and know if I deceived him.

It was time to come clean.

"Yeah, Daryl. I think it does matter. And I have something I need to admit to you as well. When we talked, that day in the NRB Cafeteria, I wasn't being entirely straight with you, either." I then laid out for him the concerns about the Stetson hat, my growing suspicion that someone had been with Fortis Henry when he'd died, and that it was even possible Fortis had been murdered.

Now it was Daryl's turn to be stunned, or at least to act that way. "You're serious?" he said. Then, after a moment's pause: "If one of us had been with him, wouldn't they have said something?" There was another pause as the light dawned. "Um. That's why all these questions."

"I don't know what to think, Daryl," I said, seriously trying to sound apologetic. "It seems possible that any one of us who were there that day could have been somehow involved. Me included. You're not the first person I've asked about this who was there that day. I've come to the point where someone needs to contact the Yakima County Sheriff's Office and lay it out for them."

"I see."

"Why'd you report him? To the Truth Spotlight folks?"

"I kind of told you that, when we spoke that day. What he did to get that cost-share money sucks. I know, it happens all the time. But it should stop. It ends up diverting NRCS cost-share money away from the most strategic uses. And it demeans the work we all do. The Districts need to face up to this and straighten it out. It can sometimes be subtle, but I've been watching this happen for years. I guess I've just had enough. I basically knew he'd find out about it. I didn't ask that Truth Spotlight guy to keep me out of it; somebody was going to have to speak up in public at some point if it was going to stop. And I got to say, what with this district elections bill up in the legislature, I think the districts are beginning to appreciate how this kind of thing can damage their credibility and screw up the great work they do."

"I'm not sure that's how they see it."

He scoffed. "Probably not. Not at the moment. They're just going to be mad at me. Probably my bosses here at NRCS will too. Everybody likes the cozy District-NRCS partnership. But they just can't keep doing business like this without it coming out, maybe some time when the consequences will be a great deal worse."

I couldn't help but agree with him. At least generally. But there was another question I needed to ask. One I knew he wasn't going to like: "So, OK, but all that aside. There's more to this for you, isn't there?"

"What do you mean?"

"Well, you obviously knew Fortis Henry was getting ready to report you to your bosses over some materials you submitted with your Supervisor application to the Conservation Commission."

That stopped him cold, so I continued. "You'd publicly embarrassed him over the supposed misuse of his position, so he figured turnabout was fair play, right?" Again, no response. "Maybe he had misused his position, but he figured you'd also misused yours. Did you talk with him about it? I'm betting he was more than happy to let you know what *he* was about to do."

"We had talked about it, yeah," Daryl said carefully. "But it was no big deal."

Again silence. Given what I'd just told him concerning my suspicions about Fortis Henry's death, he might not want to elaborate on his own possible motive to kill the man. But then, suddenly, with one of those faint flutters of accomplishment, I saw the whole thing. I believed I already knew what might be in Daryl's NRCS personnel file that he wanted to remain unmentioned.

"But it *was* a 'big deal,' wasn't it? In fact, it was critical. Because you've done this before." I was very close to turning a friend into a possible enemy. Not a great thing to do considering I liked him. I also still needed Daryl's help on the Conservation Heritage Priority Bill. And maybe on other legislation in the months and years ahead. Nonetheless, I pushed ahead. I'd been honest with him. Now he needed to reciprocate.

"What do you mean?" he said. But he was beginning to sound defeated.

"Come on, Daryl. It's right there in your personnel file isn't it?" Maybe my guess would turn out to be way off the mark. But I decided right then to take the shot: "You've already been reprimanded once for this same kind of thing, right? Probably did something you shouldn't have to help Didi Harris."

He continued to stay silent, so I went on: "You're in hock for that new farm of yours. $535,000 is a lot of money for a family guy on a government salary. I know you bought it a couple of years ago on a real estate contract from Didi Harris's dad Truman. Why a real estate contract? Why not a bank mortgage? Because you couldn't get a bank to loan you the money. Truman Harris is a rapacious real estate developer by all accounts. Even loaning you the money for your farm would have taken some convincing. He's in the business of developing and selling real estate, not lending people money. I'm betting the person who convinced him was his daughter Didi, your State Representative. She's also working that conservation futures tax bill that pertains directly to your NRCS duties under the Federal ACEP program. If her bill passes, it will strengthen ACEP here in Washington. Maybe you even asked her to do it. She is someone who doesn't take 'no' for an answer. I bet you did something stupid in her last campaign. Endorsed her or something, referencing your NRCS title. And you got in trouble for it.

"You and I both know if Fortis Henry had complained to NRCS about your application for District Supervisor, it would have been a second "misuse of position" offense on your record. Could easily have cost you your job. Debts, a kid with medical needs, a new business—you need your job. Tell me about it, Daryl. Do you really want me to dig it up on my own?"

"OK. OK, that's enough," Daryl finally said. "I hear you. You're right, at least mostly." Through the ensuing moments of silence, I could hear him breathing deeply over the phone. Finally, he said: "You don't need to spell it out. That day at his house last December, I planned to ask him after the meeting, or I guess 'beg' would be closer to the mark, to 'beg' him not to report me. It was a bullshit complaint, but with the other thing on my record, you're right, I'd have been in the shit. If I lost my job, there's no way we could keep the farm. But it never happened—he was dead before I ever had a chance to make my pitch.

"So, yeah, you're right, Sandy," Daryl continued. "But I never even got a chance to talk to him that day. I got there late. First time I saw him was when we all went out there and found him floating in that damn lagoon. Sure, I disliked the guy. But that doesn't mean I killed him."

CHAPTER NINETEEN

Friday, March 24, 11 a.m.

Inspired Guesswork

DARYL WEBER DID SEEM TO HAVE a serious motive. With Fortis Henry dead, there was no report to his bosses about his problematic application to the Commission. I still, of course, had no real evidence that he, or for that matter, anyone else, had actually committed murder. Or that he'd been with Henry at the time he died.

My conversation with Daryl convinced me, however, that I finally needed to report what I suspected to the proper authorities no matter who might find an official investigation embarrassing. I had too much cause for concern to keep quiet any longer.

On that horrible day at the end of December, all of us but possibly one had believed that Fortis Henry had died in nothing more than a tragic accident, perhaps just a simple slip and fall. The pond was in use and quickly filling up, but without the safety fence, it was still, essentially, a dangerous construction site. There had been no real investigation. The only police officials I recalled being present were two uniformed Sheriff's deputies, but I couldn't remember their names. The Yakima County Sheriff's website didn't make it at all clear who one would contact to report a suspected crime— all they provided was a general number. I hesitated to call that number because I'd very probably end up having to explain myself to a series of intermediaries before finally convincing them that I needed to speak with an actual detective.

I did, however, know someone to ask. Lieutenant Nathan Wilson of the Washington State Patrol was someone I trusted. He led their Special Investigations Unit and seemed likely to have acquaintances in the Yakima County Sheriff's office. Given our history, of course, I fully expected a call to Lieutenant Wilson would have its own challenges.

He almost laughed outright when I explained the purpose of my call. "You're telling me you suspect this guy, Henry, was murdered. You've been, what, 'looking into it' and now you want to talk with a detective?"

I understood, sympathized even, with his tone. Just a couple of years earlier, I'd been a suspect in the murder of a Washington State Senator. I'd spent several weeks asking questions and trying to clear my name without "interfering" with Lieutenant Wilson's official investigation, all to Wilson's deep frustration. In the end, we'd solved the crime and I believe I ended up earning some grudging respect. But to find myself embroiled in another murder so soon after the last incident must have seemed to him, as it certainly did to me, deeply ironic.

"Yeah," he said, filling that one half-inch syllable with yards of meaning and undoubtedly shaking his head. "Well, the guy you probably want to talk to is Detective Tracy at the Yakima County Sheriff's Office. Ricky's a friend of mine. A good man. Knows what he's doing. We served together in Tacoma PD some years back. Let him know I sent you. He'll help you out." He provided me with a direct phone.

"Thanks, Lieutenant. That's a big help. I'll say 'hello' from you."

"You do that. And, Dalton, just one word of advice. Not that I think you'll pay any attention."

"All right." I knew what was coming.

"Try to stay out of it this time," he said wearily. "Don't get personally involved. Let the Sheriff's Office do their job. Ricky's a good man. Knows his stuff. Just tell him what you know, and leave the rest to him, OK?"

"OK, Lieutenant. Thanks for the help. I appreciate it. I also hear you. And I'll do as you say."

"I hope you do, Dalton. For your sake, if nothing else."

I didn't take offense. Maybe I flattered myself in believing that I'd essentially solved that previous matter. But my "help" had also probably made his life more, rather than less difficult. I fully intended to take his advice this time around and, after passing along my concerns, would stay completely out of any ensuing investigation.

It wasn't until I was leaving a message on Detective Richard Tracy's voicemail asking for a return call that it hit me, about his name. I was reasonably sure his professional colleagues called him "Ricky" instead of "Dick" for a reason. I'd need to remember that if I ever had occasion to call him by his first name.

While I awaited Detective Tracy's return call, I tried to get some work done on my weekly reporting, but I couldn't keep my mind on it. I began thinking about the other person whom I'd been told had provided information about Fortis Henry to Truth Spotlight, Linda Cunningham. She, too, in our conversation about Fortis Henry hadn't been forthcoming about her own involvement. She could easily have mentioned that she'd helped Truth Spotlight with their story. From what Ronnie Johnson had told me, it sounded like Linda's help had been willing and significant.

In Linda's case, however, my suspicions leaned toward political motives. She seemed like a manipulator; someone who controls events by pulling strings behind the scenes. I could easily imagine her knowing that the district elections issue was simmering there beneath the surface and recognizing that discrediting Fortis Henry would almost certainly energize support for election reform, adding yet more pressure on Fortis and getting him off her back. Once Daryl Weber tipped off Truth Spotlight and Ronnie Johnson gave his friend Linda a call, she must have been all too happy to help.

She and her leadership saw torpedoing the Fortuna Package as a very big deal for their organization; having Fortis inside their group, subverting their efforts, was the last thing they needed. And as the person expected to guide their efforts, also the last thing Linda needed as well. Linda and WSAIC were involved in Olympia-gamesmanship at a level I seldom thought about. I had to admit that if WSAIC came to be seen as instrumental in killing that Fortuna legislation, and if they could do so despite all the best efforts of Washington's Democratic Governor, their reputation as a "player" in Olympia would be greatly enhanced. My work, and the small groups and interests I represented never gave me occasion to play legislative politics in that way. But it was definitely a move Linda might find appealing. By discrediting Fortis Henry and getting him in hot water with his own conservation district political base, she'd marginalized him and taken his support for Fortuna off the WSAIC map.

That might also have eliminated any real motive by her for murder. It did, however, seem like a reasonably good explanation for why she'd apparently been unwilling to come clean with me about her relationship with Fortis Henry. Finally, realizing that I was spinning in circles with these speculations, I managed to focus on the work at hand and did, ultimately, buckle down and get out my weekly client reports.

It was late that Friday afternoon when I got a call back from Detective Tracy.

"Yeah, well I pulled the file on this thing when I got your message. You know it's closed, right? An accident?"

It wasn't the most hopeful beginning. But I dove in: "That's why I'm calling, Detective Tracy. It seems like it's never really been investigated?"

"Nope. From what I see here, wasn't any reason for it. Apparently, you think maybe it should have been?"

I sure as hell didn't want to get into whether some kind of *mistake* was made. "No, no, I'm sure that made absolutely perfect sense at the time. It's just that some things have come to light, some stuff that wasn't known or considered when it happened." Then I decided I'd better put my ace on the table. "I guess you know Lieutenant Nathan Wilson? With the State Patrol here in Olympia? I flew some of this past him and he thought you might be interested in taking another look."

"So, you said in your message that you're a lobbyist or something. How is it that you know Nate?"

"Well, um, I worked on a case with him here a couple of years ago. The Senator that got murdered in his office. Maybe you read about it?"

"Yeah, I did. You 'worked' with him, huh? So how was that? What was your connection with it?"

Now he was leading me into shaky ground. "I was, I guess you could say, a suspect."

"Hmmm. I see."

I wasn't at all sure he did. "I, um, helped him find the guilty party."

"Yeah. Well, I'll tell you, Mr. Dalton. After I got your call I got in touch with Nate. He told me all about you. All in all, he seems to think you're OK. So why don't you just fill me in on why you think this accident was really a murder?"

So he already knew how I was connected with Lt. Wilson. Tricky guy! Who knew what Lt. Wilson might have told him about me?

That was, however, the best opening I was going to get, so I went for it. I explained who was there that day and, without going into detail, pointed out that any one of us could have done it and how all of us (me included) had reason to dislike the man. And, specifically, how it didn't make sense that Fortis Henry have been out there by a muddy, newly-constructed dairy lagoon alone wearing a $600 spotless white Stetson cowboy hat.

As I outlined my case, what I got back was a series of noncommittal "OKs", "I sees" and "Uh huhs." Before long, my story started to sound, even to me, hopelessly weak and speculative. That's why

I ended with: "I guess that may not sound like much to you. But I just felt like I should tell it to somebody official rather than keeping it to myself."

"You know this matter's closed, right?" he said in response.

"You mentioned that, Lieutenant."

"Been almost three months, at this point. No chance of any forensics, fingerprints, DNA. Body's gone. People forget. Even if you're right, it's a little late to do much about it."

"Like I said, Lieutenant, it seemed like I ought to say something."

"Oh yeah, you did the right thing to call. Yeah, that's for sure. Just, well, I'm not sure what to do with it. Case is closed, you know?"

It struck me that trying to explain what I knew in a phone conversation with a busy public servant late on a Friday afternoon was probably a fool's venture. If I was going to do this, perhaps I needed to do it right. I asked if he'd mind meeting me in person sometime the following week. I manufactured other business in Yakima and said I could arrange it to coincide with whatever appointment would work into his schedule. Very reluctantly, I thought, he agreed to a meeting the following Thursday at 10 a.m., nearly a week away. It would be a long drive for me, but at that point, I felt I had launched this thing and ought to follow through properly. It seemed worth the drive. By the following Thursday, I should have things in Olympia under control.

That evening, Sherry and I got together for our planned dinner after dropping David off for the evening at the home of a school friend. I slept over at the office and at about nine on Saturday morning, I grabbed my laptop and set out for home in Seattle in miserable traffic and a heavy pouring rain.

I was rounding the curve just north of Martin Way when I first saw that the traffic ahead had stopped cold.

CHAPTER TWENTY

Saturday, March 25, 11 a.m.

Cautionary Event

WHITE.

Bright fluorescent lights recessed into an institutional drop ceiling.

I was in bed. There was some kind of rough fabric across my forehead.

Sherry was there. She looked worried.

"What . . .?"

"You're in Providence St. Peter Hospital," she said. "You've been in an accident."

Then I remembered.

It was Saturday and I'd been on my way home . . . until the crash.

"But, how . . .?" Then I recalled being loaded into an ambulance. Waking up in the hospital. She hadn't been here then and I'd fallen asleep again.

"You were pretty groggy, and they didn't know who to call," she told me. But your phone was on and somebody decided to look at your contacts and recent calls. I think they maybe just hit redial, because they ended up calling me."

Last thing I remembered before the accident was having called her as I was getting on the freeway. It was raining hard and the traffic was bad. I'd wanted to tell her how much I'd enjoyed our visit over dinner the night before. I'd ended up leaving a message.

"Jesus, my head hurts," I said.

"They think you may have a concussion. A few bruises, but nothing else too significant. They want to check you out a bit before they send you home." Her smile was a mix of relief and concern.

The last thing I could remember was stopped cars just past the Martin Way exit. The heavy Olympia traffic had opened up and everyone was getting back up to the speed limit. Then, suddenly, it was all brake lights, squealing tires, and crashing metal.

"Oh God!" I said. "Was anybody else hurt?"

"There was a fatality accident ahead of you. You seem to have been caught up in the aftermath somehow. They say your car is pretty badly smashed up."

"I don't remember any of that."

"Probably isn't surprising. I wouldn't worry. You apparently talked to one of the police officers who responded at the scene before you passed out in the ambulance. They told the EMT that your car would be towed to an impound lot."

"Christ!"

At this point, an ER doctor showed up and started asking me questions, like could I count to ten, how many fingers did I see, and who was President of the United States. I must have answered correctly because, after taking down some notes, he told Sherry and a nurse that I needed to rest but I could probably go home soon. The next time I was awake it was maybe an hour later and I was feeling better, especially when I realized that Sherry was still seated there next to my bed in one of those uncomfortable chairs they provide for visitors in hospital rooms.

As I thought about it, I realized that, other than my dad, she might be the only person I knew who was likely to come visit me in a hospital room. Or to help make sure I got home afterward. I knew a lot of people, but I guess I didn't have that many actual friends. I was damn lucky they'd chosen her to call and very glad they hadn't called my dad.

They released me that same afternoon. Rather than taking me back up to my Seattle Condo, Sherry drove me to my office in Olympia. At least there I'd have someone to look in on me instead of being stuck in some big, anonymous building in Seattle. There was something quite comforting about having Sherry look after me.

She stopped in a couple of times, but the rest of that weekend I just moped around my office trying, with limited success, to get some work done. Thankfully, they'd saved my laptop and kept it safe with my other personal effects, so I had that. But when she was gone, I found myself feeling low, maybe just missing her attention. On Monday morning, I contacted my insurance company and walked my bruises downtown to pick up a rental car. I also contacted the State Patrol about my own car. Because it had been a fatality accident, the State Patrol was doing a complete investigation. When my car was ready to be released, they'd let me know. Then, I concentrated on getting myself organized enough to get back on the hill to work.

It was the following day, Tuesday, when I got a call from a Sergeant Nakamura, the State Patrol accident investigations officer I'd spoken with along the side of the freeway after my accident. He had a few questions for me about the accident, but when we were done, he set my mind at ease: "You'll have to work with your insurance company, of course. But, at this point, I can't see any fault on your part. It looks very much to us like you were simply in the wrong place at the wrong time."

I hadn't been worried. But hearing him say it made me think perhaps I should have been. "That's good to hear," I said. "I guess I'm going to need to figure out what to do about my car."

"Well, that's the other thing I wanted to discuss with you. Um, would you mind telling me how long you've owned this vehicle?"

What was this? "Of course not," I said. "I bought it new. I've had it for, maybe two years. Something like that. Why do you ask?"

"You a car buff, or something? Or maybe some kind of electronics or computer tech?"

I had to laugh. "Furthest thing from it. I'm a lawyer and a lobbyist. The closest I come to cars is on my daily commute. The only computer work I do is typing reports and searching the internet. What's this about?"

"Have you had any problems with your car lately? Had it into the shop. Or noticed anything out of the ordinary?"

"No. Not at all. None of that. It's been nearly a year since my last regular service, but everything's been fine."

"Well, sir, when our team looked over your car after the accident, we found an unusual 'dongle' plugged into the OBD port under the dash."

"Whoa . . .," I said. "A what?"

"A dongle. There's a place behind a plastic flip panel under your dash where mechanics plug in to access your onboard computer. It's called an 'onboard diagnostics port,' an 'OBD port.' Your car had this dongle plugged in there. We're wondering what it's for."

"And a dongle is . . .?"

"Well, to us, it looks like it's a transmitter/receiver, Bluetooth, that would allow remote access to your onboard computer. Am I understanding correctly that you weren't aware this thing was there? Your car hasn't been in the shop?"

"You're absolutely correct. I bought it new two years ago. Wouldn't I have seen it there?"

"On some cars, yes. On yours, it's underneath the dash and behind a plastic panel. Pretty well hidden unless you looked for it."

"I take it this is not standard equipment."

"No, sir. It is not. This is more like hacking equipment. At least that's what it looks like to us."

"Hacking?" I definitely didn't like where this was going. "So, what does that mean?"

"Well, it's hard to say. But one of the things it could mean is that somebody had your car set up for remote diagnostics. Or um, conceivably, to remotely control or to change or disable some operations. So . . ., I take it that somebody wasn't you."

"It certainly was not." I thought about what he'd said. "Are you saying you think that's what could have caused this accident?"

"Well, we certainly had that thought. It's why we've been looking at it. But it doesn't look like it. We don't see how it could have happened that way. The initial accident occurred before you ever came along. It looks like you were sideswiped by a skidding truck. We're convinced this had nothing to do with our accident, but, well, if this thing isn't yours, then you certainly might want to give some thought to how it got there. And why. There's probably some simple explanation. But I've got to say, it isn't impossible that you could have been targeted for some kind of mischief further down the line. A dongle's not the only or, these days, even the best way to hack a car. But it's probably the easiest."

I thought a moment about what that meant.

"Is there any way to tell where this thing came from? Fingerprints, or, I don't know, whatever . . . ?"

"It seemed unusual, so we checked. No fingerprints. No serial numbers. The equipment isn't all that unusual—available lots of places, including the internet. No good way to run a trace."

The idea that I'd been driving around like that gave me the shivers. "What about the car. You say you're done with it?"

"Soon. Maybe another couple of days." The Sergeant paused, and then continued: "You're sure you have no idea why that dongle might have been put into your vehicle, Mr. Dalton?"

"Absolutely sure."

"Or who might have put it there?"

"No idea."

"Well, since it was in your car, and we don't have any further use for it, what would you like us to do with it?"

"Um, I don't know. I guess I ought to keep it. Do you want to send it to me?"

"All right. I can do that. As soon as your car is ready for release. You still reside at the address on your license and registration?"

"I do."

"Fine. I'll send it to you in the post. Take a couple of days."

"Thanks, officer. I, um, appreciate your help."

"As far as the car is concerned, I can tell you it looks to be a total loss, or nearly so. Your insurer will have it evaluated. That's just from what I've seen."

"I guess I'll have to see what my insurance company says."

Yeah, well, thanks for your time." Again, a moment of hesitation. Then: "Um, also, maybe a piece of advice?"

"Sure."

"Honestly, if it was me, I wouldn't go near that car again without having the onboard electronics completely checked or, better, replaced. I'm just saying . . ."

That was certainly sobering to hear. "Thank you," I said.

"Yeah. No problem. Meanwhile, you might give some careful thought, to where that dongle might have come from. If what you're saying is true, maybe someone had something in mind for you and it could just be that it wasn't something good."

CHAPTER TWENTY-ONE

Wednesday, March 29, 9 a.m.

Tabled Motion

BY WEDNESDAY MORNING, I was already regretting my decision to drive over to Yakima the following day. I had the Senate hearing on our Conservation Heritage Priority Bill coming up on the coming Monday afternoon, with an executive session probably to follow immediately afterward. It was looking like a busy week. I really couldn't afford to take a day off to make the long drive to Yakima and back.

It was, therefore, actually a relief when, I got Detective Tracy's call asking if we could reschedule. When he suggested a date late the following week I immediately recognized it as just another demonstration, if any were needed, that he really didn't consider our meeting to be a priority. If that were true, I had to wonder why I should spend most of a day going to Yakima for what would probably turn out to be nothing. There was something else as well: I'd been giving some thought to how little I looked forward to explaining the murder motives of several of my closest colleagues. It seemed different if he looked into it and discovered those kinds of things himself. I was OK with that. But I wasn't especially happy about, in effect, ratting out a bunch of people I considered to be friends. Suddenly I was having misgivings about getting into all that in person with this guy. Somehow, it felt like I might be better able to control the conversation on the phone—maybe limit the damage.

I made a snap decision: "Do you think it might be easier if we just took the time and tried to do this over the phone."

"Sure," he said, rather too quickly I thought, and then added: "Could've done it last week far as I'm concerned."

I kept myself from rising to the bait. "When would you suggest?" I said.

"We could do it right now. I got to be out of here for another meeting in half an hour. That do it?"

I thought it sounded a bit tight and I was tempted to just call it off—to tell him if he was OK with a murderer running loose in his County, it was fine by me. Then, on second thought, I realized that didn't really make any sense; if there was a murderer, it was probably one of my own colleagues, right there in Olympia. That made me again question what I was really hoping to accomplish with this call. Mostly, I supposed, I wanted to shed a responsibility that I seemed to have taken upon myself for finding what I thought may be a murderer. Maybe, if he didn't care about that, I ought to be asking myself: should I?

In any case, I took him up on his offer and proceeded to explain in more detail why Fortis Henry's death seemed suspicious and might deserve further investigation. I tried hard to keep my arguments cogent and didn't go into a lot of detail about the various apparent motives—but I did make him understand that several of those who were there that day might have had strong negative feelings about the deceased. In the end, it felt to me like I'd done a reasonably good job of making my case without too badly compromising my interpersonal ethics.

"Yeah," he said after I'd begun to slow down. "I see where you're going with this. We recovered the hat. Gotta say, didn't look all that special to me."

"Well, maybe not, after we had splashed around the area to recover the body, and your guys pulled the hat up out of that pond," I countered. Then, realizing how defensive that might have sounded, I added: "Maybe someone could talk with Fortis's wife, Maryanne. See what she thinks about why he might have been wearing it."

"Could do that. Yeah." He sounded doubtful.

"You know, Detective Tracy, it really, seriously doesn't seem likely to me that he'd have gone out back, that day, stepped over that concrete footing for no known reason, and then just, what, lost his balance and fallen in?"

"Maybe. Report says it was muddy in the area, slippery. Sometimes death is just an accident—the place you found him in looked pretty muddy."

He wasn't seeing my point, so I kept trying. "Do you think it might be a good idea to have a chat with the people who were there that day? See if any of their stories seem worth following up? Check when they say they arrived? See if any of them might have had a chance to go out back when the rest of us weren't paying attention? Something like that?"

"Could do that." He paused, considering. "Going to create a lot of unhappiness in that family. Bringing all this up again. They're probably just starting to heal. Suddenly we're asking a lot of questions about some possible murder. Questions that probably aren't going to go anywhere. You do realize, even if we come up with a suspect, it's going to take some doing to prove it. If there was somebody with him out there that day, it would have been just the two of them there, you know. No witnesses. No forensics." He then drew what I took to be a deep, long-suffering breath.

Something I knew suddenly surfaced. Why hadn't I thought of it before? "You know, Detective, that dairy farm was pretty high-tech. I believe they keep their livestock under video surveillance. It's just possible they could have a video record of the area around the dairy barn that day."

"I suppose," he said, still without enthusiasm. "Probably just inside the barn. No one mentioned that at the time. Also, video surveillance typically gets deleted or copied over after a short time. If they got it, there's a good chance it's long gone after, what, three months now? There's a reason we close these files, you know. Been a long time. Doesn't help"

At that point I wanted to tell this man to just forget about the whole thing; that I was sure he had his hands full, what with shoplifting complaints and breaking up bar fights. But better judgment prevailed. I reminded myself that this guy was a friend of Lieutenant Nathan Wilson and I could need him down the road. I bit my tongue. I also had to admit that, in the course of making my explanations, I'd become painfully aware how thin it must all sound to him. My theory about what had happened, even to me, still seemed a little wild. But I was increasingly convinced there was something to this.

I had also planned to mention my accident over the weekend and the dongle. I admit I was spooked by that dongle. I'd done some on-line research and realized that most modern cars were vulnerable to hacking. Inserting a dongle was, apparently, one of the lowest-tech ways to gain control. It suggested someone who was somewhat tech-savvy, but perhaps not extremely sophisticated.

But why would I ask for help from some disinterested, bureaucratic Sheriff in Yakima for something that had happened right here in Thurston County? Even if Detective Tracy became convinced there had been a murder over in Yakima, the only help I'd likely get from him regarding that dongle would probably be a phone number for the Olympia or Lacey Police Department. I'd already, in effect, been warned and brushed off by the State Patrol

When the call was over, I did dial up my car dealer in Renton, the place that had done the warranty service on my car. They confirmed that it had been 10 months since I'd had the car in the shop. And they were absolutely certain that dongle had not, could not have been left behind by one of their mechanics. "If we'd left something like that in your car, we'd miss it. Immediately," their service guy told me. "We'd be calling you up wanting it back. And anyway, we just don't use anything like what you describe. We plug in our diagnostics, of course. But what you're talking about is quite different. Wasn't us. Sorry."

As frustrated as I was when I hung up from my call with Detective Tracy, I had to admit: I had, at least, saved myself a long, wasted day driving over to Yakima and back.

CHAPTER TWENTY-TWO

Saturday, April 1, noon

Reconsideration

THAT FRIDAY NIGHT I WORKED LATE and decided to stay over and work out of the Olympia office on Saturday. It was a surprisingly nice day. I called Sherry and learned that she was working in her office as well. We'd both packed a snack for lunch so I suggested, as a shared lunch break, that we take a walk together along the Olympia waterfront.

"OK," Sherry finally said a few moments after we were seated on a park bench overlooking Swantown Marina on East Bay and had opened our respective sandwiches. "What is it? We're back to all these long silences? Something's bothering you again and I'm betting it's that farmer that died, right?"

That's all it took. I laid the whole thing out—mostly in one long monologue. I'd learned a great deal about the lives and motives of the people who'd been with me the day Fortis Henry died. I'd said some of this, an abridged version, to Detective Tracy. But I hadn't yet really assessed it all in the detail it deserved. All of these people had disliked him, some more intensely than others. Even within the limits of what I knew, it was clear that all of them were a good deal happier or better off with him gone.

I realized, of course, that I probably shouldn't be telling her any

132

of this. She had plenty to worry about without being sucked into my personal anxieties. By telling her about it, I was also making her complicit in my secrets. Now, my problems would become her problems. All kinds of crazy thoughts had been racing through my mind concerning that damn dongle they'd found in my car. By having this conversation, could I be putting Sherry at some kind of risk?

In the end, however, my impulse to share, and her obvious desire to know, won out.

"Have you reported any of this?" she asked me quietly when I'd spun out most of my current theories.

"Yeah, well, some of it," I described my phone conversation with Detective Tracy of the Yakima County Sheriff's Office. "He seemed pretty skeptical. Even as I was explaining it to him, I realized how weak it sounded. I really didn't go into much detail about all the 'suspects.' I told him several of us had strong reasons to dislike the man, but he didn't seem particularly interested in the details. Once he'd heard what he called my 'hat theory' I don't think he cared much about the rest of it. Anyway, I felt a bit, I don't know, disloyal, I guess, to start telling some police officer, a stranger, some complicated, personal, and compromising stuff about people I know well and work with every day, friends. Mostly, they are people who spoke with me without me letting on what I've been thinking. Anyway," I continued. "It's still just based on some silly surmise about a stupid hat. Do I really believe they're going to take any of this seriously? Any detective's first question was always going to be: 'where's the evidence?' There isn't any."

"Come on, Sandy. You're just talking yourself out of this. You have suspicions. They seem well-founded. That's enough. It's not your job to dig up evidence. It's theirs."

She was right, of course. I fell into another glum silence. Until now, I had hesitated to tell her about the dongle. It all, somehow, seemed unreal, and she had enough to worry about. Maybe it had no bearing on Fortis Henry at all. Maybe it was somebody's simple mistake, somehow. Still, I realized it was something she needed to know.

"Jesus, Sandy," she said when I explained what I'd been told by the State Patrol investigator. She was aghast. "You're just telling me this, now?"

"Well, I only found out on Tuesday. I'm still driving the rental. Anyway, there's no need for you to worry about it." Maybe it had also been a matter of wanting the whole thing not to be true. I'd been putting that damn dongle out of my mind, not wanting to face what it meant.

She thought about all that for a moment. "You think this might be somebody you've pushed over the edge with your 'inquiries' about Fortis Henry?"

"I don't know. Yeah, maybe. I can't really imagine what else it could be."

"So, you're driving a rental. How does that help? What makes you think somebody couldn't screw with that as well?"

"I guess I'm just assuming that. I do know where to look, at least. I check the OBD port all the time. I'd see it if they did it again."

"But you're saying they don't really need a dongle thing. They can just do it over the cellular network. How are you going to check for that?"

"I think they need to be very sophisticated to do that."

"And, whoever they are, what makes you think they're not? Anyway, how would they put that thing in there? You obviously lock your car."

"I've read that they can copy your entry code when you push the unlock button on the little transmitter on your car key. They just have to be somewhere nearby when you show up and unlock your car."

"So, easy, in other words. And, anyway, this didn't work. They could come after you in some other way too, right? Maybe they settle on something low tech—like a gun, a knife, an iron pipe."

"I guess so."

With that, suddenly the possibility that I might have put her in danger became much more real. She could be at risk even this evening, by me driving her around in a rental car that could also have been tinkered with at some point over the past several days.

"Oh, Jesus," I continued as it hit me. "I haven't been thinking. I'm really sorry if I've put you in danger . . ."

She gave me a frustrated look then waved it off. "Yourself. You're putting yourself in danger. And it's not just about the car if they're going to try something else. This can't continue," she said.

"I know," I said. She had become emotional. I reached over and took her hand in mine, but I didn't know what to say.

"It's that Fortis Henry thing. It's got to be. Somebody's angry that you're asking questions."

I wasn't sure. Could it really be that my probably-unsubtle inquiries into Fortis Henry's death could have alerted the killer and made me a target? Until I'd spoken with Daryl Weber, I'd never been explicit. Still, I had to admit that any of the people I'd questioned about this over the past few weeks could have been put on alert, particularly if they were, themselves, Fortis Henry's killer.

I finally took Sherry home and got on the road for a long nervous hour's drive back to Seattle. I was feeling horribly guilty for being responsible for her distress. After being with Sherry, my Seattle condo seemed cold and empty. It also seemed, somehow, dangerous.

After a restless Sunday, and a good deal of thought about the dongle and what it meant, on Monday morning I got on the phone with a security firm and had a basic electronic surveillance system installed at my Condo unit and had the one at my office in Olympia upgraded. I also spent a couple of hours on-line researching advice for protecting yourself from intruders and from threats of death and injury. When you Google something like that you can count on a lot of wild speculation. I sure as hell wasn't going to be signing up for Kung Fu classes or converting my bedroom into a steel-reinforced safe-room. But this was unfamiliar territory.

I did learn a few useful things about protecting myself. I needed to be able to drive. I couldn't close myself up in the Condo, lock the door, and never go out. But I did begin paying more attention to my surroundings when I was out in public. I did *not* buy a gun. I flashed back to when my dad taught me how to use a rifle on a hunting trip during a fishing closure one summer in Alaska. And to my brief small arms training in the Navy. Would a gun keep me safe? . . . No. No, I thought, shaking my head to myself. I'm not buying a handgun.

I was angry with myself. I'd been stupid to have taken Sherry and David out in my car, rental or not, without considering that it, too, could be sabotaged. I was also now angry to the core with whoever might have placed that dongle in my car and who was placing me and might also be placing the people around me at risk. As the next few days wore on, I steadily built up a cold, hard knot of fury in my stomach. It kept me awake at night and, during the day, it filled my mind with angry thoughts when faced with the common minor frustrations of living.

I could, of course, simply back away. But I was beginning to see all this in another way as well. Ignoring the matter might be the most dangerous course I could take. Perhaps figuring it out was the only real way I could protect myself. I couldn't go through life checking under the dash, looking down every alley, or expecting the barrel of a gun to appear in the open window of every passing car. Now that this first effort had failed, who knew what other threats might lay in wait for me over the coming weeks and months?

One thing this seemed to confirm, however, was that someone might very badly want to stop me from looking further into Fortis Henry's death. And that provided a new and convincing argument that, if I looked, there might be something to find.

I had to be careful. But if I wanted to end the threat, I ended up convincing myself all over again that I needed to solve this murder.

CHAPTER TWENTY-THREE

Monday, April 3, 8 a.m.

Disrupted Proceedings

OUR SENATE HEARING on the Conservation Heritage Priority bill was that Monday afternoon and it was all I had on my mind when I arrived in Olympia on Monday morning. As I stepped through the front door of my office, however, the phone was already ringing. I hung up my jacket and took my laptop into my office while Helen answered.

After listening silently for what seemed like an unusually long time, she finally said: "Hold please. I'll put him right on." Then to me, after pressing the 'hold' button: "Call on one," followed by: "Good luck." She sounded mildly amused.

What now?

It was Maryanne Henry on the phone. And she was angry. "What the hell do you think you're doing?" were the first words out of her mouth. Whoa, where was the comfortable, demure housewife I recalled meeting over in Yakima a few months back? Or, for that matter, even the well-spoken professional educator who'd recently testified here in Olympia at that hearing on Howard Oxley's tech education bill? This was definitely a "new" Maryanne Henry; one who launched into what I could only describe as a "tirade" about clumsy policemen and stupid questions and "ruining" her daughter's life.

I finally managed to say, "I'm not sure I understand what I--"

"Oh, no. Don't give me that BS. You understand, all right. Did you even begin to think what the hell would happen? How dare you?"

It took a few moments, but I was finally able to ascertain that she'd apparently had a visit from a couple of officers from the Yakima County Sheriff's Office. That came as a considerable surprise. Was Detective Tracy actually investigating? I'd been convinced he'd intended to blow the whole thing off.

"Right in the middle of our goddamn wedding rehearsal." Maryanne continued. "Some detective. And his sidekick in full uniform. Pull up here in their big police car. Asking us questions like we're a bunch of criminals. All but accused me of murdering my husband. Jesus, Dalton, what are my daughter's new in-laws supposed to think about that?"

Slowly I ascertained that Tricia Henry had been married over the weekend. I gathered that the ceremony had been conducted right there at the Henrys' home in the same impressive front room where we'd all showed up for our meeting that unfortunate day last December. On Friday afternoon Tracy and one of the Sheriff's Deputies had stopped by to make some inquiries. Maybe they weren't as tactful as they could have been. Nor as discerning about what was going on there. I couldn't imagine that there'd been anything particularly heavy-handed about what they'd done, but their timing certainly could have been better.

And they had, obviously, mentioned me.

"I am so sorry," Mrs. Henry. "I hope you know I'd never have anticipated something like this," I finally was able to interject. "I'm also quite sure nobody thinks you or anyone in your family is guilty of anything. And I definitely agree that the detective should have been a good deal more tactful and understanding."

"Well, I'll tell you what. They sure put a damper on my daughter's wedding. It's all anybody talked about on Saturday. All Tricia's friends. And Tony's. The families. The kids are off for a week's honeymoon on Maui—it's their spring break. Can't imagine they're going to be able to enjoy themselves much, considering what happened at the wedding. What on earth are you thinking about, Dalton. Fortis is gone. Buried. It was an accident. Rob Thomas told me you were asking questions about this, but to bring in the police . . .; what on earth are you thinking, dredging all this up now?"

She seemed to have calmed, slightly. And I sensed I might, possibly, get some answers of my own. "What did they want to know?" I asked as pleasantly as I could manage.

"Wanted to know if anyone was with Fortis that day, when he went out back. How the hell should I know. I was cooking muffins for your meeting. Any of you folks that were here could have gone out back."

"I see."

"And his hat. They wanted to know about Fortis's hat. What is that about? Like, how much did it cost? When did he wear it? Why did he have it with him out behind the feedlot?"

"What did you tell them?"

"I don't really know why he had it with him out there. It was a good hat, maybe his best. Fortis loved his hats. But they were for dress, for when he went into town or something. He had an old 'Darigold' baseball cap he wore when he worked out in the barns."

"I understood he'd been out earlier. To the market?"

"Yeah, he went to the SuperRite, down by the freeway to pick up a few things. He came inside and left them for me here on the dining room table. I was in the kitchen, but he just called out that the stuff was there, and he was headed out back for a few minutes. Then he disappeared again. That's how I knew he got back from the store."

"Well, I want you to know I'm really sorry for the disruption of your daughter's wedding. It shouldn't have happened like that."

"No, it shouldn't," she said. Then, perhaps mollified somewhat: "I suppose those Sheriffs couldn't have known what was happening, here."

"Well let me at least offer my congratulations. We all met your daughter, briefly that day we were there in December. She seemed like a delightful young woman. You should be proud."

"I am. She's known Tony for years, childhood sweethearts. His family are dairy farmers as well. His dad and older brother run their Shulkin Creek Dairy down toward Sunnyside, maybe you've heard of it. Tricia and Tony graduate from WSU this summer. She's getting her certificate in elementary education. And he's majoring in Agriculture. I couldn't be happier." She then paused. "I'm sorry I gave you such a hard time, here. Maybe it isn't your fault. I hope you can understand how disturbing this all has been for us over the past couple of days. I wanted to make a good impression on Tony's family. Good people. Tony's brother works with his dad and, come June, Tony and Tricia are going to move in together, here. Tony's going to help me run our dairy. It's actually kind of a parent's dream."

"I do understand. And I'm really sorry for how this happened."

"You know," she said then, thoughtfully. "Fortis kept his hats, work and dress, on a rack there by the side door. That's how we usually come and go when we're using the car or going out back. I think he'd almost certainly have changed hats before he went out to do some kind of chore out back. Like I said, he was really fussy about his hats. So, yeah, I guess it's a little strange. But I still don't understand what that could have had to do with what happened. That detective was talking about, maybe, it not having been an accident. How does which hat he was wearing have anything to do with that?"

"Maybe it doesn't," I said. But I was thinking she probably deserved a better explanation, so I continued: "It does, however, make one wonder if, possibly, he kept it on because he was with someone. A guest, perhaps. Someone he was just going to talk to. Or meet with. Or, maybe, someone he wanted to show around."

There was a pause, then: "Oh," she said. "Yeah, I guess. I don't think anybody had yet arrived when he got back from the store. Maybe, though. I guess that's possible."

Then I suddenly remembered I had another question. "Uh, when that Sheriff's Detective, Tracy, was there on Friday, did he ask you if you have video surveillance out in the dairy barn?"

"Yes. Yes he did. He was very interested. There's several cameras out there. It all goes on disk. Fortis used to study those videos all the time. Said he could tell a lot about how the cows were doing by watching them and knowing how they spent their time."

"Any chance you have those records from back in December?"

"Yep. I copied off the stuff he wanted on a thumb drive and gave it to the Detective."

Apparently, I'd had more impact on Detective Tracy than I'd thought at first. I wondered if he'd let me know what, if anything, showed up on that thumb drive she'd given him. Probably not, I guessed.

An hour later, Janice and I were on the Hill, outside House Hearing Room B hoping to catch up with a couple of Legislators when a hearing let out. Janice and Helen had both overheard my side of that strained conversation with Maryanne Henry. And I'd had to explain.

"I've got to admit," Janice said above the clatter of voices echoing off the marble walls of the O'Brien Building's busy ground floor hallway. "Something like that, a couple of clumsy policemen showing up at *my* wedding rehearsal; I wouldn't have been pleased, either."

My own wedding, over a decade earlier, had been a civil ceremony at the Whatcom County Courthouse. Susan and I had wanted the least possible bother and celebration. We'd just wanted to be married and we'd gotten it done in the most expeditious way we could. I'd lost Susan to a traffic accident only a year later, so key events of our brief marriage had become quite fixed in my memory. "Anyway," I said, knowing just how old and fossilized I probably sounded: "It does seem like kids, these days, make a lot bigger deal of weddings than we did when I was younger."

"You're right about that," she said. "Weddings can cost a fortune. Flowers, photographers, catering, fancy venues, travel, dresses, websites. It all seems like it gets way out of hand. At least Tricia Henry was getting married at their home. Keeping it small."

It all did make me feel guilty for causing the disruption they'd experienced. I could only wish Maryanne's daughter and her new husband the best.

CHAPTER TWENTY-FOUR

Wednesday, April 5, 11 a.m.

Inspired Political Conjecture

OUR CONSERVATION HERITAGE PRIORITY BILL had made it through its Senate committee late on Monday afternoon and was headed for the Senate floor. Right after the hearing, Senator Fang had called an Executive Session and, with most of us still in the room to watch, they'd passed it out of Committee with a positive referral and no dissent. Even Senator Lance (L.C.) Chambers had voted for it. Whatever I'd said to him had, apparently, worked.

The brief respite that followed gave me some time in the office to clear off my desk. It also allowed my thinking to return to Fortis Henry's possible murder and, hearing nothing further from the Yakima Sheriff's Office, I found myself reassessing one of my "suspects," about whom I felt I needed to know more.

The Washington Association for Wildlife and Recreation (WAWR) offices were just a short walk from the Capitol. I'd called ahead and spoken with Lou Dwyer's assistant, so I knew she was in. I had not, however, made an appointment. I wanted to surprise her.

The receptionist directed me down a hall to their coffee room where I found Lou at a small table relaxing with a cup of coffee and casually studying a complex, half-completed jig-saw puzzle that looked to be a picture of some kind of medieval castle.

"Still a couple of weeks to go," I said. It was just 15 days to the end of session.

She looked up at me in surprise and then grinned sheepishly. "Short-timer attitude. I've got no right to be dinking around in here. With the budget, the worst is yet to come." She shook her head. "I guess I'm finding it hard to face the pile of work on my desk. You here to see me?"

Other than her, the room was empty, so I took one of the hard folding chairs on the other side of the little table. "Yeah, Lou. I am. I've got a question that I'm hoping you're going to be willing to answer for me." I paused to lend some gravity to what I was about to ask. "You know a guy by the name of Ronnie Johnson, right?"

She'd picked up a piece of what looked like castle wall and was beginning to lay it down in a likely place on the board, but my question stopped her cold. "Ronnie Johnson?"

"Uh huh. Runs Truth Spotlight, over in Yakima?"

She looked me in the eyes, glanced toward the coffee room door, and frowned. Then she rose. "Come on, Sandy. I need to face my messy office sometime. Now's as good as any."

She'd been right about her office. It was cluttered with files, books, reports, and discarded paper that overflowed the recycle bin beside her desk.

"OK, have a seat and tell me what you know," she said, closing the office door and then taking her chair behind the desk.

"Well, I know Ronnie Johnson had a bunch of 'spontaneous' tip-offs about Fortis Henry's cost share deal, all at about the same time last Fall. I know you very much needed Fortis Henry to back away from his plans to start up a separately-funded farmland acquisition program; in effect, he was stealing a program, and some support, that you and your board very much want to keep. I know you work very closely with NRCS and Daryl Weber on farmland easements and that Daryl was, at least initially, also motivated to stop the kind of insider dealing Fortis was engaged in. Although Daryl was perfectly willing to be identified as Ronnie Johnson's source, you thought it'd be better to remain anonymous considering your Board President is Hans Fortner. He and Fortis were friends, both were on the Yakima County WSAIC Chapter Board. My guess is, you knew Hans wouldn't approve of you pulling strings to discredit Fortis. By doing that, you'd be likely to alienate a lot of your organization's scarce and treasured farmer allies, so you asked Ronnie Johnson to keep your name confidential. You'll be happy to know he did. At least so far."

As I'd been speaking, I'd watched Lou's initial anger slowly turn to frustration, and then to resignation as each of my guesses apparently hit their mark. I waited while she took her time formulating a response.

"So, what's this all about, Sandy? Why are you doing this? Why do you care? Things are going fine. It looks like your Conservation Heritage Priority Bill's maybe going to pass. I think we're likely to get our WWRP budget request. What's the big deal with Fortis Henry? The man is dead. Why can't you let all this stuff rest?"

"The man was murdered, Lou," I said, mustering all the certainty I could.

She stared back at me, staggered for a moment. Then: "You're kidding, right? Murdered? Hell, he had an accident. You were there—we all were. Where's this coming from?"

I wanted to believe her sincerity, she *seemed* caught off guard. Then I recalled what Rep. Rob Thomas has told me about his upcoming primary battle. I looked at her, considered what she was saying, and then, finally, put the pieces together. "You're backing a Democrat over there this next time round, aren't you? In Rob Thomas's District. That's what this is all about. With all this Donald Trump stuff going on, you figure a 'D' could have a shot. It wasn't that long ago that Yakima voters elected a 'D'." Lou and WAWR had never been shy about endorsing and backing candidates for the Legislature who seemed likely to support the State's wildlife and recreation program. I was willing to bet Rep. Rob Thomas was never likely to back a WWRP appropriation. No Republican from that district would.

From her look, I knew I'd hit the mark.

"And you'd be quite happy if your favored Democratic candidate faced some crazy, hard right-winger in the next general election. Someone, anyone, other than a nice, popular, reasonably moderate conservative like Rob Thomas."

She shook her head, but what she said was: "Uh huh."

"I hope you know what you're doing," I told her.

She looked chagrined. "I hope so too, Sandy," she said. Then her look hardened with a question of her own. "So that's why you came by, today? You think one of us murdered Fortis Henry and you're wondering if it was me?"

"It could have been any one of us," I told her. "It sure as hell wasn't me. And if it wasn't you, then you, like me, have a very big interest in knowing who it was."

When I left her, she was still thinking about that. I didn't mention my conversation with Detective Tracy.

I wasn't sure who had actually initiated the District Elections Reform Bill—maybe it had been Linda Cunningham. But I was increasingly thinking it likely that it was Lou. She was a pot-stirrer who had any number of WAWR-friendly legislators who'd have been happy to sponsor that bill. Whoever it was, I was sure Lou was, quietly behind the scenes, nurturing and supporting that bill. She'd first discredited Fortis Henry through Truth Spotlight, and then used that as an excuse to advance a bill that she had to know would put Rob Thomas in an impossible position, one that was unpopular with the conservation districts who supported him and that could set him up for a primary defeat that would, in turn, expose their district to a Democratic takeover. Very involved. Very clever. And a big risk for Lou; I was morally certain her boss (and Fortis's friend), Hans Fortner, knew nothing about it.

Before leaving the building, I sat down in their waiting room, pulled up the Access Washington website on my mobile, and looked up the District Elections Bill. Sure enough, it was prime-sponsored by a Democrat from North Seattle, someone I knew to be a regular ally of WAWR and who would, ordinarily, have little or no interest in conservation districts or their elections. That made me all but positive it was Lou that had been behind that bill, probably from the very start. She'd done it knowing that if she was discovered, she'd have made a powerful member of her own Board very unhappy. As well as a lot of conservation district supervisors.

While I had the bill status on screen, I also checked the votes on that bill in executive session in House Local Government Committee. I was not surprised to note that Rob Thomas had been reported absent. But later, on the House Floor where he knew he needed to be counted, I saw that he'd voted in favor. That was the measure of how spooked he must be by his anticipated right-wing primary challenger.

I bet the conservation districts were very disappointed when that bill got through the House. They were doubtless scurrying to fix things in the Senate.

I also bet there were some tense moments ahead in the Thomas household.

CHAPTER TWENTY-FIVE

Thursday, April 6, 9 a.m.

Appeal to Authority

I'D BEEN SURPRISED AND MORE THAN a little confused when I'd learned that Detective Tracy had actually been making inquiries. That was something, at least. I was still convinced, however, that he'd be little use in helping me find whoever put that dongle in my car. There was nothing solid to suggest Fortis Henry and the dongle were in any way connected—just my own rank speculation. The dongle was my problem.

And it was a problem with which I needed some help.

Following a quick call and a brisk walk across Capitol Campus, I was led down those same long, well-polished, echoing hallways at State Patrol Headquarters that I vividly recalled from my brief work with Lieutenant Nathan Wilson a couple of years before. Wilson was a career professional; the head of the Patrol's Special Investigations Unit. He was anything but an effusive guy, but the handshake and smile I got this time around was a good deal more cordial than on our first encounter just over two years earlier.

"So, how'd it go with Tracy?" Wilson asked me as he ushered me through his office door.

"He is looking into it, from what I hear," I said. "I didn't think he would. After we talked, I figured nothing would happen."

Wilson smiled broadly. "That's Tracy," he said. Doesn't like to get expectations up. But don't you worry. He's a sleeper. First thing you know, he'll surprise you."

"I hope so," I said sincerely. "I've certainly run into a dead end."

"So, is that what brings you in, today? You know, there isn't much I can do about some non-highway related murder. Especially over in Yakima."

"I know, Lieutenant. It's something else, something I think is related. But I can't see Detective Tracy being interested. And it is 'highway related,' at least in a way."

With that, I explained about the dongle that had been found in my car a week-and-a-half before. "The accident was here in Lacey and I'll admit this thing has me spooked. I think I need help with it and I don't know who to turn to."

"You think it's related to this death over in Yakima?"

"Yeah, I do. I mean, it's the only thing I can think of. Up till a week or so ago, I hadn't told anyone what I was thinking. But maybe I haven't been all that subtle. Especially if one of the people I've talked to is the killer. I have, after all, been asking some pointed questions."

He smiled at that. "I bet you have." Apparently, I still deserved some payback. "You obviously think you raised someone's hackles?"

"It's all I can think of."

"God, Dalton," he said, shaking his head. "It may seem strange to you, but I actually know people who go their entire lives without becoming involved in a murder investigation. And I'm a police officer. Why you?"

I laughed at the thought. "I don't know, Lieutenant. But I could sure use some suggestions about how to make it end."

"Well, I do have to confess, that business with this dongle thing, it's worrisome. It sounds like something that might require some technical skills. Anybody on your list seem like a candidate?"

"Nope. Not really." I filled him in on the possible motives of the people who'd been there that day, including myself, and then added Fortis's wife Maryanne to the list, although I really didn't think she was a prospect. She'd been in the kitchen, out of sight, but she'd come out to answer every time one or another of the rest of us had come to the door over the roughly half an hour before the meeting was to have started. I supposed the "accident" could have happened before any of us got there. She could be misleading us about when Fortis got back from the store but there could, easily, be a store clerk or someone to confirm when he left. Or a security camera. Anyway, why would he wear his special hat out back for his wife? Why would she do this the day she knew she had visitors coming over—alternative suspects? I didn't believe it, even if the most likely suspect is always, supposedly, the spouse. In this case there were just too many others who had problems with the man.

"I don't see any of the people who were there having any special electronics or tech experience."

"You said Sgt. Nakamura was the Patrol investigator you talked to, from your accident. Did he mention tracing the gadget?"

The offending dongle had showed up in my mail at home a few days after my accident. I took it out of my pocket and laid it on Wilson's desk. "He didn't think it was possible," I told Wilson. "They're too common. Available everywhere."

Wilson picked it up and turned it around in his hands, studying at it with interest. "Hmm." Clearly it even had the Lieutenant stumped. "Your car have that new, automatic parking function? The one where it will parallel park the car for you?"

"No, but I don't think that's necessary. Apparently, lots of a car's controls are now electronic."

"So, this thing is a transmitter/receiver, Bluetooth or something? Seems like, for this to work, the killer would need to be nearby. Follow you around in another car. Maybe look for an occasion when you're at risk. And then apply your brakes or sabotage the power steering or something. Presumably whoever it was would want to make sure the accident was bad enough you'd either be killed or at least messed up enough to stop looking into things."

"You're not making me feel any better, Lieutenant."

It didn't get any better from there either. I left Wilson's office feeling more at risk than when I'd arrived. He wrote down some notes about the dongle and promised to let me know if some kind of trace might be possible, but neither of us had much hope. All he could suggest was that I might touch base, again, with Detective Tracy in Yakima and tell him about the dongle incident.

Later that same day I did just that. And was blessedly able to get right through to the Detective. As Lt. Wilson had suggested, I let him know about the dongle.

"This happened, when?" he asked.

"Saturday before last. In the morning."

"Hmm. So, we talked about all this that following Monday. Seems like you might have mentioned it. What, it slipped your mind?" He sounded at least mildly irritated. Maybe he had a point.

I answered truthfully but carefully: "Honestly, Detective Tracy, when we spoke, I had the distinct impression that you were uninterested. I didn't think you planned to do anything. I was actually quite surprised when I got a call from a very angry Marianne Henry on Monday morning after your visit to her home last Friday."

"You need to keep me informed, Mr. Dalton." It sounded very much like he was speaking through gritted teeth.

"I also wasn't sure you'd be interested in a personal threat to me that had taken place over here west of the mountains. Wasn't sure you'd think it was related or that you'd have any interest in investigating it. I am sorry for not being more forthcoming."

"This isn't the only thing you haven't shared with me." It was a statement. It occurred to me that Lt. Wilson might have given Tracy a call following my visit this morning.

"If you mean that I've made some inquiries on my own over here in Olympia, I have. At this point I've spoken with everybody who came to the meeting that day. I had other reasons to talk with them, but I did make sure Fortis Henry came up. As you know, all of them had cause to dislike Fortis Henry. And not one of them, at least so far, has been questioned by you. Their motives were one of the things that made me start thinking about all this in the first place."

"Yeah," he said, sounding a trace sardonic. "I gather that." He *had* been speaking with Wilson. Probably that was just as well. "And I gather that it includes you, right? You had your own bone to pick with Mr. Henry?"

Naturally, it would come to this. "Like every other person there, Detective Tracy, I had significant differences with Fortis Henry. That is, in fact, another of the reasons I contacted you in the first place. I didn't want it to later appear that I had information about this and kept it to myself."

"Uh huh. Well, be that as it may, I'd have you over here to make a statement on this if I thought there was anything to it. At the moment, all I see here is some remotely plausible supposition. We'll keep our eyes open, but I don't really see this going anywhere at the moment."

"You did, however, think enough of it to go out and question Maryanne Henry. Did you think she sounded like a suspect herself?"

I wasn't sure he was going to answer. But he did: "Nah," he said with finality. "I don't see it. We asked around about her a bit. Nothing. No motive. She teaches high school. History and social studies. Is involved in the community, in politics, on non-profit boards."

"Like the Secondary Educators?" I asked.

"Yeah, that's the one. But we can't see anything that would make her a suspect. Other than that, like you, she was there."

"I see," I said. But something he said made me wonder: "You said she was involved in politics. Do you happen to know if she's worked on Rep. Rob Thomas's campaign?" It seemed logical given that Rob Thomas was also her brother-in-law. I hadn't forgotten that he had mentioned to her my questions about Fortis's death.

"Yeah, that's what we heard. Seems like his campaigns are more-or-less a family affair. Last Fall she did some kind of volunteer work or other."

"Um, there is one other thing. Did you, by any chance, check out the video record from the dairy barn? See if there was anything on it of use?"

"Nothing. Bunch of cows. Eating, craping, laying around. Dullest surveillance videos I've ever seen, and that's saying something. The cameras don't cover the area beside and behind the building."

I could tell from his tone that I wasn't going to get any further help from this quarter.

Then he confirmed it. "I think if this guy Henry was killed, or if someone was out there with him when he died, it's going to turn out to be one of your friends right over there in Olympia. You're going to have a devil of a time proving it. And if someone put that dongle in your car, that's who it's going to turn out to be. I'm sorry to say, Mr. Dalton, but with nothing more to go on, it's going to be hard for us to make this thing a priority." There was a finality in his voice that made it clear this conversation was probably the brush off from the Yakima County Sheriff's office. I couldn't count on any further help from them.

If all this was going to get sorted out, it would have to be me that sorted it. Until then, I needed to watch my back.

CHAPTER TWENTY-SIX

Friday, April 7, 7 a.m.

Seismic Shift in the Political Landscape

RIDAY MORNING, THE STORY WAS ALL OVER THE NEWS.

Fortuna was in trouble.

I was on I-5 headed for work somewhere south of Tacoma when my current audiobook ended and my sound system defaulted to the morning news. Fortuna's collapse was the headliner on the 7 a.m. report.

Howard Oxley's Fortuna was actually an umbrella corporation that owned controlling interests in several other interrelated enterprises. Best known among them were Fortune Technology Products, a Texas-based manufacturer of well-regarded Fortune computers, Fortune-Soft, which produced a great many popular phone and computer applications, and Fortune Biologics, a more recent acquisition that developed and manufactured various commonly used diagnostic devices in the field of medical technology and did medical research.

Fortuna had recently paid over a billion dollars for the firm they'd immediately renamed Fortune Biologics. It was a very public acquisition that had bet heavily on the Portland-based firm's cutting edge research into fabrics, plastics, and other specialized materials that could interface between the human body and high-tech implant hardware, materials that could overcome the body's seemingly inevitable rejection of foreign materials. This morning's Wall Street Journal was reporting the failure of what had been one of Fortune Biologics' most promising lines of human-tech interface research. Worse yet, the news hadn't come from Fortuna officials. Instead it had been initiated by a courageous whistle-blower who had been, reportedly, faced with both corrupt promises and grim threats before finally going public. It was not the kind of story likely to engender investor confidence.

Fortuna's stock was in free-fall.

At the Washington State Legislature, this was obviously big news. The Legislature had passed, or was about to pass, several statutory changes designed to encourage Fortuna's investment in their new computer-farm in Eastern King County. There were also appropriations on the cusp of passing. Most of those would have been finalized over the course of the coming week before the Legislature adjourned. With this news, the whole Fortuna Package would be on hold. That computer farm was probably history with the big, institutional partner-investors likely to lose interest. Most of the appropriations could still be fixed; the money could easily go elsewhere or simply be zeroed out. But some of the bills had passed and had already been signed by the Governor.

Now it all looked to have been a very big mistake.

In recent years, the Legislature had found it difficult to meet state constitutionally mandated funding requirements for public education. The Legislature was under a court order requiring dramatic increases in that funding. The State budget was under stress. Even so, the tax breaks and other financial incentives provided for Fortuna had made sense at the time they'd been voted through only because the economic impact of their computer-farm investment was projected to generate other new tax revenue that would, hopefully, more than make up for the loss. Now, all that was in doubt.

When a law is changed to incentivize business investments, those changes don't typically just apply to a specific business enterprise. With artful crafting, they can be targeted somewhat. But, of legal necessity, those changes have to apply to everyone who is similarly situated. So, for example, when the government improves a reach of highway for the workers at a new factory, everybody can use that highway. When they change development regulations to allow a business to be built on land that is, perhaps, otherwise zoned, other developers may also find a way to use that opening to develop other, similar land. When they provide a break under the tax laws so a company, like Fortuna, can sell intangible electronic services at a reduced rate under the State's B & O tax, other local firms that sell similar services will also pay at those reduced rates.

Unfortunately, it isn't as easy as just, somehow "cancelling" the new legislation. The repeals have to pass through the legislative process just like the initial bills did. Besides Fortuna, there were a lot of other people who had also supported passage of those new laws, people who would also benefit from them. What were legislators supposed to say to them: "Sorry, Fortuna's gone bust. We made a mistake. Your needs weren't really important enough for us to have voted through that new road or the lower taxes we promised you. Too bad!"

The Governor, who had strongly supported the Fortuna Package, and the legislators who'd already voted through much of it, were deeply embarrassed. They could be in for some political repercussions.

I have to admit to being deeply grateful that none of my clients would be directly affected. I was betting there would be several legislators who would be spending their next few weeks concocting plausible explanations for some of their recent votes. Fortunately, I wouldn't be among the lobbyists who'd be receiving calls to help them with their talking points. Of course, maybe the researchers at Fortune Biologics had something else up their sleeves, or maybe Howard Oxley could pull something new out of his hat and Fortuna would weather this.

But when you read the financial pages, it didn't sound good. And the one thing that was absolutely certain: Fortuna's computer farm investment was dead.

CHAPTER TWENTY-SEVEN

Saturday, April 8, 4 p.m.

Unscheduled Revelation

SATURDAY WAS THE DAY Sherry and I had arranged to meet for the dinner I'd promised in appreciation of her looking after me following my accident.

Sherry's son David's school was holding a "technology fair" that afternoon. David had built a very cool battery-powered electric motor that used wire-wrapped steel bolts as electromagnets and a piece of PVC pipe as a rotor and commutator. It was a lot of fun seeing all the kids' projects. David's little motor ran like a champ. I took a picture of it. Afterward, we delivered David to the home of his new "debate partner." The two of them planned to spend the afternoon researching their arguments for a classroom debate the following Monday. Their topic: which were better, team or individual sports.

Needless to say, dongle or no, Sherry drove.

It was late afternoon when Sherry and I finally sat down at the Falls Terrace Restaurant near the old Olympia Brewery in Tumwater to catch up. At that early evening hour, the place was still mostly empty. We got a nice table by the window overlooking the falls. It was a quiet, comfortable place to eat but before the waitress had even left us with our menus, I could tell Sherry wanted to talk.

"I have something to show you," she said when we were alone. She pulled her phone out of her purse, brought something up on the screen, and then slid it across the table.

It looked like a copy, or perhaps more correctly, a photograph, of a printed email message. It was addressed to Aaron Nicolaides; I didn't recognize the sender. The subject was: "Bad news." What followed was a brief, to the point account of the research disaster that had been behind the recently reported collapse in Fortuna stock. Bad news indeed.

"Yeah," I said. "I saw the news yesterday. I bet there are some worried people, about now."

"Look at the date," she said, pointing.

I did. Then I understood.

"Where'd you get this?"

"I took it myself. With my phone."

"When."

She reached over and pointed at the screen. "Then," she said.

"You've had this all this time?"

"Uh, huh. I didn't, you know, think it was all that important. Not till yesterday."

I reread it. Aaron Nicolaides had received this message over a month-and-a-half ago, back in late February. That had been during the thick of the debate on the Fortuna incentives bills. Naturally, some of those bills had passed through House Technology and Economic Development Committee, one of those for which Sherry was legal counsel. But she had a point. Unless you were very familiar with this specific research and with its importance to the company, all you'd have taken from reading this back in February would have been that some research wasn't going to pan out. Not, necessarily, that it was such a big deal.

"How'd you get it? Why'd you snap the picture?"

"I don't know. They were acting strangely. Nicolaides, Drum, Fernandez, and Bob Springfield." Springfield was Drum's Legislative Assistant, and Fernandez's district was where Fortuna's new computer farm was to have been built. Fernandez was, therefore, one of the Fortuna Package's biggest supporters.

"I was looking for an empty room," Sherry continued. "I had some folks scheduled to come in about a bill. Actually, it was Howard Oxley's Tech Education Bill and your friend Stoney was one of them. You probably remember, he was a big supporter. Anyway, when I walked past our little conference room on the second floor, Nicolaides and company, the four of them, were in there with the door open. They were arguing about something and then, they sort of closed down when they saw me walk past. Something about the whole situation didn't look right to me. Like, furtive or something."

"But why'd you end up with this?"

"Well, as I approached coming up the hall, I heard Drum say something like: 'This doesn't make a goddamn bit of difference.' Then, as I was passing by, I saw him drop this paper in the wastebasket by the door. He was kind of dramatic about it, as if to say: 'Who cares.' Like I say, it just seemed strange. When they saw me walk by and glance in, they looked like kids caught smoking in the schoolyard.

"I went looking for another room for our meeting." she continued. "Everything was also in use upstairs, but when I came back down, I walked by that same conference room again and they were all gone—the room was empty. I guess I was just curious. I reached in and pulled this memo out of the wastebasket and took a snap of it with my phone before dropping it back in. Then I went out to reception. Stoney and the others had arrived. I took them back to that same room for our meeting. I'd been asked to help draft an amendment. Your friend Stoney's a real hard charger, by the way. Even after we all met, he had to come back and continued pressing his case, one-on-one, at my office, make sure I got it right.

"Anyway, when I came by that room again later in the day, I noticed the wastebasket was empty. That seemed odd at the time; the cleaning crew doesn't come in till evening. I didn't know what to think. Then I basically just forgot about it. Until today."

"Wow," I said. "That all sounds to me like those guys knew exactly what this memo was all about, how important it was." Nicolaides, Drum, and Fernandez had been leading the fight together for the Fortuna Package for the past two or three years. Drum and Fernandez were fellow Democrats who'd worked closely with Nicolaides since the days when he'd been Speaker of the House. The three of them were obviously a tightly knit team.

"I know. I think they knew damn well that the bottom was going to fall out at Fortuna. Those guys kept it a secret."

"Obviously they wanted those bills to pass. Maybe they figured it wouldn't turn out this bad. Didn't want to spook the legislators. Or their other corporate investors."

"Yeah, I guess. Jesus, Sandy. What should I do about it?"

"Now, you mean?" I smiled at her and shook my head. "Well, that's up to you. But I'd be awfully inclined to keep it to myself. Unless somebody asks about it. Does anybody else know you have this."

"No, I don't see how. I haven't told anyone. Didn't seem important."

"Well, you could report it, of course. But if you do, it's going to make a lot of people very unhappy, including one of your own Committee Chairs. I'm not entirely sure what the upside is. I mean, everybody knows about all this now, so there's nothing really to expose unless you want to embarrass Nicolaides, Drum, and Fernandez. They'd come out looking horrible. But I'm not sure why you'd want to do that."

"I suppose," she said doubtfully. "Those guys have caused a lot of grief."

"Look at it this way," I said. "When you saw this thing back in February you didn't really think much of it. There was no way for you to know its significance. That's exactly what they're going to say too. Even if, as you suspect, they knew its importance, they're just going to claim they had no way of knowing what impact it would have. At this point the thing is moot. I'd say what you do now is just keep your head down and do your job. Maybe I'm wrong, but that'd be my advice."

With that, our waiter came, and we ordered. I could see that Sherry had relaxed. I didn't think she had anything to worry about, and it certainly seemed pointless for her to make this memo known. Maybe, later, if this memo came to light, people would be angry to realize that the entire Fortuna debacle, the passage of that now worthless incentives package, could have been avoided.

But I sure couldn't see any reason Sherry needed to place herself at the center of all that when she'd had absolutely no way to know what might have been coming.

CHAPTER TWENTY-EIGHT

Monday, April 10, 4 p.m.

Debate and Passage

Late on Monday I was back up in the Senate Gallery, this time watching what I hoped would be final passage of our Conservation Heritage Priority Bill. I had the Governor's office sewed up. So this was the big day, do or die.

Janice and I had spent several hours that afternoon, working the Chamber doors, sending in messages, and exchanging texts with our champions as well as with queasy supporters and vacillating fence-riders. We believed we knew where we stood but, as with elections, the only poll that counts is the vote on election day.

Janice, Stoney and I were seated side-by-side on a gallery bench watching the laborious legislative process slowly work itself out on the Senate floor beneath us as we waited for our bill to be called. I knew, of course, that this was very important to Stoney but I was a bit surprised to find, when the votes were finally in and the bill had blessedly passed, that I'd been holding my breath as well. I was proud of this bill and of our work in passing it.

Afterward, Janice had to head back to the office, but Stoney and I went downstairs to the Capitol Dome Deli, and then took our coffees and our mini-celebration outside the building onto the Capitol steps into an unseasonably warm April afternoon. While he made a couple of calls to his Conservation Heritage Farms Association colleagues to let them know the news, I took a seat on a granite step, soaked up some welcome sun, and took in the view.

As I sat there appreciating the moment and looking across the flag plaza toward the Supreme Court Building, I became aware that Stoney was holding out his phone in my direction. Someone wanted to talk to me.

"Mr. Dalton?" It was Ed Nowak, the guy who'd been our witness. He was one of Stoney's Board Members. "I just wanted to thank you for your help with this thing," he said.

"It's my job," I said.

"Hell of a lot more 'n that," he said. "My daughter and her husband are going to be really happy about this."

'Your daughter?"

"Yep. She and my son-in-law been working here on my place for several years now. Great kids. But them working here, it just hasn't been working out. Daughter finally, took a job checking in a grocery here in town. Son-in-law's still been giving it a serious go, but we all know it wasn't going to work. Farm just doesn't earn enough. I been wanting to give them the farm outright and just step away. But the farm's all I got—I couldn't afford to retire. This thing you guys passed changes all that. Now maybe we can make this work."

"Well, it should be me thanking you, Ed. Your testimony that day really set things up. Not just anybody could have done that. I'm sorry to hear you're thinking about quitting farming."

"It's past time."

"Your daughter and her husband plan to keep farming?"

"Oh yeah. 'Till the money runs out,' as the say. They got all kinds of ideas. Want to go organic. Start one of those 'subscription' deals where people pay ahead for a weekly box of groceries. Want to get some kind of 'Salmon Safe' certification—use it to help sell stuff at the Farmers Markets. With this bill, they'll get 'cost-share' help with some of the salmon stuff. They're going to do just fine."

"You think getting this bill passed will help?"

"It's the only way it could work. Place just doesn't bring in enough money for me to retire and for them to support their family. Even with me still working, we been barely making it. Now I'll be able to sell my development rights, put on a farming easement, pay off a few debts and use what's left to finally retire. I can give them the farm outright and they'll be in a great spot to make a go of it on their own. Place stays in farming - no goddamn developers. This changes everything. It's going to make all the difference."

After I'd given Stoney back his phone and he'd finished his calls, he joined me and the two of us sat back to recapitulate and savor the victory. "This is going to be a big help," Stoney said. "I want to make sure I've properly thanked you myself. I feel like you've given us exactly the right guidance at every stage. I'm sure our members are going to remember and appreciate your work, Sandy. I sure will."

"I think you and your farmers have done something to be proud of. I'm glad you let me be a part of that."

"I'm curious about something. You seemed so positive about our prospects, right from the start. I come down here a good deal, as you know. But I find this place depressingly unpredictable. Were you really sure we could pass this thing?

I had to laugh at that. "Not at all sure. But it felt like the politics might line up. There wasn't any big appropriation to complicate things. Nobody who passionately hated it. Some good, well-intentioned people who liked it a lot, both sides of the aisle. Mostly, it was a damn good idea. Just seemed worth a try. We did have a few hurdles."

Now it was his turn to laugh. "Not to mention people dying on us."

At that moment, I realized I needed to come clean with him about what I'd been up to on Fortis Henry's death. The fact that the Yakima County Sheriff's Office had been looking into the matter, and my role in that, were likely to become known. I needed him to hear it from me.

"There's no reason you'd know this," I said. "But I'm not so sure Fortis just died by accident that day. I think it's possible he had some help."

It took a moment for that to soak in. Then: "Help? What do you mean, help?"

"As in I think he may not have been alone when he fell in the lagoon that day."

Again, he needed to think about that. "Jesus, Sandy. What are you saying? You think he might have been . . . pushed?"

Then I filled him in on why I thought he might not have been alone and explained briefly how everybody there that day had it in for him for one reason or another. Including the two of us.

"I'll give you the thing about the hat," he said when I was done. "The guy was a 'dandy,' far as I'm concerned. I wouldn't go an hour with a freaking white hat before it had grease or dirt or something all over it. That was a nice clean dairy, but there's no way he or anybody could of worn that hat working out there in the mud with a bunch of cows and kept it spotless. No way." He gave it some more thought. "Still, it's a lot to take in. Idea that one of our group might have killed the man. Then they, what, just came in and joined the rest of us without saying a word?" He was shaking his head. "Have you reported this to the police?"

"Yakima County Sheriff's been looking into it. I don't believe they've come up with much, however."

"So, you've been thinking about this, since when? Since clear back in December?"

"No. Maybe a couple of months, though. It just hit me one day along about February. About the hat. And all the reasons to dislike the man. I'm well aware there isn't much to go on. I just can't seem to leave it alone."

"Well, I guess we did it without him. Without Fortis, I mean. Probably doesn't do any good to get all knotted up trying to guess who might have been involved. Main thing is, we got the damn bill passed. Right?"

"Yeah," I said. "There is this one other little problem, though. I think I may be at risk. I think, by looking into this, I may have pissed somebody off." Then I told him about the dongle in my car.

There was a long pause, then a look crossed his face, like he'd remembered something. He didn't share it, instead he said: "God, it's hard to imagine somebody in our group, one of the people that was there, could be behind something like that."

I certainly had to agree with that.

CHAPTER TWENTY-NINE

Tuesday, April 25, 11 a.m.

Final Action

IT WAS A CLOSE CALL, but even with a lot of last-minute budget adjustments and a change of course on some of the Fortuna bills, they'd still, somehow managed to adjourn the Legislature in time to meet the State Constitutional limit on a Regular Legislative Session.

The conservation district elections bill had passed, but it had ended up amended in the Senate much like Miles Morgan and I had discussed several weeks earlier the day I'd stopped by the Conservation Commission. Rep. Rob Thomas would, presumably, be relieved since the watered-down version of the bill probably passed muster with his conservation district constituents and with his wife while the passage of a bill, weak or not, gave him cover to argue that he'd supported the necessary reforms.

The Conservation Commission also got their budget request. Some of the money originally intended to cover Fortuna's requested improvements to State Highways 202 and 203 managed to find its way to the Commission instead. Some of those savings also went into a slight increase in the WWRP appropriation as well. I was thankful for both.

Rep. Didi Harris's increase in the Conservation Futures taxing authority died in the Senate, the victim of tax fatigue and of a robust opposition campaign led by Linda Cunningham and her league of WSAIC-approved, five-star legislators. The connection between the bill and the needs of the agriculture industry her organization represented were, in my view, vague—in my view, it would have helped farmers rather than hurting them. But the bill's defeat did demonstrate the WSAIC's continued clout. With the Fortuna package dying on its own, she'd presumably needed some other victim on which to flex her political muscle.

The expansion in my clientele to include agriculture had already generated some new inquiries for the coming year. And, with the Legislature adjourned, I finally had the time to buy a new car and return my rental. My old car had, as predicted, been totaled. Early on the Wednesday following adjournment, I'd Ubered over to Ballard to pick up my new Subaru Forester in a miserable, pouring rain. With my anticipated new clients, it seemed likely I'd be spending some time on the road over the coming months; I definitely needed a decent car. I had, however, opted for something simple this time; something without a bunch of fancy computer-generated special features. Yes, it did, however, have an on-board-computer. Apparently, there wasn't much choice about that. For what it was worth, I had been assured by a puzzled but helpful young salesman at Carter Subaru that the computer was protected and the ways it could be hacked were minimal.

I happily turned in out of the rain to park my new car in the enclosed garage beneath my condo building in Seattle. As the elevator carried me up to my home office I was aware that I should be spending this morning working rather than buying cars. I was feeling unsettled. My relationship with Sherry was my most dependable friendship and now that the session was over, she'd be back working with the Olympia law firm that employed her in the off-session. It felt disappointing that, in the months ahead, it was unlikely I'd have occasion to get together with her.

It had been nearly four months since Fortis Henry's death. I'd done everything I could to find his killer. Other than having discovered some troubling undercurrents in the motivations of several of my colleagues, however, all I really knew was that the killer, whoever it was, had apparently become desperate enough to try to take me out of the picture.

Or so it seemed after that dongle turned up. I'd taken precautions, but I was vulnerable. If someone wanted to kill me, they could have done so easily, many times over, since my accident. Yet it had now been a month since we'd found that dongle; a month with no apparent further attempts. Why?

My Seattle condo is on the fourteenth floor of a 20 story, mostly residential building in Belltown. I have a reasonably nice view of Elliot Bay and the Seattle waterfront. I should have been working. Instead, I was sitting there in my home office absently staring out the window at one of the green and white Washington State Ferries that come and go from Coleman Dock and connect Seattle with the other side of Puget Sound. I always found it restful to watch their slow, stately progress across the bay.

I looked forward, for sure, to some time off over the coming summer. In another couple of months I would be off on a planned canoe and hiking trip before I launched into my usual fall regime of building my client's public and legislative support in anticipation of the next year's session. I should have been using the time that day to think through their strategies for that. Instead, I'd been playing Spider Solitaire and absently nibbling at the last, broken remnants from the bottom of a mostly empty bag of corn chips.

My mind wouldn't leave it alone. I still kept returning to the horrible discovery of that body floating in the dairy waste lagoon, and to my own unsettling reaction to finding Fortis dead. I still needed to understand.

What was I missing?

For the umpteenth time I worked my way through the suspects. And yet again, while all of them had cause to have killed the man, none, including Maryanne Henry, felt right for the crime.

Moreover, not one of these people seemed to have the kind of technological skills or interests to make them seem likely to use a car computer as a possible murder weapon.

The heavy rain from earlier in the day had finally ended. The fast-moving cirrocumulus clouds had slowed and opened up allowing the welcome sun to break through. The blustery winds had calmed and, aside from a slight remaining swell, the surface of the Sound had grown smooth and quiet. Beneath my window, the paved city streets were already drying under a warming sun.

It felt very much like that fateful morning over at Fortis Henry's home outside Yakima. I had a sudden clear vision of standing in the Henrys' front room, looking out his front window at the view across the Yakima Valley, and waiting for our host to arrive.

That's when it hit me. Something I'd never considered. I initially dismissed the idea; it couldn't be. But, then again, maybe it could.

Suddenly I believed I might know who'd actually killed Fortis Henry.

I considered what I'd learned in the weeks since. It fit. The more I examined it, the more certain I became.

Spinning around in my chair, I went on-line and tracked down answers to a few of my remaining questions. Then, after some further reflection, I did the only thing I could: I dug a battered business card out of my wallet and got on the phone.

"Tracy here," was the curt but efficient answer of my reluctant acquaintance in the Yakima Sheriff's Office.

"Detective, this is Sandy Dalton, the lobbyist. I'm calling about the Fortis Henry matter."

"I know who you are, Dalton. What is it this time?"

It was clear that I needed to carefully consider my words. Even so, the message I delivered probably seemed disjointed and rambling. Especially since, as I made my explanations, more clues leapt out at me. By the time I was through, I was entirely certain I knew the culprit. And I thought I knew how Tracy might prove it.

After answering a few of his questions, I had one of my own:

"So is this enough for a search warrant and to bring someone in for a few questions?"

Always hesitant to tip his hand, Tracy was slow to respond. He hemmed and hawed a bit, but when he answered, he said what I wanted to hear. "Yeah, I think it might be," he said.

I knew what I'd given him was a long way from hard evidence. Detective Tracy had been right, the day we'd first spoken, when he'd suggested that a savvy culprit might just clam up and come out of this fine. So, I made a suggestion, a way he might approach the interrogation. And what he might look for in his search.

Tracy's response was a quick laugh. "I think you'd better leave that to us," he said

"Will you let me know what you learn?"

There was another long pause. "If I've got anything to tell you, I'll give you a call. Meanwhile, given what I'm told about you, let me give you some advice: At this point, you need to just back away from all this till things sort themselves out. You may be onto something here but you need to leave this to us. You do something now, you could just screw this up. You understand, right?"

That sounded very much like Tracy was again bouncing back some of what he might have heard about me from Lieutenant Wilson. On the upside, Wilson had probably also told him I could be relied on.

All I could do now was wait.

In the end, I heard it on the news well before Tracy actually called me back. The first report on the arrest appeared the following day in the on-line edition of the *Yakima Herald-Republic*. In what one might possibly describe as my "frenetic" stomach-churning web-browsing that morning, I found it right away. The story was picked up by *The Seattle Times* and, later in the day, it was in their Wednesday print edition on an inside page.

Fortis Henry's death had been a homicide.

And his killer had been found.

CHAPTER THIRTY

Wednesday, April 26, 3 p.m.

Surprise Amendment

MAYBE I'M A GLUTTON FOR PUNISHMENT, but I felt like Detective Tracy owed me. So, I left him a message around noon on Wednesday. I was still working at home when he finally called me back at around three that afternoon. By that time, I was feeling a bit left out and put out. I knew he was probably a busy man but, even so, I suppose there might have been a trace of petulance in my voice when we finally connected.

"You wanted him caught. Right?" he said. "Well, we caught him."

It seemed to me I deserved a bit more than that. I had, after all, identified the culprit.

"The papers say they had a fight?"

"Uh huh."

"Over the daughter, Tricia?"

"Uh huh."

"Come on, Lieutenant. You can at least let me know if I was right about all this. If it played out the way I told you yesterday. Surely you owe me that?"

"Yeah, I suppose. You weren't far off. Happened just about as you suggested. An argument. Bit of a shoving match. Once Henry fell in, the perp says he tried to help, but there wasn't anything he could do till it was too late. Afterward, he just came back to the house and decided to say nothing about it."

The rest was largely as I'd surmised and what I'd learned from the sketchy early newspaper reports.

The person I hadn't accounted for, that day, the person responsible for Fortis Henry's death, was his then future son-in-law, Tony Dykstra.

When I'd first remembered that Tony Dykstra, too, had been present the day Fortis Henry died, the thing that had caught my attention was recalling the casual, motherly way in which Maryanne Henry had, that rainy day, told him to "wipe your feet, young man." I had glanced at his feet; they'd been wet. And there had, in fact, been a bit of mud caked around the soles of his leather Nike walkers.

Then I remembered I'd been puzzled by Maryanne's having come over to Olympia to testify on that bill back in February. Obviously, she was continuing with her teaching profession, but who was going to run the dairy business? Later she'd told me that would be her new son-in-law with his fresh new degree in Agriculture. Tony's older brother was already working with their father in their family's dairy down in Sunnyside. As a second son, like Daryl Weber, Tony might need to chart a future of his own. He was young, and maybe he'd need some strategic guidance, from time to time, but as a stand-in to help manage Maryanne's dairy farm, he was perfect.

By the time we all stepped outside for our short trek out back to look for Fortis Henry that fateful day, the rain had stopped. The sun was breaking through the clouds. The nice clean pavement in the Henry Dairy's parking lot was already beginning to dry.

So, if he'd just driven in, where had Tricia's boyfriend picked up that mud?

Then I'd recalled my conversation with Janice Burdel about the trend toward extravagant weddings. She'd mentioned how people created wedding websites. I took a look. There was no separate website, but Tricia Henry's unrestricted Facebook page openly shared all kinds of personal information about the newly wedded couple, including proud mention of Tony's remarkable 3.8 grade point average; clearly a bright kid. It also confirmed what Maryanne had told me: Upon graduation, Tony would be joining the Henry Dairy of Zillah, Washington, as "Associate Farm Manager."

Tony's own Facebook page was also openly public, if less extensive and not nearly so current. At least as of when his page had last been revised, Tony's plans had included graduate school in Agricultural Sciences at Texas A & M. There was no mention of an anticipated wedding. Obviously all that had changed since he'd last updated.

Tricia's much-newer page contained several of the expected formal pictures taken by the couple's professional photographer. But she'd also posted many informal shots snapped casually by friends and relatives on their phones. The Henry home had been filled with wedding guests. But their front room was still a limited venue. It all looked to have been a nice, low-key, in home wedding. But I had to ask myself: What had become of Tony's ambitious plans for graduate school? When had the couple decided to wed? And why a modest, home-wedding for the daughter of such a locally prominent, financially successful, politically and socially connected family?

Unfortunately, linked to that question was another. Somehow, the wedding seemed to follow rather quickly after Tricia Henry's father's death. Why marry in April when both of them would be graduating in early June? Back when we'd first met this couple at the Henry home in December, there'd been no mention of marriage. Tony had been introduced as Tricia's "friend," certainly not as her "fiancé."

Perhaps I should be ashamed to say so, but all that had caused me to take a closer look at those wedding pictures, especially the informal, candid ones taken by friends and posted immediately afterward, the ones that had been less-carefully vetted for preservation for posterity. I'm anything but an expert in such things, but even I could tell. In some of those pictures the signs were unmistakable. Tricia Henry was pregnant at the time she and Tony wed. It seemed likely that meant that, back in December, her pregnancy had only recently become known. Since the child had obviously been kept, that meant that, along about Christmas or New Years, its anticipated birth would have become a likely, even necessary, topic of family discussion between Tony and his future in-laws.

It would have been an unplanned pregnancy that was to end up requiring a hurried wedding. There might even have been consideration given to Tricia needing to drop out of school early. Tony had, apparently, been planning to go all the way to Texas for a graduate degree. Had he been planning to take Tricia with him? All those issues might easily have led to a heated discussion between the unborn child's father and the soon-to-be father in law. Given Tricia's father's likely protectiveness for his daughter, it seemed quite possible that Tony and Fortis had had a lot on their minds that day in late December.

According to Detective Tracy's account, that was, in fact, what had happened.

I also recalled Tony mentioning, that morning at the Henry home, that he'd stopped off on his way there to pick up a few snacks for the coming New Year's Eve party. That stop seemed highly likely to have been made at the very same small local grocery down at the freeway exit where Fortis had also gone to run his errand in anticipation of our meeting. As was his habit, Fortis had donned his good hat before going out in public.

Both he and Tony would have been at the same, local minimarket at more-or-less the very same time.

If they'd run into each other there (as it turned out they had), they'd likely have agreed to come back to the farm to talk. (I'd also considered it possible that they might have just happened to pull into the Henry Dairy driveway at about the same time.) In either case, their encounter would have marked the beginning of a very uncomfortable conversation between them, a conversation they couldn't have in a public place and that neither of them wanted to share with Tricia's mother. Since Maryanne Henry was busy working away in the kitchen of her home, and since the rain had stopped, they had taken their discussion out back, down beside the dairy barns and, ultimately, up the newly graveled access driveway to the edge of the new dairy waste lagoon behind the farm. Both were lifelong veterans of dairy farming—the location of that conversation wouldn't have seemed unusual to either of them.

That's when the argument had culminated in a pushing match and Fortis Henry had lost his life.

The capper for me, the one item that had cemented my certainty that Tony Dykstra had to be the killer, was a further detail I'd also gleaned from Tricia's Facebook page and from a glance on-line at the Washington State University curriculum. Tricia had proudly mentioned on Facebook that her new husband was soon to graduate with one of the popular majors in the general field of Agricultural Science: Agricultural Technology and Production Management. That, too, rang a bell.

Even before I'd seen that, however, I'd figured that, while the Henry Dairy might be a leader in its use of technology, I was sure that nearly any large, successful, modern dairy would utilize the same general livestock management systems, namely placing trackers on each animal and assembling and assessing the resulting data by computer. As the son of another successful local dairy farmer, Tony Dykstra would be entirely familiar with such systems. Those systems would also be bread-and-butter in a college curriculum for an Agricultural Technology and Production Management major; surely there'd be classes on wireless electronic tracking technology likely to be of interest to a young, up-and-coming dairyman, particularly one anticipating graduate school.

Tony Dykstra would have exactly the kind of technology interests that might suggest to him the possible use of a dongle to hack an enemy's car.

I also remembered Maryanne Henry mentioning that Rob Thomas had tipped her off to my inquiries. Maryanne could easily be the source from which Tony Dykstra had heard that I was becoming interested in Fortis's death. In any case, Tony's family traveled in the same circles as several of the people I'd spoken with about it. Their home and dairy was also in Rep. Rob Thomas's district. They would be active in WSAIC and would also know Linda Cunningham well.

Once Tony knew I was investigating, he could easily have driven over to Seattle or Olympia to hack my car. I left the car every day in the open driveway at my Olympia office. And my condo garage in Seattle, while inside, was not especially secure. Once the dongle was in place, he could return later, at any time, follow my car until he saw some hazardous situation when he could take over control, and either kill me or at least divert me from further inquiries.

Even the lack of renewed threats over the past month was consistent. My lack of progress, his return to school in Pullman, and his and Tricia's marriage, might have either dissuaded him or occupied him with other priorities.

The only time I'd met Tony Dykstra was the brief encounter that day in the Henry front room. He'd seemed like a nice kid. I knew there was a big difference between a semi-accidental death during a heated argument and a clever, cold-blooded, methodical plot to kill or disable someone by sabotaging their car. But I really had no idea what he might be capable of. It had to be him. He was the only one of the people involved who was even faintly likely to have had the technical skills to pull it off.

There was something else I suspected as well; something I hadn't shared with Detective Tracy. I thought it possible that Maryanne Henry had known or suspected, early on, exactly what had happened that day out at the dairy waste lagoon. She, too, had noticed Tony's wet, muddy shoes on the day in question. More than anyone, she might have also wondered, right away, why her scrupulously neat husband had been wearing his expensive hat out in the dairy barn that day. As Tricia's mother, she may well have learned of her daughter's pregnancy well before Fortis knew of it; maybe Tricia had confided in her mother or maybe Maryanne had noted the symptoms. If so, she'd have been quite conscious of how any interaction between Fortis and Tony could become a confrontation. When she saw Tony at her front door, that day, with Fortis seemingly out back and likely to return to the house at any moment, she must have been fully alert to what could happen if they met.

And suspicious about it afterward.

Finally, Maryanne considered Tony to be a good "catch" for her beloved daughter. Perhaps, after Fortis's death, Tony had actually confessed to her what had happened. Maybe he'd made his explanation, thrown himself on her mercy and asked her forgiveness. She might easily have kept the whole thing quiet for him and for her daughter.

And she might have tipped Tony off to my inquiries.

Again, Tony Dykstra had to be the one.

"Did Maryanne Henry know what he'd done?" I asked Tracy, without elaborating. Even if Maryanne Henry had provided some help to the young man after-the-fact, I found it hard to bring myself to place her in legal jeopardy.

"We believe she did. No way to be sure, though."

Tony and his new wife, Tricia, were still in school at Washington State University. On Tuesday evening, when Tracy and his colleague had driven to Pullman and gone calling, Tricia had been alone and preparing dinner in their recently rented, temporary apartment in Pullman town. The two detectives had gone back out to their car and caught up with Tony as he arrived home twenty minutes later. Rather than take him upstairs to join his wife, they'd decided on a solo interview in the back seat of their Yakima County Sheriff's vehicle.

"Did he know about the security cameras," I asked.

"Knew all about them. They have them at his family's farm down near Sunnyside."

"You did use that, then?" When Detective Tracy and I had talked on Wednesday afternoon, I'd known, as he must have, that even if we were right, we would have little or no hard evidence of a crime. There'd be no way to actually prove Tony Dykstra's presence with the victim out behind the barn that day. We'd need a confession. I'd suggested a strategy for getting that confession.

"We used it. But it didn't go like we figured."

"It didn't?"

"Kid's a bit too smart for his own good," Tracy explained. "When we sat him down in the car, we did like you and I talked about. We just acted like we had him dead to rights. We told him we had the whole thing on disk. He just kind of smirked at us, like he knew that was bullshit."

"He knew?"

"Exactly. So, I say to him: 'You seem pretty damn sure of yourself.' And he says: 'You got nothing on those cameras. They're just inside the barns.' And I say: 'And you know that because . . .?' And then he gets all flustered. That's when I figured he'd probably been talking to Fortis Henry's wife. So, I just hit him with it, straight up: 'You and Maryanne Henry had a chat about all that, right? About what's on those cameras?'"

"And . . .?" I asked.

"That's all it took," Tracy said. "Apparently the possibility of implicating his new wife's mother and new boss wasn't something the kid was prepared for. Maybe his wife, too. She might also have known about it. He just didn't want to go there; he, basically fell apart. Dumped out the whole thing. 'All an accident,' etc. etc. By now, I guess his lawyer's probably informed him that he should have kept quiet. Unfortunately for him, it's now just a bit too late. All on car and body cam."

"What's going to happen to him?"

"Not up to me," Tracy said. "But I'd guess he'll be charged with something fairly light. He might do some jail time, but not much. At sentencing, it'll be a convincing defense case for leniency: The death was mostly an accident. He's the son of a pillar of the community. He's young and foolish but has a good, productive life ahead. Recently married with a young child on the way that will need a father. Not likely to be repeated. Etc., etc."

"What about Maryanne? Accessory after-the-fact and all that?" I saw the whole picture. Maryanne had known all about her daughter's pregnancy. She'd had all the facts. She'd figured it out early on. As I'd guessed, Tony had probably confessed it to her, explained that it was all just a horrible accident, and begged her forgiveness. By that point, the couple might already have been engaged with the wedding scheduled.

Maryanne had a pregnant daughter close to graduation, a highly eligible, soon-to-be son-in-law, and an approaching "shotgun" wedding. The last thing she wanted would be to have her daughter and her new husband starting out their life together with him in prison. She also had no husband and maybe limited personal interest in dairy farming; she needed someone to help her run the family business. Tony might be young, but he was smart and capable. She no doubt believed his story. With his help, she could continue her own profession as a teacher and education advocate. She'd probably twisted Tony's arm and that's when his plans for graduate school went up in smoke.

"Not my concern. No way to prove it without the kid's testimony," Tracy explained. "At this point he's clammed up, but he'll plead out. We've got his confession and too many of the pieces. He goes to trial, a jury may not be inclined to be so lenient."

"Should be some challenging conversations soon in the Henry and the Dykstra households. Interesting to see what happens with the marriage."

"Also, not my concern," Tracy said with finality. "There's always plenty to do without getting involved in the aftermath." The depressing cynicism dripped from his voice.

"Thanks, Detective. I appreciate you taking me seriously when I probably looked like some hyper-engaged meddler."

"It did look pretty thin," he said. I guessed "hyper-engaged meddler" was exactly how he'd have described it.

"Well, I appreciate it. It's a big relief to have this sorted out. Maybe I can finally start getting some sleep at night."

There was a long pause at that. "Oh yeah," he said. "Um, about that. About the business with the dongle and all."

"Yeah?"

"Kid says it wasn't him."

CHAPTER THIRTY-ONE

Wednesday, April 26, 4 p.m.

Added Revelation

66WHAT?" I SAID.

"Says he didn't have anything to do with your dongle business. Doesn't know a thing about it. We grilled him on it; pretty hard. He just denies it, flatly. Says he's been over in Pullman going to school for the past couple of months. Hasn't gone anywhere near the West Side. We can't be absolutely sure he didn't slip over to Seattle or Olympia at some point, of course. But from what we're seeing from his credit card records, his class times, the school's records, and what we're told by his fraternity brothers, it sounds right. Bottom line is, he's believable. From his reaction when we braced him with it, I just got to say, we're convinced."

"Oh Christ," I said.

"Also, nothing came of the search. He has a laptop and a phone, of course. Nothing in there to suggest the kind of hacking you're talking about. No special software. No extra transmission or Bluetooth equipment. Nothing whatever to link him to that. To be honest with you, Dalton, I think you need to figure that he didn't have anything to do that dongle stuff. That has to be somebody else."

"You believe . . ."

"I do. We do. It looks like your dongle hasn't got anything to do with this."

I couldn't believe it. It didn't make sense. Perhaps, in the moment, the more important matter was that the young man had confessed. The mystery of Fortis Henry's death was solved. The killer was in police custody. And, not insignificantly, it wasn't one of my close colleagues in Olympia. That, at least, was a huge relief.

I hung up the phone and leaned back to consider what I'd just learned. I did feel pleased to have it solved. But I also felt profoundly dissatisfied. It was hard to believe Tony Dykstra had nothing to do with that dongle. If not, I was back to square one. Was I really going to just go on with routine, continue my life, all as if nothing had changed? My mind was in turmoil—I had tasks I should be working on right that moment. Instead, I was sitting there without a clue what to do next.

It had been several weeks since I'd stopped by for a visit with my father and I realized I really wanted to see him. It would only be a matter of weeks now before he'd head north for another Alaska fishing season. Also, he had a right to know how things had turned out with the case that he'd helped me figure out early on.

The news that the killer was caught was something he'd be happy to hear.

HALF AN HOUR LATER I was back at Fisherman's Terminal in Ballard, stepping off the worn planking of Dock Ten and swinging up over the bulwark onto the front deck of the "Shirley J." I found Dad on his stomach down in the engine room replacing an oil filter on the old General Motors 6-71 diesel that powered his boat. When he looked up and saw me, the happy smile I got triggered a swell of emotion. Soon, he'd be gone again. I needed to treasure my time with him. The recent loss of another husband and father of my acquaintance should be a message: one never knew when things would fall apart.

We were, almost immediately, back up in the pilothouse, seated at that familiar well-worn galley settee table. I had a hot cup setting in front of me filled with, what else, black bitter coffee that had been brewing on the stove since six that morning.

Dad was, I think, quite pleased by my news. I walked him through the whole thing, what we'd discovered and what had happened over just the past couple of days.

I hadn't told him about the dongle. Maybe that was wrong, but every time I'd considered doing so, I'd found I couldn't. Couldn't visit him with one more worry on the eve of his departure for fishing. I'd been so sure that dongle had to have been planted by Fortis Henry's killer. Now all that was up in the air. When I told him about the call from Detective Tracy, he just nodded as if he'd fully expected, all along, that I'd get to the bottom of the thing.

He was the one to change the subject: "Last time we talked," he said, leaning back with his old, stained coffee mug and a sly smile. "It seems like I remember you were seeing that young woman again, the one you dated some years back?"

"Oh that," I said. "Yeah, I still run into here from time to time . . ."

"Serious?"

I had to laugh. I would never dream of inquiring into details about my dad's private life, but, obviously, it was perfectly OK for him to ask about mine. "No. Just colleagues," I said, wondering as I said it if that was really true.

"Have I ever met her?" he asked.

"I doubt it." I remembered the photos I'd snapped the day Sherry and I had picked David up after his technology fair event. One of them was of Sherry, David and me with David holding his little electric motor. I brought it up on my phone and showed it to Dad. "That's her son, David with her," I said.

"They look nice," he said. "You all look happy."

I was about to tell him not to get his hopes up—Sherry and I were just friends. But, right then, in that instant, something clicked together in my mind. Sherry, the phone, the picture, what she had told me over dinner after we'd dropped David off at her neighbors that afternoon. Everything jelled in a sudden flash of insight. I stared across the table at my father, seated there in this warm, cozy pilot-house. I was startled; frozen in thought and then in fear as drifting puzzle pieces I'd allowed myself to ignore began to snap together.

I'd known, of course, when I'd headed over here from my condo half an hour ago that this thing wasn't really over. I'd automatically continued with my newly acquired habit of watching other people for unusual behavior. When I'd climbed into my new car I'd checked under the dash. As I'd made the drive, I'd watched in my mirror for anyone that seemed to be following. When I'd pulled into the Fishermen's Terminal parking lot, I'd looked at the vehicles pulling in behind me, checked for cars that might be backed into nearby parking spaces with drivers waiting "innocently" behind the wheel. I'd scanned the sidewalk for people who might seem out of place, who were loitering, who suddenly turned away when I looked in their direction. Over the past month, these had become skills for simple self-preservation that, with luck, I'd never need. Habits that, if enough time passed, perhaps I'd, one day, be able to forget.

But without Fortis Henry's killer to blame, I had to reconsider the possible source of my fears. Nothing else added up. It might be conceivable that, in the middle of a tough, angrily contested legislative session I could have stepped on someone's toes, maybe without intending it. Or I might know something critical without understanding its importance. But none of that seemed likely. Somehow, when I'd believed it was Fortis's killer, the threat seemed comprehensible and manageable somehow.

Without that, everything was in the air.

Suddenly, with my dad's mention of Sherry, and seeing him look at that picture on my phone, I'd had an extraordinary thought, a deeply disturbing one. The more I considered it, the more convincing it seemed. And the more shaken I became.

This wasn't over. Not by a long shot.

"Sandy! Sandy, you OK?" My dad was staring across the table

trying to figure out why I'd suddenly stopped talking. Why was I sitting there, like an idiot, with my mouth open but no words coming out?

"Oh, shit. Stupid! Stupid! Stupid!" I said. I bumped against the settee table as I stood and almost knocked over both our coffees.

My dad was sitting back, looking increasingly concerned.

"Dad," I said. "I, um, I've got to go. I'm really sorry, but I just realized I . . . I need to go. Nothing to worry about. I'm sorry. I'll give you a call, explain later, OK?"

Without a backward glance, I picked up my phone and left the pilothouse. I hurried up the side of the boat, leapt over the bulwark, and rushed down the dock leaving, I'm sure, a deeply bewildered father peering after me.

As I hurried toward my car, I pulled out my phone again and dialed furiously.

Holy shit! It wasn't me that was at risk. This wasn't about me. It never had been.

This was all about Sherry.

CHAPTER THIRTY-TWO

Thursday, April 26, 5 p.m.

Pre-Adjournment Frenzy

I-5 WAS A MESS.

Sherry wasn't answering her cell and she wasn't answering at home.

I'd left a message before I realized that, in my panic, I wasn't thinking straight. It was a weekday. She was back working at the law office downtown. Of course, on a weekday, at five, she'd probably still be at work.

I'd forgotten the name of the law firm that employed her but brought up my contact list and, with some difficulty, managed to come up with the number.

But Sherry wasn't in. She'd been there earlier. But now she wasn't answering her line. The receptionist suggested that maybe she was headed home. Considering the time, that seemed quite possible though I knew she typically put in long hours when she worked at the law firm. I left her a message there and then called her home again while, at the same time, narrowly avoiding a collision with a slow milk tanker-truck working its way over into the left lane presumably in preparation for the left-hand exit to I-405 near Southcenter. There was obviously a sound reason the State of Washington prohibited the use of cell phones while driving, but that was, at the moment, the last thing I cared about.

Maybe I could pass him on the right. No, now an old green corolla was moving into that lane.

It had been nearly three weeks since Sherry had told me about that damn email that had been sent to Fortuna's lobbyist Aaron Nicolaides. I should have seen this immediately. But I'd been so wrapped up with Fortis Henry, so worried about my own damn personal safety, that I'd neglected to think about hers.

I'd completely missed the potential significance of that message.

I'd known the obvious from the start, of course: that the Governor and the legislators who had supported and voted for the Fortuna incentives would now be in for very a rough ride. Probably also the lobbyists who'd pushed them. They'd all have some serious explaining to do, especially the elected officials. They'd have to justify how they'd passed legislation that had turned out so badly. They'd all plead ignorance, of course. How could they possibly have predicted this? In the end, maybe that would work for them.

But what about the people who had actually seen it coming?

At the time Sherry had first seen that message, all she'd taken it for was some mildly concerning news about Fortuna. Whoever had sent it to Aaron Nicolaides, Fortuna's legislative lobbyist, that person, however, had to have had a very good reason for doing so. One had to ask: why would Fortuna's lobbyist be interested in minor problems with some arcane line of medical research?

There could only be one reason: because it was important for something currently happening in the Legislature.

Sherry had said Nicolaides, Drum, Fernandez, and Drum's Assistant, Springfield, had been acting suspiciously in the meeting she'd observed the day she walked by in the hallway. And that Drum had dropped the memo into the wastebasket with the comment that it made "no difference." Obviously, they'd all known that it could make a very big difference.

A huge financial investment of this kind, depending on

participation by several large, publicly visible corporate partners, would hang by a thread until it was final. This one
depended on favorable action by the Legislature which hung, in
turn, on public good will and the perceived public benefit to the
State of Washington. Even a small hitch in Fortuna's financial
stability would shake that support and unsettle their investment
partners. This research disaster was, obviously, much more than
a mere "hitch."

With Nicolaides' encouragement, however, the little cabal
in that conference room that day made a conscious decision to
keep quiet about it and to go ahead with promoting the legislation needed for the Fortuna investment. In effect, they decided
to purposefully mislead every legislator they dealt with from that
day forward. Not to mention their corporate partners and the
Washington public.

Given what had happened since, that decision could now
destroy them, the person who'd sent the message, and anyone else
who'd known about the failure of that research and who had tried
to keep it hidden. They'd all now be claiming that they'd had no idea
about this—a claim clearly put to the lie by that email memo. A col-
lection of powerful people with unlimited money, with boundless
connections, and with a powerful motivation to save themselves.
Some of them would be employed by one of the largest high-tech
companies in the world—people who, sure as hell, would know
how to use a freaking dongle. They'd wanted that incentives legislation passed regardless of the risk to Washington taxpayers. But if
that memo became known, they might have to face some serious
consequences, political, financial, and even legal.

Critically, from what Sherry had told me, there was no reason
to believe anybody was aware she'd seen and copied that memo.

But what if she'd been wrong?

When I'd shown Dad that picture on my phone, I'd remembered
what Sherry had told me over dinner about that day. When she
had set off in search of a room in which have a meeting, one of the

people she'd been planning to meet with, who she'd been expecting at the Committee Offices that day, and who'd joined Sherry back in her own office after their meeting, had been Stoney. The bill he'd been there to discuss had been Howard Oxley's Tech Education Bill.

I also remembered that the day that bill had come up for a hearing, instead of meeting over in the Capitol Dome Deli, Stoney had insisted on joining me at the hearing. I'd just figured he was planning to play it safe with the traffic getting there or to keep tabs on me. Now it seemed, maybe, not. Why would Stoney be taking an interest in a Tech Education Bill?

Maybe the answer was that what he was really interested in was Oxley and the Fortuna Package.

Then, with a start, I realized something else that had been obvious: Stoney was a substantial landowner and small-business entrepreneur up in the very same Eastern King County community where Fortuna had planned to build its new computer farm facility. Of course, he'd have an interest in the Fortuna legislation.

But was there, perhaps, more?

The I-5 southbound evening commute was, predictably, down to stop and start. I pulled out my mobile again. I'd been to Stoney's farm on a couple of occasions, so it wasn't hard to find it on the map provided on the King County parcel search website. According to the County's records, the owner was Stoney Creek Investments—that would surely be Phil (Stoney) Stonington.

Fumbling, a bit, as I drove while also thumbing a search, I found a link to the King County Recorder's Office. And there I found the very answer I had feared: Stoney Creek Investments had, some two-and-a-half years earlier, been paid the sum of $60,000 for a one-year option to purchase, for $4.7 million, some 73 acres of undeveloped land along State Highway 203 north of Carnation. That option had been renewed twice over the ensuing two years. The buyer: None other than one Fortune Real Estate Services, Inc. – Fortuna.

Then everything made sense.

Despite his earnest support for farmland protection, Stoney stood to make a nice windfall on his land sale. To be fair, most of Stoney's land was forest, not farm. Even so, there was no way, given the usual rigor of King County's disciplined zoning, that 73 woodland and a few agricultural acres would be worth $4.7 million—at least not before some legislative enactment changed the zoning laws. Moreover, I knew Stoney owned a couple of small business properties in downtown Carnation itself, a town that would prosper and properties whose value would greatly inflate if the Fortuna deal went through.

As active as he was in politics, I could also be quite sure Stoney had an ongoing relationship with his own State Legislator, none other than Rep. Jerry Fernandez, my nemesis on the bill that would have killed our commercial fishing vessel insurance pools. Fernandez, after all, represented the legislative district where Fortuna planned its project; I hadn't been at all surprised that he was with Nicolaides and Drum when Sherry ran across their little meeting, last February, in the O'Brien Building.

There was yet another, in an endless series of stops and starts in the traffic. I took another in a series of deep breaths to calm myself.

My friend and client, Stoney, was into this Fortuna calamity up to his ears.

There was something else. Sherry had told me that one of the reasons she knew Stoney, was that he was that he was good friends with a fellow House staff member. I'd assumed she'd been talking about a committee staffer. But could that friend have been Drum's legislative assistant, Bob Springfield? I believed I recalled that Springfield was from Carnation. He was quite possibly known to Stoney. Maybe he'd been recommended to Drum by Fernandez. Or by Stoney himself. Springfield had also been present in the room when Nicolaides and the two legislators had been discussing the memo. Springfield was probably Stoney's principal staff contact connected to the key legislators working the Fortuna Package.

As the pieces fell into place, it just got worse and worse.

Finally, I thought about that day Sherry had run across the Nicolaides, Drum, Fernandez, Springfield mini-caucus in that room down the hall from her office and had taken that picture. After snapping the picture, she'd met with Stoney's group on the Tech Education Bill and then she and Stoney had returned to her office. I pictured the layout of her tiny office, with the desk pushed up against the outside wall, the open laptop completely visible to anyone in the room, the cell-phone charging cradle beside her computer, also facing back into the room. I knew it was her habit to slip her phone into its cradle when she was in the office. If she'd done that, it would awaken. A light brush with a finger, or the back of a hand, and it would revert to the last item she'd had open, her picture of that incriminating message. Anybody in that room would have a clear view of everything on her desk. And even if Sherry was seated at the desk, she could be completely unaware that they were watching.

Maybe that was pure guesswork, but it all added up: Stoney's obvious self-interest in Fortuna, his relationship with Springfield, his presence in the room at the critical moment. Perhaps most significant of all, in our many conversations since, he'd never mentioned anything about the Fortuna matter to me. He'd been consciously keeping it all under the table. There might be an innocent explanation, but I wasn't seeing it.

As I was passing Federal Way, traffic began to break up, but by the time I'd reached Tacoma, it had slowed again. It was all I could do to keep from slamming the steering wheel with my fist in frustration.

If Stoney had mentioned to Springfield, or to anyone on the Fortuna team, that Sherry had a copy of that memo, she would have been in danger from that moment on.

She'd be in danger right now.

Initially, of course, Nicolaides, Drum, Fernandez, Springfield, maybe Stoney, and whoever else had known about the impending research failure and its possible political significance, would have known that, at some point, that failure would become public. Fortuna's lobbyist, Aaron Nicolaides, wouldn't have been told about it if there hadn't been a very real and immediate concern. They'd probably asked his advice on what to do about the pending legislation. In any case, they'd all have known that if or when Fortuna's research collapse became known, it would become big news.

If they knew what Sherry had done, knew she had that memo, they'd have had to face the very real possibility that, when Sherry heard that news, she could realize the memo's importance. She could then become a big problem

I hadn't a moment's doubt that my dongle demonstrated exactly what they'd decided to do about it.

Why my car rather than hers? The answer was easy; I'd have seen it if I hadn't been so close to the case.

If they had "dongled" *her* car and used the thing to cause a serious accident, the subsequent police accident investigation would doubtless turn the thing up, just as it had in my accident. Then there'd be an intense inquiry over who might have put it there and what they might have had to gain. That investigation would focus on Sherry, on the matters she was involved in, and on the people with whom she worked. People like Nicolaides, Drum and Fernandez.

For the past few months, Sherry and I had been seeing a lot of one another. We weren't romantically involved, but anyone could have known of our relationship and would probably have assumed we were dating. They'd have realized that, if you put a dongle in *my* car, and caused an accident when Sherry was with me, I'd be the focus of attention. Once the dongle was in place, all they needed to do was wait until we were in my car together. Nobody would suspect that a bureaucratic lawyer for some legislative committee, a mere passenger, could possibly have been the target.

But a lobbyist like me must certainly have made many enemies. Probably, we were both very lucky that we'd been so busy, this past Session, that we'd gotten together only very occasionally. That must have been a big frustration for the perpetrators. If it hadn't been for my fortuitous accident on my way home from Olympia that rainy Saturday morning, their plan would, sooner or later, have worked. They might have made their move the very next time Sherry and I went out together.

I had wondered why there'd been no repeat attempts following my accident. Maybe the "Fortuna conspirators," whoever they might turn out to be, had decided to back off. But there was another possibility as well, one that was much less comforting. Perhaps, until Monday's news, the perpetrators were just taking their time, seeing no hurry, cooking up an alternative strategy. They'd want to get it right after their first failure. But, with the news of Fortuna's collapse, the whole matter would have suddenly become urgent. Now they'd realize that Sherry could, at any moment, remember that memo and realize its significance, exactly as she actually had done.

Unfortunately, she'd only told me. I had "helpfully" suggested she keep it to herself.

How could I have been so stupid?

For the past week, every single moment following Friday morning's news about Fortuna's tumbling stock, Sherry had been in grave danger. Who knew what they might have in mind for their next try? Quite possibly something much more direct, dangerous, and certain.

Meanwhile, I'd been dinking around with Fortis freaking Henry! Speculating on theories, suggesting suspects to the police, and today, having a friendly chat with my father.

What a dumb shit I was!

Traffic slowed again as I approached Fort Lewis/McChord. This drive was taking far too long. I'd left my messages, but I had to do something more. I got back on the phone and called Sherry's Olympia law office again on the chance she'd returned. It was now after five-thirty. This time, someone else answered the phone. Considering the time, it might have been one of Sherry's colleagues working late after the receptionist had left for the day.

"Oh, yeah," she said. "I think Sherry was dropping by her office at the Capitol to pick up a few things before heading home."

This momentary lead collapsed when nobody answered the phone at the Committee offices in the O'Brien Building. Session was over. It was late and past closing. She might even be there but, as someone not presently employed by the Committee, she might not answer. Sherry was also still not answering on her cell.

Everything seemed to be falling apart.

Then I made the only other call I could think of.

"Wilson!"

Nothing could have felt more friendly than the clipped, cold, officious voice of Lieutenant Nathan Wilson answering his phone at the Washington State Patrol. Thank God he was still in his office. He'd picked up on the first ring.

"Lieutenant, this is Sandy Dalton. I've got a problem."

"Of course," said Wilson.

This was no time to scan for signs of the man's deeply buried humor, assuming it existed. "I have a friend," I hurried on. "Sherry Sebold. I think she's in danger. She's a lawyer with a Legislative Committee during Session. Off-Session she works for a downtown law firm. Right now, I think she's on her way home from work and may have stopped by her Legislative Committee staff office in the O'Brien Building."

"OK."

"I don't know who else to call, Lieutenant. I'm stuck in traffic on I-5. I'm afraid for her life." Given his position in the Patrol, this wouldn't necessarily be his problem. But the Washington State Patrol is responsible for security on the Washington State Capitol Campus. He had authority, he knew people, he was on site, he could get something done. At least he could if he wanted to. I wasn't entirely in left field with my call.

"I see. OK, I'm listening. Slow down and take it from the top."

That's what I did. He already knew about the dongle. I just needed to explain why the situation might, suddenly, have become exigent.

All the time I was talking I was fighting to keep calm, to be cogent, and not to honk my horn at the stupid asshole that had just cut into the left lane in front of me and was now creeping along at ten-miles-an-hour with a space wide open in front of him the length of two football fields. The whole time I was talking I was thinking about all the ways Sherry could be at risk.

For that matter, I suddenly realized her son could also be at risk. If the perpetrators knew about the photo Sherry had made of that memo, someone might decide they wanted to talk to her and get hold of any copies before disposing of her. David could become leverage. It was a Thursday evening. I looked at the time. David would be finishing up with one of the after-school events he often attended.

"You say Sebold has left work," Wilson asked me when I finally slowed down enough for him to get a word in.

"I think so. Usually she works later than this. But they said she was headed over to her office at the O'Brien Building to pick up a few personal items before heading home. I told him where her campus office was located. "It's also possible she'll stop off to get her son. He may be at risk as well," I said. I had no idea who, exactly, we might be dealing with, but it seemed like it could be someone very sinister with deeply powerful interests behind them. I admit, at that moment, I was probably more than a little frantic.

"I think he's at a 'computer club' meeting," I continued. "He goes for a couple of hours on Tuesdays and Thursdays, at the school after classes are over. Christ, somebody needs to call the school and make sure he doesn't leave with somebody he shouldn't. His name's David Gavick, it's his father's name . . ."

"Dalton! Dalton, calm down, will you?" I shut up. "I'm on it," he continued. "I'm sending an officer over to the Committee office right now. Tell me the name of the school. And do you have Sebold's picture?"

I gave him the name and location of the school. And I did have that selfie of me. Sherry and David. "Wait one," I said. I brought it up on my phone, got Wilson's cell number, and texted it to him. "It's on its way."

"Good. I'll call the school. And . . . yeah, I got the photo. I'll make sure this goes out to all the duty officers. We'll get it to the Sergeants-at-arms at the Capitol as well. Maybe they'll see her when she enters or leaves the O'Brien Building. Relax. We got this."

I wasn't so sure.

"David's school. If he's still there . . . could you have an officer ask them to make absolutely sure David is safe and that he stays safe. If he heads home on his own, we need to make sure he doesn't get waylaid somewhere."

"I'm already on it. You're going to need to tell me more about where all this is coming from. From what you're saying, it doesn't sound related to that Yakima murder we talked about, right?"

"No. I think that's over," I said.

"OK, you just relax, drive carefully, and get here safely. We'll see to your girlfriend and her son. When you get here, you can fill me in on the details. I'm sticking my neck out here, Dalton. So, I hope you have a damned good explanation."

"I do. I'm going to head to her office at the Capitol when I arrive. But I'll give you a call and explain everything, OK?"

"I'll be dying hear it."

Again, was that humor? Irony? Who could tell.

CHAPTER THIRTY-THREE

Thursday, April 26, 6:05 p.m.

The Crunch

IT WAS AFTER SIX when I walked into the House committee staff offices on the second floor of the O'Brien Building. When I arrived, Sherry was right there in her usual office talking with an unfamiliar uniformed State Patrol Officer. They both looked up expectantly when I walked in.

"Sandy!" Sherry said when I appeared in her doorway. She looked just fine. I was washed with a massive flood of relief at seeing her there, safely in her office. On the desk behind her was a half-filled "banker's box" containing books, papers, and a few personal photographs. She was looking confused, but she was obviously unharmed.

"This who we're talking about?" said the officer, "P. Dumfries" according to his nametag. He was probably wondering why the hell he'd been called over here.

"Yes. Officer Dumfries, Sandy Dalton," Sherry made the introduction and we shook hands briefly.

"What's this all about," Sherry asked me, looking very confused.

It was just at that moment that Bob Springfield, Representative Drum's Legislative Assistant, fortuitously appeared in her office doorway; apparently, he, too, was there on an off-Session errand.

Sherry had once told me he spent nearly as much time down here on the second floor with the Committee staff as he did up on the fourth floor manning his own desk in front of Drum's actual legislative office. "Hey, Sherry," he said, obviously curious about people here so late in the evening and about the presence of a uniformed police officer. "What goes?"

In an instantaneous flash of insight, I suddenly realized that, right there, right then, that was going to be our moment of truth. Other than my dongled car and a lot of suppressed anger, all I had was a long, twisted chain of supposition. If I was wrong, it wouldn't just be me looking like a fool. Sherry's legislative job and reputation could also be at stake.

I didn't know much about Bob Springfield other than that he was originally from Carnation, over in Eastern King County. Springfield was a recent political science graduate from Pacific Lutheran University in Tacoma and was interested in a future in politics. I assumed he lived in Olympia, at least during Session. He was clearly committed, judging from his presence here at this hour and off-Session.

I looked quickly around the room. I knew, perhaps intuitively, that what was about to happen to me and to Sherry, could depend on these next few minutes. If I did what I was considering, Bob Springfield was about to get some valuable post-graduate political science experience. There was a lot on the line. It was a big risk, but I didn't really see a choice.

I decided to take the chance.

"Hello, Bob," I said, very gravely. "It's good of you to join us. Please come in and take a seat." I aimed him over in the direction of a small, well-worn, half-couch at the side of the tiny office, reaching out my arm as if to collect and guide him—not really giving him a choice in the matter. "I'm afraid we have some important issues to discuss."

He glanced nervously over at that State Patrol officer, then at Sherry, then at me, and then, with a deeply worried look, he moved over and perched nervously on the front edge of the couch. In that brief moment, watching his face, I knew I'd been right in my assessment of him and in my understanding of what had happened. I was about to take a huge risk, but I'd also spent years of my life reading people's reactions and divining their point of view from what little I knew about them. I was fully aware that I'd have but one shot at making this work. My guesses needed to be flawless. From this point forward, everything depended on what I was about to do.

The first step was to get that State Patrol Officer out of the room.

With a glance, a nod, and a slightly raised index finger in Sherry's direction, by which I hoped to convey to her that I had this in hand and that she should follow my lead, I turned to the Officer: "Um, Officer Dumfries, I wonder if I could ask that you step outside into the hall and give us the room for just a few moments. It was really good of you to come over here. I think you may be needed still. But it would helpful if you'd give us some privacy. Maybe you'd be willing to stand by, just outside. Maybe help make sure we aren't interrupted? It will only take a few minutes, I promise."

Dumfries was clearly taken by surprise. I hoped he wasn't offended by my request. I badly needed him to agree. He glanced at Sherry who, thankfully, nodded her confirmation. Maybe it also helped that it was Lieutenant Wilson, a respected senior officer at the Patrol, who had asked him to come over here. For whatever reason, thankfully, he did as I asked. "I'll be right outside," he said. When he was gone, I shut the door.

Now it was just Sherry, Bob Springfield, and me. The last thing we needed, at this point, was to have someone reading this nervous but well-educated young man his Miranda rights. I did, however, want a record of what we were about to do. So, when I'd turned to close the door, I'd used that opportunity to pull out my phone, set it to voice record, and replace it in my shirt pocket.

I'd been carrying the dongle Lieutenant Nakamura had found in my car around with me ever since I'd showed it to Lieutenant

Wilson when we met a couple of weeks earlier. It had been in the glove box, first of my rental, and then in my new Subaru. When I'd left my car in the lot a few minutes earlier, I'd expected to have some explanations to make to Sherry and maybe to some other officials of the State Patrol. I'd grabbed it and put it in my pocket.

I pulled it out and laid it silently on a side table right next to where Springfield was seated. Then I turned one of the empty chairs around to face in his direction and sat. In the cramped space of the tiny office we were only a few feet apart. With as much serious drama as I could manage, I paused, pointed significantly at the dongle, and said: "You want to explain that?"

Springfield looked up at me, at Sherry, at the closed door outside of which he knew there was a waiting State Patrolman, and then back at me. He was like a trapped animal. I just waited him out.

"Um, no. I mean, what's that?" It was evident from his manner that Springfield had either seen that dongle before or, at the very least, that he knew exactly what it was and why I was asking.

"I see," I said. I sighed deeply and sadly. "That's too bad. I was hoping perhaps you didn't know what it was and what it means. But I see that you obviously do."

"Well, no, I mean, um . . ."

I just shook my head pityingly.

He shut up. Then he mustered some courage and continued: "So what does that thing have to do with me?"

We'd been extremely lucky. It had seemed entirely possible, that all Springfield and the others had done was pass information along. Fortuna's cover-up of their failed research project and the fact that it had taken a "whistle blower" for the information to finally come out spoke, in my view, to an unethical company leadership, the kind of business climate that can lead people to do desperate things. The dongle, the threat to Sherry, it all could have been something orchestrated and known about only by higher-ups in a dysfunctional Fortuna hierarchy. If that had been the case, I think our chances of catching them out would have been minimal. But it now appeared that there might be answers to be had much closer to home. I wondered just how involved Springfield was, personally. Maybe very involved. Clearly, he knew something about what had been afoot.

"Mr. Springfield, here's the situation," I said. "You have a choice to make, about your future. I'm sorry, but you're going to need to make that choice right now." I held up a finger. "Before you say anything more, before we open that door and bring that officer back into this room, you need to decide which of two things is going to happen. Either you're going to make this right, or you need to plan on going to jail for a very long time. Unfortunately, you need to decide quickly, because that State Patrolman isn't going to be patient for very long out there. You need our help. But, when he returns, it's going to be out of our hands."

There was a helpfully coincidental cough, then some footsteps and the sound of some low voices coming from the other side of the door. Then more footsteps. And silence.

"Sherry," I said. "Do you still have handy a copy of that memo you came across back in February. The one that foretold Fortuna's current misfortunes?"

Sherry opened her briefcase, pulled out and unfolded a paper copy of the memo, and handed it to me. I laid it down beside the dongle on the little table beside Springfield's couch and smoothed it flat for him to see.

"So, as you can see, Bob, your secret is out. It's not going back in the bottle, at this point. You understand that, right?"

He nodded grimly.

"We know that Representative Drum, Aaron Nicolaides, and Representative Fernandez saw this memo, and then kept it and its obvious implications, a close secret while their Legislative colleagues here, Republicans and Democrats, voted to adopt costly public support for what was a doomed project. We also know that, when they realized Ms. Sebold, here, had seen this memo, they began taking, shall we say, steps to silence her. We know you were there and knew about that."

SUSPENSION OF THE RULES

"I didn't . . ." he began.

But I held up my hand and interrupted. "Just hold on a moment, till I'm done, OK? I want to help you here, so don't say anything until you have the full picture, OK." Springfield nodded, and I continued: "So we know what I've told you. And we know from Phil Stonington that you knew Sherry had a copy." With that last point, I was taking a huge chance. Out of the corner of my eye, I saw Sherry start at that news. I desperately hoped I was right, but there was no real choice for me but to use everything I had.

"That's what we know." I continued, relentless. "Here's *your* choice: You can deny everything. In effect, that will make you a willing part of their criminal conspiracy. You can then go to prison with them for a very long time for attempted murder." I paused to let that sink in. I thought he looked to have turned very pale. "Or," I said. "You can explain to the two of us right now, and in a few moments, to the Officer outside, how, when Stoney told you that Ms. Sebold had a copy of this memo, you informed Mr. Nicolaides, Mr. Drum, or Mr. Fernandez of what you'd learned. Then, we will assume, I hope correctly, that you had *nothing* further to do with this whole matter. That's right, isn't it?"

I suspected Springfield's role could have been a great deal worse. For all I knew, he might have been the person who actually installed and planned to activate that dongle. Or he could have been a go-between with hired muscle. Whatever his actual role, I was also sure Nicolaides, Drum, and Fernandez would implicate Springfield the moment they thought that might help them save themselves. Springfield needed to see a way out. This might be the only one he had. In my experience, people also want to talk their way out of things, even when they shouldn't.

To my immense relief, Springfield jumped at the opening.

"No, I didn't. I just told them what Stoney had said. I had no idea what they did after that."

I pointed at the dongle again. "But you know now, right?"

He looked dejected and then angry. "Not until Tuesday.

Representative Drum brought me into his office Tuesday afternoon. Nicolaides and Fernandez were there. They'd told me back in February that I needed to keep quiet about what I'd seen. And I had. But this time, they were, like, deadly serious. They scared the shit out of me."

"So how is it that you know what this thing is?" I pointed at the dongle, again.

"I've read about them. On-line. Seen pictures. There are, like apps for your phone that use them with a Bluetooth, that can tell you all about your car." He was very uncomfortable.

"There's more than that, Bob. You're going to need to tell us, or this is likely to go very badly for you. What do you know about this dongle?"

Springfield sighed in resignation. "One day near the end of Session I heard Representative Drum talking on the phone. My desk is only a few feet from his office door upstairs. I hear him all the time when he's in meetings or on the phone."

"OK."

"He was talking to Aaron Nicolaides. My phone has a readout on it that shows who the current caller is. Nicolaides is with that big Law Firm up in Seattle; it shows up as 'Morganthau.' When I see that, I always know it's Nicolaides."

"So, let's have it. What did he say?"

This was a big hurdle for this loyal and, who knew, maybe even basically honest, young man. I wanted to believe what he'd said so far. But this, a direct betrayal of his employer, might be a very big leap. He sat in silence for a moment, obviously uncertain.

So, I primed him: "You know you don't have a choice here, right?" I aimed a thumb at the still-closed office door. And at the law-enforcement presence outside it. "So far as I can see, you're not in any real trouble. Not yet. But if that's to continue, you need to own up. You do that, and I think you'll come out of all this just fine. It's up to you."

He sighed. "They were talking about Sherry." He nodded in

her direction. "Drum said they needed a 'solution.' He said the 'damned car gadget' wasn't going to work and that they needed to do something 'more direct.' I didn't like the sound of any of that. Now, you're showing me this dongle, and it seems like, well, like I know what he was talking about. You've got to believe me, I didn't have anything to do with any of that."

With that, with the copy of the memo, and with what Sherry had seen, we had them. It wouldn't be enough, on its own, to convict. But it was convincing, plenty good for what we needed to remove the danger. It would serve as "probable cause" in investigating a criminal conspiracy formulated here on the campus of the Washington State Capitol. A conspiracy among officials of State Government. Dealing with a matter of State legislative policy. So it would soon be a new problem for my long-suffering friend, Lieutenant Nathan Wilson of the State Patrol. Regardless of how his investigation went from this point forward, and no matter how deeply they'd end up probing the internal morass that was obviously the Fortuna Corporation, Nicolaides, Drum, and Fernandez personally were in for some serious problems. Once Sherry handed that memo, on paper and on flash drive, over to Officer Dumfries, and I delivered up my recording of this meeting, she and I would be out of the woods.

I looked at Sherry as I stood up and we exchanged very relieved smiles. She hadn't said a single word during the entire exchange. Now she was shaking her head in what seemed to be amazement and mild disbelief.

As I stepped over to open the door, I looked back at the starkly worried face of Bob Springfield, a young man who had gotten himself deeply mired in something for which he had seemingly been completely unprepared.

I didn't know what the future truly held for Bob Springfield. I had no way to know if he'd been the least bit truthful. Maybe he'd just been taking my lead and looking for a way out. Somehow, I wanted to believe him. I guessed some future jury might, one day, also be inclined to believe him.

Conscious that my phone was still recording our conversation, however, and hoping to keep our young witness securely enfolded within the story he'd just told, what I said was: "Don't worry, Bob. You'll be OK. You tell the police what you just told us. You tell them the truth about everything you know. You're going to come out of this just fine."

EPILOGUE

Sunday, May 10, 4 p.m.

IT WAS ONE OF THOSE RARE SPRING DAYS when the sky clears for a brief foretelling of summer. The soft beach sand beneath our feet at Priest Point Park had been warmed by the slowly setting sun. Sherry and I sat on a dry, bleached log and watched David patiently practice his recently acquired skill at skipping rocks across the quiet water.

The fallout from Sherry's revelation of the now infamous Fortuna memorandum was finally settling down in the press. But as long as State Representatives Thomas Drum and Jerry Fernandez were still in office, the Washington State Legislature was bound to be an awkward place for the woman who had blown the lid off of what the press had, somewhat unoriginally, dubbed "Fortunagate."

The State Patrol didn't discuss their ongoing investigations in public, of course. So far, nobody had gone to jail. I suspected that Nicolaides, Drum, Fernandez, and whoever else they might have worked with at Fortuna might well escape criminal prosecution even though the placement of that dongle in my car had definitely been an "act in furtherance of a criminal conspiracy" whoever had actually put it there.

I also suspected that Fernandez, in particular, might have had a good deal to do with the choice to target my car. He had been absolutely livid following the embarrassing defeat of his mean-spirited marine insurance pool legislation. I guessed he'd have been perfectly happy to include getting rid of me as a part of any plot they'd hatched to silence Sherry.

Even with Springfield's, Sherry's, and my testimony, however, proving any of that was going to be challenging. Until this morning, I'd been convinced the only penalty they'd suffer would be whatever they lost by way of public distain and possible electoral defeat.

But I'd turned out to be wrong.

That morning's Seattle Times financial pages had reported on an FBI/SEC probe into insider trading in Fortuna stock linked to the research failure at Fortune Biologics and the "ill-fated" legislative incentives for Fortuna's now dead computer farm project. The article mentioned two unnamed "elected public officials," and a "Fortuna lobbyist" as among the investigative targets. It wasn't hard to guess who they were. All three of them had owned Fortuna stock. And not one of them had, apparently, had the discipline to keep themselves from selling it once they'd seen that email memo. Not only were all three likely to suffer consequences for insider trading, but by selling their stock, they'd all essentially acknowledged their understanding of the significance of that memo. So much for their pleas of ignorance.

The article didn't mention any "legislative staffers" so I assumed Bob Springfield wasn't included, a good sign for him.

I could only hope that a certain East King County farmer, and still-current client of mine, would not turn out to have also sold Fortuna stock. If he had, it would greatly diminish his innocent explanation for why he'd told Springfield about Sherry's possession of that email message. He'd apparently seen it pop up on Sherry's phone when they'd returned to her office that day. The message mentioned Fortuna and its subject was "bad news" so, of course, he'd read it and then had asked Bob Springfield about it. Springfield had told him it was "nothing to worry about" and Stoney's story was that he'd then forgotten all about it.

Springfield, however, had definitely understood the significance of the memo and of Sherry's possession of it. And he'd passed the information along.

Other than recklessly covering their financial backsides, Nicolaides, Drum, and Fernandez been incredibly cool in keeping their secret. They'd pressed forward with their legislative incentive bills presumably under instruction from Fortuna. When they learned that Sherry had intercepted their memo, they'd made their fateful decision to dispose of her.

We had no way to know how far up in Fortuna's hierarchy the plot had gone or who else might have been involved. Despite the wholesome public image of its CEO, it was clear Fortuna was a troubled organization. Public disclosure of a major research debacle had been forced upon them at huge personal risk by a courageous whistle-blower. They'd continued pursuing government incentives for a business investment even after they knew that investment might well be doomed. They were willing to mislead partner-investors by failing to disclose material information about their own financial stability. They'd certainly made a poor choice in retaining their lobbyist. I personally believed they might be capable of anything.

With the damaging email now in the hands of the police, and the truth publicly known, whatever had been their previous plans for Sherry, they would no longer be viable. Sherry and I might not be popular in some quarters, but at least neither of us seemed likely to be in further danger.

Nicolaides, Drum, and Fernandez had been cool but, when it came to their own pocketbooks, they'd all three apparently panicked. With the evidence of the memo matched up with indisputable financial records documenting their stock transfers, they wouldn't be squirming out of that insider-trading charge so very easily. No matter what happened, both legislators had been sufficiently disgraced that they'd almost certainly lose their committee chairmanships. Their prospects in next year's elections looked dim.

The whole mess would, however, continue to complicate Sherry's life as House committee legal counsel. Little wonder she was seriously considering a job change and perhaps moving into the active practice of law before the start of the new Session next January.

I also knew exactly who had caused all this.

That person would be me.

"We had no choice, Sandy," Sherry had told me more than once since that day over a month earlier, when I'd pried open Bob Springfield's reluctant testimony. With my actions that day, I'd also offered up Sherry and the entire matter for police and public inquiry. "If we hadn't gone public, we'd still be at risk," she'd said. I knew it was true. But that wouldn't alleviate the unpleasantness she'd had to endure from some of her more short-sighted colleagues.

Out there on Budd Inlet, a commercial salmon troller was passing, plowing north up Puget Sound, probably leaving a moorage slip in Olympia's East Bay Marina and, considering the season, maybe headed for Southeast Alaska. It had a long trip ahead. Maybe in a few weeks it would be fishing alongside the "Shirley J." along the shores of Yakobi Island in the North Pacific.

The distant thrum of its engines drifted across the quiet inlet. It awakened vivid memories of fishing with my dad. Of beating north across Queen Charlotte Sound against a fresh Northwester. Of idling through the narrow, rocky entrance at Deer Harbor before dropping anchor in quiet, protected water beneath tall, stately Sitka spruce. Of pulling in a powerful thirty-five-pound chinook salmon and hearing the solid "whump" it made when it landed on the back deck. Or of unloading a hold full of fresh, iced fish at low tide beneath a dripping wet, barnacled pier in Sitka Harbor.

That, in turn, reminded me of my grandparents' idyllic farm in North Central Washington. Of neatly tilled soil ready for planting. Of the distant hum of my grandfather's tractor working the fields. Of the big, brown, dreamy eyes and huge wet noses of my granddad's cows nuzzling my arm through the boards of the fence along the pasture just beyond their barn. Of the creamed "young spuds" my grandma used to fix with the sweet little immature potatoes we'd harvest by hand from along the edges of the field in early Summer.

Those days seemed far away. Yet, at the same time, they seemed very recent and immediate. Those were days in lives still being lived by the fishers and farmers I represented here in Olympia; people whose livelihoods were no longer generally perceived as mainstream by the modern world. More than ever before, they needed someone making sure their business and way of life wasn't forgotten in an age of jet planes, computers, and self-driving cars.

Today, however, under an idyllic sunny sky, with the cries of gulls and the occasional happy screams of children playing further down the beach, and with the white marbled dome of the Capitol clearly in view on its hill above Olympia down the inlet to the south, I was mostly focused on the future. After several months of accumulating evidence, I'd finally realized something obvious—something I should have seen a great deal sooner.

Sherry had only recently concluded that this might be a good time to step away from working for the Legislature. I needed to know what she had in mind.

"Have you found a law firm yet?" I asked her.

She shook her head. "I really don't think I want to move to Seattle," she said. "If I don't however, that limits my options."

"Are you thinking about trial work?"

"Yeah, some. Wouldn't mind doing some personal injury cases. But I'd also like to try some general in-office stuff. Some contracts, domestic relations, estates, small corporations; a community practice."

"You probably wouldn't get that with a big Seattle firm anyway."

"I know."

"Do you have any interest in government relations? I'd bet there are firms that would welcome someone with your background in legislative policy."

"I don't know. I haven't thought about lobbying. But, sure, maybe, as a part of something broader. Might be interesting. It would help keep me here in Olympia. Keep David near his dad and from having to change schools." She paused and looked thought-fully in my direction. "What's this?" she said. And then: "You're doing that thing you do, aren't you? With me. Right now."

"Thing . . .?"

"You know what I'm talking about. You're trying to get a read; to figure me out. What's with the questions?"

I knew exactly what she was talking about. I smiled and came to the point: "So, here's a thought," I said. "You know Janice is leav-ing, right?"

That stopped her cold as she thought for a moment about what I'd said. She sat up and turned to face me. "What are you suggest-ing, Sandy?"

"Well, there's no reason my practice couldn't expand some to include some general legal work. I might round things off a bit myself as well. With a bit of legal work, I could make better use of my own time and staff when the Legislature isn't in Session. I have people in the fishing industry asking me to write contracts, handle maritime accident cases, draw up S-corporations, all of it. The insurance pools sometimes end up in litigation. Since the end of Session, I've already had calls from the agriculture industry. I'm just referring all that elsewhere. It's a fair amount of work. If I had someone in house, we could do all that stuff ourselves."

"We?"

"Yeah, why not? You and me. I'm guessing, with your contacts on the Hill and in the world of business and technology, you've got a built-in clientele yourself. Would you be interested in a partnership?"

"A partnership? Really? You're serious?"

"Sure. It will take time for us to build up the practice enough to make any real money. But it seems like we'd have a good head start."

"Wow. You are serious." She hesitated briefly. "You think, at first, we could come somewhere near what I'm earning now?"

"I think we should. We'll keep our overhead low. It all seems doable to me."

She didn't think long. "Well, then, yes. Absolutely. I can't imagine anything more perfect."

I was thrilled with her answer. My heart was skipping, but I'd only taken the first small step. She looked very appealing, sitting there on that weathered log watching her son play on the beach nearby. I'd stopped short of this step for far too long. So, I went for it.

"There's something else I've been thinking about as well. Maybe something I shouldn't suggest given that we're about to go into business together."

"OK," she said, questioningly.

"Have you got any big vacation plans this summer?"

"Not really." She was studying me, now, openly curious.

"Well, look, I've got this trip planned. A canoe trip up in the "Bowron Lakes up in BC. You ever been there?"

"I've heard about it. Never gone. Place sounds incredible."

"You been in a canoe?"

"Yeah, once or twice, a long time ago. I'd love to do more."

It was a preposterous long shot, but I couldn't have asked for a better opening. "Why don't you join me?"

"Join you?"

"Sure. Why don't we go together? You got the time?"

She thought about that. "Yeah, well, I've apparently got a new job and a business partner I'd need to consult. But, the more important matter is that I've also got a young son. When are you going?"

I was pleasantly surprised. She was actually considering it. "Late July," I said.

She gave that some thought. "I bet I could shift things around with my ex. He takes David for a few weeks each summer. They'd probably both be fine with it." Then she looked at me: "But you must have plans yourself," she said. "You with some other people?"

"I'm on my own."

She gave me a look like she knew what that might mean. Then she said: "Um, I looked into it once. They have some kind of limit, right. On the number of boats and people?"

I smiled. "I already have a reservation. I think you can add a person if you already have the reservation for a boat."

I could see she was wavering. It was a big step. Her answer could end up confirming what we both knew. Over the past few months we'd been skirting the line between mere "colleagues" and something that could become much more serious.

"Look, we've known each other for a long time. You know me well enough to know I'm a perfect gentleman, right?" I said. "We can take separate tents and gear. Make of this trip whatever we want. Mainly, Sherry, I just think it would really be enjoyable to do this together. If you're interested."

"Well, in that case," she said with a smile bright enough give me butterflies. "That sounds like the best idea I've heard in a very long time."

ABOUT THE AUTHOR

D ON STUART HAS OVER 20 YEARS of lobbying experience in the Washington, Oregon, and Idaho State Legislatures and in the U.S. Congress. He served as Executive Director for Salmon for Washington, a trade group representing commercial fishermen and fish processing firms (1990-96), Executive Director for the Washington Association of Conservation Districts, a professional association representing local governments assisting agricultural landowners (1997-2000), and Northwest Regional Director for American Farmland Trust, a national environmental organization protecting local farmland from development (2000-2011). Don was also the campaign manager and public spokesperson in the successful defense of a Washington statewide anti-commercial fishing ballot initiative (I-640) in 1995 and he ran for the U.S. Congress in Washington's First District in 1996.

Don is also a former Alaska commercial salmon troll fisherman (1962-65, 1980-89), a formerly practicing Seattle trial attorney (1972-79), and was a Lieutenant in the U.S. Navy Judge Advocate General's Corps during the Viet Nam War (1968-72). His opinion column on fish politics appeared monthly in the Fishermen's News from 1990-96. He is the author of Barnyards and Birkenstocks: Why Farmers and Environmentalists Need Each Other, published by Washington State University Press (2014), and of The Washington Guide to Small Claims Court, published by Self-Counsel Press (1979).

CPSIA information can be obtained
at www.ICGtesting.com
Printed in the USA
BVHW081649041022
648644BV00014B/618